THE FLESHMARKET VAMPIRE

By

M.T. O'Neill

Dedication

For my wife Lalita.

You are my everything. I love you x

CONTENTS

CHAPTER 1

With the cold night air biting at her lips and cheeks, Mercy soared above Edinburgh's Old Town, gothic in its splendour and dramatic in its beauty.

Brightly lit sandstone buildings, charred black by centuries of industry pumping soot into the air and coating the town, passed below. Layer upon layer of building and rebuilding throughout the ages had resulted in a mishmash of architectural styles, and a multitude of closes and alleyways which now lead to nowhere. The city was in the process of being enveloped in the haar, the thick, gunky, low laying fog which would often roll in from the North Sea, just a few miles away.

Mercy reached one of her regular darker alleys just off a main road, set herself down, and joined the human revellers. Visibility was diminishing and people in the distance had become misty, poorly outlined silhouettes. Taking in the nightlife on her usual nightly stroll, she stopped outside the Surgeon's Hall Museum and smiled as she studied the facade; a Neoclassical building in the Greek Revival style, it bore six large pillars as a dramatic welcome to visitors.

I remember when it was just an empty plot of land, before the Surgeons' and Barbers' old collection got so big it needed an entirely new building to house their curiosities.

She passed closed shops and the residential flats above which lined the streets, and she smiled at each partial conversation from those passing her, allowing the briefest snapshot of their lives.

She raised her hand in greeting when the familiar figure of Franky appeared from around the corner of the next block. He returned the gesture.

"Hey Franky. Thanks for meeting me tonight. How goes it?"

"No bad. How's yourself?"

"Aye, fine, just out for a walk. Taking in some air, I love the haar," she said staring off into the ethereal white bathed in an orange hue from the streetlights. "How are you?"

"Aye, I'm fine. The haar looks nice but the damp air isn't good for my lungs. I was just checking on some people. You know Auld Bert? He's dead. Knew him for years," he said with slumped shoulders.

"When? Any idea of the cause?" she asked.

"You and your sense of empathy, Mercy," Franky said, shaking his head. "A few weeks ago. I think it was the wee cold snap we just had. I only just found out."

Mercy pursed her lips and nodded.

"And Auld Bert isn't the only one. Annie's dead as well," Franky said as he ruffled his dishevelled brown hair with his hands.

"What happened to her?"

"Disappeared like the others," Frank replied.

Fucking hell, Gabriel!

"You know I had nothing to do with it, don't you?" she asked.

"I know, and I trust you," he replied. "It's bad enough when it happens to normal people, but when it happens to mine... you know they can't fend for themselves. And they're targeted more than most."

"I know," she said, stuffing her cold hands into the pockets of her denim jacket.

"I know we've spoken about this before, but I really need you to do something about this. Now more than ever. I don't know what you *can* do. You're such a bloody mystery all the time, but I know that you get things done. Whoever is doing this has to stop."

"I know, Franky. I know. I'm on it."

"Good. Anyway," he said and puffed out his sunken cheeks, "will you have a job for me anytime soon?" he asked with hope in his voice.

"Actually, I do," she replied. "His name is Thomas Briggs. Forty-five. Lives in Stockbridge, near the supermarket on Comely Bank Road apparently. He's a person I'm interested in. Find out all about him. The usual. Here is his picture a contact of mine gave me. You'll find it useful," she said and handed over a file containing a pen, blank pieces of paper, and a photo.

"Did this contact bring him to your attention?"

"Aye," she replied. "Call me when you have something for me."

"Aye, will do."

"Do you need anything in the meantime?" she asked.

"Some spending money would be handy."

"Here," she said, digging into her wallet and producing £100 in 10s.

"Cheers. I'll be in touch soon," he said as he took the money and walked away.

Mercy continued her journey, approaching the crossroads between North Bridge and the Royal Mile. The headlights of the cars illuminated those who passed by along with the eerie whiteness of the fog. A car momentarily highlighted the hazy figures of four young men as they stood over a homeless old man sitting cross-legged under a raggedy tartan blanket.

She focused on the conversation as she approached.

The four men were laughing.

"Come on, we'll find you someone, and if you win, you'll get… what?" one of them said as he turned to his friends. "£100? Yeah? Does £100 sound good, mate? We'll make it a fair fight. We'll find you someone as skinny and haggard as you!" he said as his three friends sniggered.

Mercy picked up her pace as the bully nudged the homeless man with his polished shoe.

"Hey there," she said, distracting the bully and his friends. She smiled a sweet and friendly smile.

"Well hello darling! What can I do for a fine girl like you?" the bully replied with a grin, sweeping his perfectly coiffed hair to the side.

Mercy maintained her smile. She stared at the three young men behind the bully, smug grins smeared on their faces.

"You three; stand still like statues and stay silent."

The bully's three friends stiffened their posture with expressionless faces.

"And you," she addressed the bully, her smile fading. She pointed at the two-foot-wide portion of brick wall between the large glass windows of the closed shops. "Smash your face off that brick wall with full force repeatedly until I tell you to stop."

The bully walked to the wall and repeatedly slammed his head against the brickwork.

The delicious smell of blood filled the air. Mercy pulled out her signature vivid red lipstick as the face of the bully started to leave bloody smears on the wall. She reapplied another coat of lipstick using the darkened shop window as a mirror, ensuring there were no smudges, and then straightened her half-up, half-down ponytail. She then turned back to the bully.

"Stop."

The man stopped and turned to face her. His nose was broken and wedged to the side of his face. There were deep cuts above both eyebrows and blood dripped onto his white shirt.

She licked her lips.

"Where do you live?" she asked.

"The Shore," the bully replied.

"That's a few miles away. Take your shoes and socks off and give them to the homeless man."

The bully complied and removed his expensive leather shoes.

"You three," she addressed the bully's friends. "You are all going to go to the centre of St Andrews Square in the New Town, and you're going to kick the shit out of each other. You're not going to stop until the police arrive. All four of you are going to forget me *and* this meeting."

"Hey! These are size 9s! My size!" the homeless man said, studying his new footwear.

"It must be your lucky day," she said. "And as for you," she addressed the barefoot bully whose expensive cotton shirt was becoming increasingly stained red. "You are going to walk home and you are going to kick every lamppost you pass with full force with both feet. If by the time you get home all your toes aren't broken, you're going to break them yourself with your own hands. Now, all four of you, fuck off."

The bully and his three friends walked away in silence without registering one another. They crossed the North Bridge over Waverley Train Station and disappeared into the fog.

Her attention returned to the homeless man who was giggling at the men who were wandering away.

That's a new face. I don't recognise him.

"Thank you, young lady!" he said with a broken-toothed smile.

"Young lady?" she asked with a smile as she dipped her hand into her black denim trousers. She withdrew her wallet and produced a crisp £20 note.

"'Old fishwife' if ye like, hen," he responded, his smile morphing into a mischievous grin.

"The air is damp tonight. Have you got a place indoors?" she asked as she pressed the note into his palm.

"Emmm, no hen," he said as he unfurled the note to look at it. "Awww, that's really generous of ye!"

"Want me to put you in touch with someone?"

"Naw, naw, it's OK, hen. It's no too cold tonight," he said, his smile widening.

The sound of car tyres screeching in the distance and a woman briefly screaming tore her attention from him.

She followed the direction of the sound onto the High Street section of the Royal Mile and onwards to Cockburn Street, pronounced "Coeburn". She followed the cobblestone-covered road as it wound down a steep slope and turned to the left.

In front of her a black taxi was stopped in the middle of the road, its hazard lights flashing. The driver was hovering over someone as a couple of revellers rushed over.

Mercy casually strolled over to survey the scene, the smell of blood once again fresh in the air. The driver was on the phone and a well-heeled elderly couple were perched over a man in his late teens lying on the cobblestones. Slender in build, with short light brown hair, the man stared intently to his left. He then looked up at Mercy.

His desperation was all too familiar. His heartbeat rang strong in Mercy's ears.

"Stop… him," the man said.

Mercy turned her head in the direction the stricken man had been staring: Fleshmarket Close.

She approached the close and peered down the set of steps. In the distance was the unmistakably gothic appearance of Gabriel, walking with his arm around his latest meal.

Gabriel then grabbed the woman and disappeared into the darkness of the night sky.

Sparing a second to ensure there were no eyes on her, Mercy shot into the air. Hovering a few hundred feet above the Old Town, Mercy scanned the skies for Gabriel, but he was gone in the haar. Whilst still in the air, Mercy turned her attention to the man. Now unconscious, with more people having arrived, she continued to stare from her hidden place, cloaked in darkness and fog.

Christ, it was like looking at Josef again. That expression on his face as he looked up at me. Only Josef would have had the guts to go after Gabriel like that. Is this sorry guy the opportunity I've been looking for?

"If you live, you're going to change everything," she said with a smile as the flashing lights of the ambulance approached the scene.

CHAPTER 2

Danny retrieved the jacket hanging over the back of his chair, all the while smiling at the girl dancing on his table.

"You heading home honey?" she shouted over the music.

"Yeah," he replied. "Have a good night."

"You too, doll!" she replied and continued dancing.

Danny looked over at Aurelia and smiled. Whilst swinging her coat over her shoulders, Aurelia continued to dance along with the man playing a trumpet on the next table.

As he donned his brown leather aviator jacket, Danny's eyes remained fixed on her. She was happy and vibrant.

"Ready?" he shouted over the blaring noise of the upbeat big band cabaret music.

She nodded and shuffled over to him and grabbed his forearm.

"Sorry," he said.

"Don't worry about it," she replied, her eyes sparkling.

They left Bohemia with full stomachs and light heads, and headed out into the cool Edinburgh night air.

They stepped onto the pavement of Market Street, directly across from the entrance to Waverley, Edinburgh's main train station. The haar had set in and most of the train station was no longer visible in the fog.

"How's your headache?" Aurelia asked as she squeezed his forearm.

"It's OK," he lied. "I feel better for being out in the fresh air."

"We'll just take a slow walk home and the fresh air will help."

Aurelia clutched the crook of his forearm and they turned to their left, passing under the stone archway of Fleshmarket Close, the alleyway which ran alongside Bohemia up the steep hill towards the Royal Mile, to the small upstairs flat they called home.

They strolled up the first of several sets of steps which comprised the bottom of Fleshmarket Close. The far end of Fleshmarket Close, up the hill, was shrouded in fog.

"I'm sorry, Aurelia," he repeated.

"I told you not to worry about it. I'm just proud of you for trying. Besides, you lasted almost the entire night! That's really good! You've come on so much since we moved to this city, so be proud of yourself. Mum would be proud of you," she said with a smile and gripped his arm tighter.

Danny smiled and nodded.

The quiet of the alleyway and the cold air had indeed helped his migraine, which was settling down from a thunderous cacophony of blinding pain to a more subtle jackhammer of blinding pain. The momentary stench of stale urine as they passed a small, boarded up inlet turned his stomach, but as they passed the makeshift urinal for drunks, the air cleared.

Twenty-first century Edinburgh was a modern bustling city of commerce and culture, beloved by tourists and natives alike. The city proudly retained all its history, advertised through its gothic architecture, tour guides, ghost tours, and tell-tale place names. Nowhere was this more synonymous than the thousand-year-old Old Town area, the original part of the city with narrow footpaths and winding alleys, called 'closes'.

"Did you know," Danny said as he gave Aurelia's arm a squeeze, "that Fleshmarket Close was given its name because all of the butcher shops were located here over 200 years ago. Racks of raw meat from freshly slaughtered animals lined the entire close, and all the fresh blood ran down the steep gradient of the close."

"Yeah, you've told me that before, like, ten times," she replied with a smile.

"Sorry," he said and looked down at his feet as they continued to walk.

"Don't apologise. I like your stories," she added before squeezing his arm.

The clacking footsteps behind them caught Danny's attention. He half-turned around to see the figure of a man dressed in black with shoulder length swept back light blonde hair, twenty feet behind them.

"That was great, that band was brilliant. Even coming off the little stage and playing on the tables, it was great fun!" she said.

"Yeah. Perhaps we can go again at the weekend?" Danny suggested as he turned back to face Aurelia. "I know that you love it when Bohemia have all sorts of cabaret acts."

"Yeah, sounds good. I had a great time anyway. A cheeky wee Tuesday night out is fun, but it's not like it's going to be our last night out again, so don't worry. Did you enjoy yourself?"

There was a whooshing sound from behind them as though a sudden wind had blown up the close. Danny craned around once more, and the man was gone.

"Um, yeah. I'm surprised at how much fun I had. After a while I just developed a bit of a migraine and started to feel wonky. Thanks for leaving early."

After the gradient of the hill eased, they climbed the final set of steps and reached Cockburn Street, a cobble stone road which cut Fleshmarket Close in two and led to the final part of the Royal Mile before the Mile became pedestrianised. They crossed Cockburn Street and re-joined the final section of Fleshmarket Close; a short, enclosed stretch of alleyway which ran under an eight-storey building and led onto the Royal Mile, and directly opposite their flat.

"Spare change, mate?" the homeless man asked as he huddled, shivering in his ragged dark blue sleeping bag. The building under which he sat offered protection against rain, but did not protect him from the cold, biting wind which blew directly down Fleshmarket Close. In the narrowness of the close, they found themselves stepping over the end of his sleeping bag.

Danny quickened his pace, pulling gently at Aurelia's arm. Aurelia pulled back and they came to a stop. She fished into the pocket of her coat, produced a small pink wallet, and handed over some coins, placing them directly in the homeless man's hand, rather than into the upturned cap lying on the ground in front of him.

"There you go, doll."

Danny scanned both ends of the alleyway and tapped his foot.

"Aww cheers, darling. Yous two have a good night, eh?"

"You too, hun," Aurelia replied, as both she and Danny stepped out from under the archway onto the Royal Mile.

"Right. Kettle on, an episode of something on the TV before I head off to bed, I think. Maybe you should just sit in your room with the lights off for a while. It might help your head," she suggested.

God, my head's killing me.

"Could I please go Javed's? We don't have any paracetamol and my head could be doing with some," he said.

"Why don't you go yourself? I'll head upstairs and get the kettle on."

"Or you could come with me and keep me company?"

Aurelia hesitated.

"Come on, I'll buy you a sweet and you can have a vape outside," he added hopefully.

"Fiiiine," she replied, along with an exaggerated sigh which advertised her jest in such a situation. "Let's go. You can get me a wee pack of chewing gum while you're in."

They rounded the nearby corner onto North Bridge and Danny stepped inside the newsagent's, Javed's. Upon stepping inside, to Danny's right there was the usual newsagent's fare, including household items, numerous bars of chocolates, and behind the counter alcohol and cigarettes. To the left was a vast array of Edinburgh souvenirs. Tartan and Scotland-themed kitsch and tourist-centric tat which was ignored by the locals, yet acted as catnip to excitable tourists.

Having retrieved both his and Aurelia's favourite chocolate bars, as well as chewing gum for her, Danny stepped into the queue. As he waited to be served, he surveyed the headlines on the various newspapers. One, however, caught his attention more than the others.

NUMBER OF MISSING CONTINUES TO SOAR.

The subheading on the front page read: *Instances of missing persons continue to increase. Council and police are baffled.*

"Next," Javed stated.

Danny's attention was brought back to the Asian man behind the counter. Danny stepped forward but another man stepped directly in front of Danny and was served at the counter.

Rude prick! I should say something! He took a breath and looked down at his feet. *No, just let it go. It's not worth the confrontation.*

The rude prick, having taken his change, left the shop without registering Danny.

"Hiya. Sorry about that," Javed said.

"No worries. Some people have no manners."

"Yup, selfish arseholes," Javed added in his broad Pakistani accent.

Danny slid his bank card back into his wallet and stepped back onto North Bridge. The cold air kissed his cheeks once more.

"Here is your chewing gum. I also got you a Boun..." he began before his voice trailed off.

Aurelia was gone.

In the foggy semi-darkness of the street, Aurelia's familiar light grey faux-fur coat and light blonde pixie cut hairstyle was missing.

"Where the...?"

Danny rounded the corner, back onto the Royal Mile.

He scanned the few forms which were present on the road, but none resembled his sister.

He dialled her number. It rang, but no one answered.

Sixty seconds later and he was standing outside the front entry door to their flat. He peered up at his windows. They were all in darkness.

Right, she won't be home. The living room light would definitely be on. OK, don't panic, Danny. She's not answering her phone, so she has probably dropped it, or left it back in Bohemia. She'll be retracing her steps,

He approached the entrance to Fleshmarket Close.

She should have bloody well come into Javed's and told me before swanning off!

He strode towards the close, which bore the name on both the pavement as well as the black wrought iron post in the centre of the entrance.

He stepped into the darkness of the alleyway. The homeless man still sat in his sleeping bag, staring directly ahead of him at the stone wall opposite.

"Excuse me mate, did you see my sister go past you a few minutes ago? She has light blonde hair and a light grey fur coat?" Danny asked.

The man didn't answer. He did not even register Danny's presence.

"Mate? Remember me? She gave you some change a few minutes ago! Mate? Mate!" Danny shouted.

Still, the homeless man stared vacantly at the wall opposite.

Fuck's sake! Typical junkie!

Danny continued down the slope of Fleshmarket close towards Cockburn Street. He neared the cobbled street and smiled; Aurelia was further down the close, across the road, walking away.

His heart lifted as a wave of relief flooded over him.

"Aurelia!" he shouted with a smile, but she didn't turn.

There was a man next to her, his arm lazily draped around

her neck. He stood in the light of the lamppost illuminating the close, but he'd still found a shadow. With black trousers, short black jacket, and light blonde hair partly tied into a ponytail, it was the man who had been walking behind Danny and Aurelia as they walked up the close. The man turned to Aurelia and spoke into her ear; his lips brushed her earlobe with each word.

"Aurelia?" Danny repeated, a look of worried confusion now etched on his face. He picked up his pace after them.

Without warning, the man violently jerked her against the wall, pushed her head to the side, exposing her neck, and pressed his head into her throat.

"HEY!" Danny screamed and he burst into a sprint.

His heart pumped jet fuel. Anger and fear clenched his fists. He laser-focused on the man.

Danny didn't pay attention to the slipperiness of the wet cobble stones as he ran across Cockburn Road, nor did he notice them shine from the headlights of the car rounding the corner. There was only the blast of the car horn, the sound of tyres screeching, and the impact of the grill against his legs.

He bounced onto the bonnet of the car and rolled off as it stopped.

The back of his head smashed onto the cobblestones.

Then the pain hit him. His right knee burned and yet at the same time was completely weak. The ribs on his right side ached. His migraine was now gone and a strange numbness took its place. The cold of the cobble stones pressing against the back of his skull was now warm. Warm and wet and fuzzy.

As his vision blurred, cleared then blurred again, he turned his head towards Aurelia.

Both she and the man in black were walking away, down the steps of Fleshmarket Close. With his arm still draped around her neck, the man looked over his shoulder at Danny. Blood stained his smile bright red.

Danny opened his mouth but no words would come. Only his neck was capable of movement as it straightened and forced the yellow-tainted fog obscuring the stars into his field of vision.

"Don't move," a middle-aged man was saying. "You're awright, son."

Looking over Danny was a man with short salt and pepper hair, a rotund face with ruddy cheeks, and a bushy moustache. He flashed the briefest of smiles, but his eyes were shot through with panic. He held a phone to his ear.

Danny winced as his head turned in the direction of Aurelia and her attacker, but they were both gone.

"Hello? Aye, I need an ambulance. I hit a guy with my taxi. He appeared from out the blue and I hit him. He's on the ground right now... Yeah, he's conscious."

An old couple had joined them, both expressing shock.

"Lift his head," the old man said.

As they kneeled over him, into Danny's vision walked a young woman. She surveyed the taxi driver, the couple, and finally Danny.

Long dark brown hair was tucked behind ears which stuck out slightly, and flowed over the shoulders of a light denim jacket. Spotlighted by the taxi's headlights, her blemish-free alabaster skin was offset by her vibrant bright red lipstick. The most striking thing about her, however, was her expression of complete disinterest in what was happening.

Danny began to swim into unconsciousness.

"Oh Christ, is that blood?" the old man's companion asked. "That's so much blood!"

"Stop... him," Danny whispered.

Her attention focused on the now-deserted Fleshmarket Close, before returning to Danny.

All the time, the girl with the red lipstick stood over them all, surveying him silently. She then walked away without a word or an expression of interest, and out of his peripheral vision.

"Don't worry, pal. An ambulance is on its way," the taxi driver stated loudly.

Danny closed his eyes. Despite the pain, he just wanted to sleep.

"You'll be alright, my dear," the elderly woman said in a gentle and soothing tone.

Then there was darkness. Thick, gunky blackness, and all-encompassing silence.

CHAPTER 3

The chattering of women in the distance creeping into his ears was a quiet, distant distraction from the darkness and peace, but soon it grew in volume. As their voices grew, so did Danny's pain.

At first it was a mild headache accompanied by a pain in his right knee, but as his senses slowly returned to him, his right ribs and left hip began to ache. The pain in his knee, however, only grew in intensity and ferocity, dragging him into full consciousness.

The stench of disinfectant irritated his senses. Strip lighting above him burned through his closed eyelids. He opened his eyes and immediately squinted against the harshness of the light.

"Fuck," he whispered with a dry, rasping voice.

As his vision grew more accustomed to the light, he surveyed his surroundings.

The blue curtain of the hospital cubicle was pulled part-way around, offering him some privacy from the bed next to him, but not from the elderly man in the bed opposite, who was reading a newspaper.

Minimal light and grey murky skies filled the entire view out of the window on his left.

Hooked onto the right railing of his bed were the bed controls and an alert button. He raised the back of the bed until he was sitting in an upright position. The pain on his hip and his knee grew further.

Where am I? How did I get here?

He pressed the call button for the nurses' station and a beeping sound began in the same direction as the voices.

A few moments later, a smiling middle-aged nurse with a kind face emerged from behind the blue curtain and pulled it back fully, allowing Danny to view the remaining two beds in the ward room.

"Hi there!" she greeted him before reaching past him and turning off the call button on the wall behind him. "How are we feeling?"

"OK," he lied. "Um, where am I? What happened?"

"You're in the Western General," she replied whilst looking at his chart, before going silent for a few moments. "You were hit by a car. You hurt your leg and got a bump on the head. You timed it right, waking up now; the doctors are making their rounds in the ward. You should be seen in the next minute or two and they'll be able to give you more details. I'll get you some water," she said with a smile.

As the nurse left, a small troupe of men and women in white coats shuffled into the room.

Good timing, right enough.

"So, Daniel Thomas," the head doctor read from a small bundle of notes. "Morning Daniel. I'm Doctor Collins," she addressed him before looking at his chart. "How are you?"

She wore a pleasant smile on a stern face.

"Sore. What happened to me? Why am I here?"

"I'm afraid you were knocked down by a car last night. I take it you don't remember what happened?"

Danny shook his head whilst grimacing with the pain which continued to burn at his knee.

"You were given stitches in the back of your head. You probably have a little concussion. You mainly have bumps and bruises and you're going to be sore for a while, however it seems that the brunt of the force was on your knee."

"It's killing me."

"That's understandable. We'll get you something more

significant for the pain. Do you mind if I take a look at it?"

Danny shook his head and rested his head against the pillow. As he closed his eyes, the pressure of the bedsheets pressing against his knee eased and a rush of cooler air hit his sensitive skin.

"Damage to the right knee with inflammation and swelling. Possible damage to the lateral collateral ligament, medial collateral ligament, and damage to the meniscus."

Bloody hell, that doesn't sound good.

He sighed as Doctor Collins briefed the gaggle of junior doctors hanging on her every word.

"Daniel?"

"Hmmm?"

"The X-Ray you were given last night showed no broken bones, and the patella – your kneecap – is intact so that's really good news. The issue is that there is likely to be damage to the tendons and ligaments around your knee, including the soft tissues in the joint itself."

The nurse returned with a plastic jug filled with water and a disposable cup. She placed them on his wheeled tray and stood in silence, her smile still fixed.

"So, what does that mean? What needs doing?" Danny asked Doctor Collins, his eyes still closed.

"Well, we need to get the swelling down as soon as possible and be careful that there is no infection in the area. Then we'll do a scan to fully assess the extent of any damage. We can then refer you to a physiotherapist, as well as booking you in for a chat with a consultant to decide if anything else needs to be done. It depends on how it heals."

"Can I try getting up?" Danny asked.

"If you think you can, sure. But please be careful as the swelling is still quite bad," Collins replied.

Danny took a deep breath and braced himself for the inevitable spike in pain. He swung his left leg out of the bed. He moaned and gurned as the pain shot through him, from his ribs and spine to hips and knee. He winced as he sat upright and gingerly moved his right leg to the edge of the bed.

He then looked down. His eyes bulged. Queasiness swirled in his stomach, threatening to make a break for his throat. Swelling had rendered the knee badly misshapen and wrapped it in a mask of dark blue and purple.

The nurse stepped in and slid her head under his arm. A junior doctor approached him, ready to support him.

His right leg remained straight as his foot landed on the ground with a jolt.

"Arghhh! Ya fucker!"

"OK, I think that it's best you get back into bed," Collins said with an expression of awkward regret.

The doctor and nurse aided him back into bed and he lay, exhausted, queasy, and in intense pain.

"Aurelia!" he yelped as a flash of her being attacked by the man with blonde hair replayed in his mind.

Oh my God! Aurelia! I forgot!

"Sorry?" Collins said, looking up from the chart.

"My sister!"

"Oh, you had a female visitor early this morning," the nurse said.

"Really?" Danny asked.

"Yeah. I never spoke to her. Considering how she was here out of visiting times, I figured that she must have been immediate family."

"Thank God," he whispered. "Is my phone here?"

I miss her. I hope that she is OK. She must be, I guess.

"I think so. It'll be in your cupboard." The nurse opened the doors of the small cupboard which sat next to Danny's head. "There you go."

"Right, we'll see how you get on this evening and make another assessment. I'll order more powerful painkillers and anti-inflammatories and we'll get you on the mend," Collins finished with a smile before she and her group moved on to the elderly man who had been reading his newspaper.

"I can't believe I only remembered Aurelia now. I was so

wrapped up in myself I never even thought about her!" Danny said as he flicked through his contacts list.

"Don't feel guilty," the nurse said softly. "You've had a real upset, and most likely a concussion, and so it's only natural you wouldn't think of other people immediately."

"I suppose. Did she say anything?"

"Well, like I said, I never spoke to her. She spoke to Annie, the nurse at the desk at the time. She only stayed for a few minutes then left."

He pressed the call button and held it to his ear.

"You'll need to tell me where she got her denim jacket. It was lovely. That big daisy in sequins on the back. My daughter would love that."

As the phone continued to ring, the nurse's words registered with Danny.

"What jacket? She doesn't have a denim jacket."

"The jacket she was wearing this morning," the nurse insisted.

A surge of worry rose in Danny.

"What did she look like?" he asked, bracing himself.

"Tall..."

Aurelia is 5'5"

"... long dark brown hair, in a half-up, half-down ponytail. Really smooth pale skin but she was wearing bright red lipstick," the nurse finished her description.

"That's not Aurelia. Aurelia is shorter, has a dyed light blonde pixie cut, and was wearing a light grey fake fur coat," Danny corrected her as the phone cut into Aurelia's voicemail.

"Did anyone else visit me?"

"No, I don't think so."

"Please ask Annie what this woman said to her."

"OK, I'll mind and ask her."

"Could you please ask her now? Please!" Danny insisted.

"OK, gimme two minutes," the nurse replied and walked off, clearly with her nose out of joint.

Danny tried calling her again with the same result. Before

long, the nurse was back.

"She can't remember."

"What do you mean 'she can't remember'? She let this woman in out of hours even when spouses aren't usually allowed that."

"All I can say is that Annie can't remember talking to anyone with that description, which is weird because I saw them talking. I dunno what else to tell you, son."

Danny sighed and rubbed his temples.

Right, think Danny. Aurelia was last seen then by me, and I think that guy was attacking her. Christ, she's missing!

"OK, what's your name, nurse?"

"It's Lucy," Lucy replied with a smile.

"Lucy, thank you for helping me, but I need you to call the police and get them to come here. I think that my sister was attacked last night."

"Oh God," Lucy replied. "OK, give me a minute."

Within ten minutes, two tall male Police Scotland officers approached Danny with Lucy in tow.

"Mr Thomas?" the first officer addressed Danny.

"Yes," Danny responded as he tried to sit up straighter, resulting in a great deal of pain.

"My name is Officer O'Donnell and this is Officer Prince. You wanted to speak to the police as you believe that someone was attacked?"

"Yes, that's right," he answered whilst Lucy raised the back of the bed for him and the two officers sat on the visitors chairs next to the bed.

The other three patients in the wards were staring intently at the scene.

"Lucy, do you mind?" Danny asked as he nodded towards the other patients.

"Of course," she said with a smile, and pulled the blue curtains around them, forming a private, if not soundproof, cubicle.

"It's my sister, Aurelia Thomas. I saw a man attacking her.

At least I think he was. I ran after them, across the road, but I didn't see a car and it ploughed into me and I ended up here."

He proceeded to recount, in minute detail, the events of the previous night before the questions came; questions which ranged from guessing Aurelia's mental state on the night to prodding Danny to repeat his account of the events.

"So, you said that you saw a man walking behind you, then you turned around a few seconds later and he was gone?" O'Donnell asked.

"Yeah," Danny replied.

"How is that possible? I've walked along Fleshmarket Close many times and at the section you are describing there are no other turns to disappear down. So where did he go?"

"I dunno."

"Then you said that he reappeared with his arm around your sister and he attacked her. Even though there were others there, for example a homeless man and an elderly couple and the taxi driver, although none of them acknowledged the man attacking her."

"I don't know what you expect me to say. I've told you what happened," Danny said.

Do they think that I am imagining it? Do they think I've gone mad?

"Are there any other family or friends in town that she might be staying with?" O'Donnell asked.

"No, she was always a bit of a loner. I guess we both are. We don't really have many friends."

Something stung inside Danny when he made the admission.

"We live together," Danny continued. "We moved to Edinburgh from Glasgow a few months ago because she found work here. We have no other family. We only had each other," Danny said, picking at his fingernails.

"OK. So, there are no boyfriends?" O'Donnell continued with his questions. "Do you have a picture of her?"

"No, like I said, we were new in town and had no ties with

Glasgow. I can email you some pictures from my phone."

"That would be great. Now, most people who go missing turn up within forty-eight hours, and so hopefully she is safe and unharmed. We'll need to search all the various places she has been, and that will include your house, the bar you were in. Also, it would be beneficial if you can look at her social media accounts to see if there have been any updates there."

"Sure, whatever you need," Danny replied.

They're not taking this seriously.

Danny rubbed his temples in a slow circular motion.

They're not even going to try. No wonder the rates of missing people are so ridiculously high in this city.

The interview finished with O'Donnell handing Danny his card and leaving with his still-silent partner.

For the rest of the day, Danny continued to move his knee as much as the swelling and pain would allow, as well as fighting the groggy head the astonishingly strong morphine caused.

In between ten-minute drug-fuelled naps, Danny would call Aurelia's phone to no avail. He checked her social media accounts. There had been no updates. He checked local news websites for any reports of a woman being attacked, however he had no luck.

As the lights on the ward dimmed, Danny received a notification that only ten percent of his phone's battery remained. Against his instincts, he turned his phone off.

"I'll ask around for a charger later," he muttered to himself as he sat his phone on the tray and closed his eyes.

Even with the stiffness, the pain, and the worrying over Aurelia, sleep came quite easily to Danny. However, it was punctuated by nightmares, all involving Aurelia being attacked and Danny being hit by the car.

He was awoken by Lucy the next morning, being her usual cheery self.

"Morning! How did you sleep?"

"Surprisingly well," Danny replied as he rubbed sleep out of his eyes. "Although with the nightmares I had, I wish I hadn't slept at all. Do you think I could borrow someone's charger?" he asked as he reached for his phone and turned it on.

There were no messages for him, no missed calls, nothing from Aurelia.

The hours passed. Danny was successful in borrowing a charger for a short period of time, long enough to recharge the phone and keep it on. After lunch he called the officer who had visited him.

"Hello?"

"Hiya, it's Danny Thomas. You visited me in the hospital yesterday. How did you get on with trying to find Aurelia?"

"Hello, Mr Thomas. Unfortunately, no luck I'm afraid. We have tried..."

The officer continued to explain the situation but his voice faded into insignificance in Danny's ear. The rest of the call was conducted on autopilot.

After disconnecting the call, Danny stared at his phone. And stared. And stared.

He took a deep breath, closed his eyes, and sat upright on the bed. There was a minimal amount of pain in his ribs.

I need to be completely silent in doing this.

He pulled his sheets off, exposing his legs. His right knee lay there, still swollen, still purple and blue. Still aching.

In screaming pain, he swivelled his body out of bed in one sweeping motion.

He gurned and stood by the bed, waiting for the pain to subside, and to catch his breath.

He bent over and collected his personal effects from the small cupboard, all the while careful not to bend his knee.

He feverishly stripped off his hospital gown, only to be relieved to find he was still wearing underwear.

He buttoned his white shirt with a dried blood patch on the back of the collar, before surveying his folded black trousers.

Now how am I going to manage this?

He dumped the trousers on the floor, waist end up, and proceeded to slide his feet into them in a comical manner. In spite of the throbbing in his knee, and the pain radiating up his leg, he tested the limits of his flexibility to gradually slide them up to his knees using his thumbs in the belt loops on the waistband, until they met resistance.

"Shit!"

The knee had swollen to such an extent, the trousers would not go any further than his thighs.

Well, I can't exactly shuffle my way out of here like this!

He grabbed the fabric on each side of the inside stitching of his trousers, at the knee, and pulled. A ripping sound echoed in the ward room. He pulled his trousers up and buttoned them. He smiled at the gaping hole in the inside seam of his trouser leg, level with his knee. Still leaning on the bed railing, he slipped into his black leather loafer shoes and gathered his possessions.

"Right. You can do this. Just ignore the pain and get out of here," he whispered.

With his first step onto his right foot, his knee buckled entirely and only his arm on the railing saved him from hitting the ground.

"Shit! Shit, shit, shit!" His face burned red and a vein on his temple throbbed. "You fucker!"

The stares from the three faces in the room burrowed into him.

"Get back to your fucking newspapers!"

One patient looked away, but the other two continued to stare.

With each step, he used anything he could get his hands on to take the weight of his right leg. With some strategic thinking, he successfully negotiated his way out of the room and into the ward corridor.

"Umm, Danny, what on earth are you doing?" Lucy asked as her eyes rose from her computer at the nurses' station.

"I'm going home."

"Danny, you are not in any condition to be leaving."

"I'm fine."

"Danny, please at least wait to speak to a doctor when they

make their rounds!"

"My sister is missing out there and the police aren't going to take this seriously. She's just going to disappear with all the others. I'm going to go out there and look myself."

"Danny, please."

"Fine!" Danny barked. "I want to speak with a doctor now. Not during their rounds. Right now."

"Fine, I'll see if a doctor can come and speak with you now. But please go back to your bed and rest."

Danny sat up in bed once more after being helped there by Lucy. This time, he was sitting above the sheets and still wore his clothes. His left leg jiggled as he ran several arguments in his head with whichever doctor would appear.

This isn't me. I'm not this rude or insistent. Lucy's only trying to help. Wind your bloody neck in Danny, you prick!

Soon, Doctor Collins walked into the room with a smile on her face.

"Mr Thomas," she addressed him as she approached his bed.

"Doctor."

"As I understand it, you want to leave. You understand that we are still unsure of the extent of the damage to your knee?"

"I understand that, but I'm still leaving. Now give me whatever I need to sign to discharge myself."

"Mr..."

"I'm of clear mind. My knee is injured, but I've not had a heart attack. I'm not a danger to myself or others. I'm leaving," he stated with resolve.

"OK," Collins conceded. "I'll get the paperwork for you to sign. I can't stop you, but with the pain you are in, and with the possibility that you could actually do further damage to your knee..."

"Then give me what I need. Crutches or something."

Danny left the hospital with a sturdy brace on his knee, a crutch under each arm, and a box of prescription painkillers.

Doctor Collins had told him to go home and rest. Danny had other ideas.

Out in the open air, he scanned the distance for a taxi rank. He waved his hand over at the first black cab in a line of four. The lights flashed at him and it made its way over. Danny took a few steps backward as the grill of the cab approached him. He began to pant. His heart started hammering and his equilibrium was unsteady. The screech of braking tyres replayed in his head.

He froze as the driver waited. After a moment, the driver opened his door, and poked his head over the door at him.

"Are you getting in pal?"

Danny silently nodded, his eyes still bulging at the driver.

The cab made its way through the town without incident, but every bump, every pothole was agony on his knee. Before long, it pulled into the side on the corner of High Street. Danny paid the fare plus tip and carefully stepped down onto the pavement. The pedestrianised section of the Royal Mile was ahead. By now, the pain in his knee had radiated upwards, and his hip was now aching.

What should have been a sixty second journey from the road to outside the flat took ten minutes. The windows were shrouded in darkness. He sighed as he lowered his head. He proceeded down the alleyway to the side of his building, into the rear courtyard and through the security door. The journey up the four flights of stairs was fraught with both blinding pain and the fear of losing his footing.

He unlocked his door and stepped inside. The flat was cold, dark, and unwelcoming.

"Aurelia? Aurelia?" he called out.

Please answer.

He was greeted with silence. He dumped his box of painkillers and the prescription letter to his doctor onto the glass coffee table. He grabbed a can of cola from the fridge and took a biscuit from the tin.

What do I do? Where do I begin?

He stood in the centre of his living room for fifteen minutes in complete silence, drinking his cola and studying the extensive sagging of the couch.

If I sit on that, I'll never get back up again.

He approached the window which offered a view of the Royal Mile. The entry to Fleshmarket Close across from his flat called to him like a siren song, beckoning him to the dark memories beyond.

Thirty painful and nerve-shredding minutes later, he had completed the journey back down the flights of stairs, crossed to the opposite side of the street and was heading through the opening of Fleshmarket Close. Soon he was into the open air of the close and approaching the same homeless man, asking a couple for spare change as they passed.

Danny shot the couple an awkward smile as they separated to allow him past.

He stood over the homeless man.

In the daylight, many more details about him were evident. The sleeping bag was rolled up and was being used as a back rest. A small home-made cross lay beside his upturned baseball cap in front of him. He was gaunt-faced and dishevelled and looked to be in his twenties with short greasy black hair, wearing a well-worn dark blue jumper.

"Awright, mate? Spare change please?" he asked as he squinted up at Danny.

"Do you remember me?" Danny asked.

"Eh, no mate."

"The other night my sister gave you some money as we passed you. I was wearing these clothes. My sister is short, has light blonde hair and was wearing a light grey fur coat."

"Sorry pal, I can't remember."

Danny studied him for a moment. His blank stare twinged with a sense of confusion, advertising his honesty.

He was probably drunk or high at the time.

As Danny turned away, the red vape pen sticking out of the man's pocket caught his attention.

"What's your name?"

"Tam."

"Tam, can I see that vape pen for a second?"

"Um, aye," Tam replied and fished out of his pocket and handed it to Danny.

"Oh God," Danny whispered.

On both sides of the vape pen, in silver swirling font, 'Aurelia' was engraved; a personalised gift Danny had presented to Aurelia not four months previously.

"Tam, I need to know. Where did you get this?" he asked. His voice was slow, soft, and nonthreatening. Belying the calmness of his exterior his heart was beating faster and a cold wave washed over him, making him shiver.

"Erm, I dunno."

"Tam, it's really important. You must have got it from somewhere."

"Honestly, I dunno."

"Tam this belongs to my sister!" he replied, this time more insistently, whilst holding the object by its end.

"Erm, I just found it on the ground next to me the other night. Can't remember how it got there. I think somebody gave it to me. I sometimes get fags and the likes, so I think someone gave me it."

"Who?" Danny persisted, his ire rising.

"I told you! I don't know!"

"Look mate, I know you were probably wasted that night," Danny replied through clenched teeth.

Tam frowned in offence.

"But she is missing, and you were the last person to see her. Now you have her vape pen. I'm not going to leave unless you tell me what I need to know!"

"Just fuck off, you prick!" Tam replied.

"No chance!" Danny replied, before making the mistake of accidentally knocking Tam's shin with one of his crutches.

Tam sprang to his feet and, with astonishing force, pushed Danny away.

Danny smacked off the opposite wall. A wave of pain racked him before his knee buckled and he landed on the ground. He screamed in pain with his knee caught under his body.

Tam grasped his possessions, including Aurelia's vape, and ran, taking with him Danny's hope. Danny grimaced and growled as he stumbled to his feet and propped a crutch under each arm.

You fucking idiot! Perfect. Just fucking perfect! Well done, Danny. You halfwit!

Danny headed home, dejected muttering escaping his lips.

CHAPTER 4

With a smile on her face, Mercy read the local newspaper and sipped her cappuccino. Humans always placed so much importance on the insignificant, convinced that anything they did meant anything at all. Each edition of the newspaper read like a macabre comedy of fools.

The doorbell rang, diverting her attention from her reading. By the time the bell rang for a second time, Mercy was down two flights of stairs and had her hand on the door handle. She opened it to see the welcoming smile of Franky.

"Awright, boss?" he asked.

"Come in," she replied and closed the door behind him.

They stood in her large, tiled kitchen. She had poured a fresh coffee for herself and one for Franky, whose legs were dangling from the large square, black marble-topped island worktop.

"Seems you were right about Thomas Briggs," Franky said.

"I thought so. My contact is never wrong. So, when can I expect to receive a final report on him?"

"Very soon," Franky replied. "You can wait, eh?" he added with a grin.

"Of course, it's not life and death," she replied with a smile of her own.

"Listen, uhh," Franky said before taking a deep breath and looking down at the mug in his hands, "I promised my people that we'd have a wee talk. It's about what I said a few weeks ago."

"Oh God, here we go," she said, her smile still in place.

"I'm serious, Mercy."

"OK, have your say," Mercy said as she took another gulp of coffee.

"Thanks," he said, his legs continuing to sway.

He cut a feeble figure, with dirty fingernails, hunched shoulders, and skeletal features borne from malnutrition rather than through genes.

"Like I said. I told my people that I would speak to you about the amount of people going missing."

"Aye," she admitted looking down.

"Is it your kind? Are there more in the city?"

"Aye. I should have kept a closer eye on them when they moved back to Edinburgh, but I've been... estranged from my kind for a very long time. I was glad to be away from all that."

"I get that, Mercy. But people are dying, and they can't help themselves," he said.

"I know. It's something about this nest. They've become more bloodthirsty. Most nests only kill enough to stay alive and strong. Any more and the human population get suspicious, and the nest needs to move on. The amount of hunting this nest has been doing shows incredible arrogance, and that's for a *vampire*. I know that something has to be done Franky, but I've told you my problem before."

"I know, I know. You cannae kill one of your own kind."

"It's the one unwritten rule we all follow. It's more than just a code of honour, it's much deeper than that," she said.

"Well, while yous are being all honourable, my people, you know, the network of homeless that you rely on, they're being fucking *slaughtered*."

"I know," she replied and shuffled on the spot.

"It's no just us they're targeting. Loads of folk have been going missing from some of the rougher areas of the city. Places the police doesnae give a shite about. They're no scum, Mercy. They're just poor. And they're being hunted like fucking animals."

"I know!" Mercy snapped.

"Then fucking do something about it!" Franky snapped back.

She glared at him and he glared right back. The ten second silence passed like an eternity.

"I'm working on it," she said, finally.

"Exactly *what* is it you're working on?" Franky asked, clearly intending to nail Mercy on the details.

"I've found someone. Someone who shows potential. Someone I can bring in and fight with us. Someone who will hunt the vampires. I saw him the same night we last spoke. He had been hit by a taxi."

"He cannae even cross a road? Aye, sounds like just the lad we need," Franky replied and shook his head.

"He had been chasing a vampire. Gabriel. That prick had hypnotised his woman. He saw her being attacked and still ran after them. The last time I saw someone rushing in to fight a vampire, it was 200 years ago. We need that kind of spirit."

"Sounds good, Mercy. But have you not thought that he was just drunk and didnae know that he was going after a vampire?"

"He knows what he saw. Whether his mind is ready to face the truth or not, he still ran to save his woman and attack Gabriel," Mercy replied.

"How did you first see him?" he asked.

"He had been hit by the taxi. He was bleeding on the street."

"Oh, for fuck's sake," he said, closing his eyes and shaking his head once more. "This guy sounds great, eh? How do you know he was even chasing this Gabriel bastard? He could have just staggered onto the road at the wrong time."

"Because!" Mercy snapped back. She took a deep breath and her increasing irritation eased. "Because he looked up at me and begged me to stop Gabriel from taking her. Like I said, he had been chasing Gabriel."

"Hmm," he replied, advertising his scepticism.

"I followed the ambulance to the Western. I followed them and got the name from the head nurse of the ward he was admitted to. His name is Danny. Danny Thomas."

"Our saviour's name is Danny-fucking-Thomas! We need a Max Thunderbolt. Maybe Axel Bullet. Fuck, I'd take a Jake Powers. No, we've got wee Danny Thomas, who cannae cross a fucking road without a lollypop lady to stop traffic for him. Well, let me give you this wee bit of advice: never trust a guy with two first names."

Mercy chuckled.

"Look, I've been watching Danny for the last couple of weeks now," Mercy continued. "The first thing he did when he signed himself out of the hospital, leg still fucked up, was to start snooping around the area where the attack happened. He's hunting Gabriel, he just doesn't know what he's up against. He went speaking to Tam McFarlane who sets up just off High Street."

"I havnae seen Tam in a while. How is he?"

"He's fine. Danny was interrogating Tam on what happened that night. Turns out Tam had a total blank," she said.

"What does that mean?" Franky asked.

"It means that Gabriel hypnotised him. I told Tam to set up elsewhere from now on, and not to go back there. I still check in on him. He's now down at the Vennel. He's doing OK."

"Good," Franky said with a sigh.

"But it shows that even with all the weirdness, and the stuff which doesn't make sense, the guy is still willing to act. True, the leg could be an issue, but I'll take whatever I can get."

"So, what's your plan?" he asked.

"I'm going to keep watching Danny for a while. He has been locked away in his house for a few weeks. If he re-emerges and continues to search, then I'll find a way of making contact and testing his resolve."

"Sounds like a shitey, half-arsed plan," Franky admitted.

"It's all about the execution," Mercy said and sipped her coffee. "I just need to watch him closely and wait. I visited him in hospital that night. He was still unconscious, but the nurse I spoke to gave me his details. If he *is* intent on finding either his woman or Gabriel, he'll make it clear."

"Well don't wait too long because this nest is killing a lot of people," Franky reminded her as he hopped off the worktop, left the coffee on the counter, and headed for the door. "Thanks for the coffee. I'll be in touch with my final report on Briggs. Get working on your Danny fella soon, Mercy, because something's going to have to give."

Mercy stared at her mug as the front door opened and slammed closed.

"Fuck!" she spat and dumped her coffee into the sink. "Danny, you better be worth it."

CHAPTER 5

The shadows had grown long as the sun had proceeded from east to west and was now setting beyond the buildings of the Royal Mile.

Danny sat on the wooden chair by the living room windows, staring at the locals and tourists passing by below, stopping only to glance at the entrance to Fleshmarket Close when someone passed through the opening of the close.

The homeless man who had been an unaware witness to Aurelia's last known moments had not appeared in the close since pushing Danny and running off, taking with him Danny's last lead.

The ticking of the wall clock in the kitchen echoed into the living room, displacing the silence in the room.

He produced his phone and highlighted the 'favourites' section of his phone book. He sighed as he pressed '1' and held it to his ear.

"Hello, Officer O'Donnell speaking."

"Hi Officer O'Donnell, Danny Thomas here."

"Hello, Mr Thomas. How can I help you?"

"Well, I haven't spoken to you in a couple of days, and so I was wondering if you had any updates?" Danny said.

"I'm afraid not. The people we have spoken to and our press release hasn't had the traction we had been hoping for."

"What about the homeless man I described to you?" Danny asked as he studied the creases in the palm of his hand.

"Well, using the description you gave us, we haven't been able to locate such a man. I understand that homeless people tend to stick to the one area. However, if he believes that he is in trouble, he may have moved to a different area of Edinburgh entirely, or perhaps moved to another city."

"So, no further forward then?"

"I'm afraid not, Mr Thomas."

Danny let out an involuntary hiss of disappointment.

"Well, thanks for your time, Officer."

"You're very welcome, Mr Thomas."

Danny pressed the disconnect button. He threw the mobile phone full force at the couch. The cushioning absorbed the impact and it fell onto the seat of the couch, undamaged.

Danny stared at the couch and then closed his eyes.

"Are you coming, Twatface?" Aurelia asked as she slumped into the couch with a bowl of popcorn in hand and her feet crossed on the coffee table. "I'm going to start the movie with or without you!" she said with a playful tone.

"Coming!" Danny replied, grabbing the freshly sliced pizza in one hand and two cans of beer in the other.

Placing the food on the table, he slumped down beside her as she pressed the play button on the remote.

They dined on cheap supermarket pizza and watched one of Aurelia's favourite and cheesiest movies. He leaned away from her and farted in her direction.

"Oh, for fuck's sake you complete twat!" she shouted, and slapped him across the back of his head.

Danny opened his eyes and smiled a pained smile.

"I won't find her sitting here," he muttered.

He glanced over at the corner of the living room, at the crutches he'd used. They now sported a fine layer of dust to match all the other surfaces of the flat.

He grabbed his walking cane and leant on it as he rose from the chair and passed the still full box of painkillers and unopened letter addressed to his doctor's practice. Beside them lay letters from the hospital consultant and physiotherapy department, both opened, but ignored. He opened his fridge and took out the pre-packed slices of cheese. They were half green, covered in mould.

He tutted and threw the pack at the swing bin. The lid clattered as it disappeared into the bin and the lid swung closed. He then lifted the lid of the three-day old takeaway pizza box, removed a slice of the half-finished pizza and swung the door shut with his cane. He feverishly consumed the slice and limped back to the wooden chair. In the last few weeks, the swelling and bruising on his knee had subsided significantly. As a result, the pain had decreased with it, however the weakness had remained, necessitating the use of a cane.

You can do this. Just man up. She needs you.

Looking out of the window once more, he nodded.

"Tonight."

11pm arrived.

The sun had set, and the city lights illuminated the Edinburgh cityscape in an array of yellow and white.

Danny opened the security door and left the building, the cool air rushing to greet him. He slowly walked up the short slope from the courtyard to the Royal Mile.

His first journey outdoors since the accident was more tiring than he expected. Unsure of where to go or what to do, he walked towards Cockburn Street and followed the winding corner down and to the left. He hobbled down the hill, a nervous smile affixed to his face.

The headlights of a passing car behind him illuminated the cobble stones.

He flinched to the side and stumbled against a shop window.

The car passed him and continued down the street and to the right, behind the building at the end of the street.

The hairs on his neck were standing on end. He panted. The sudden pain from his knee seared into his mind. A floating sensation overcame him as his head began to swim.

"Jesus. Get a grip, Danny!"

He took a few moments to compose himself.

Come on, Danny. You can do this!

His breathing and senses returned to normal, being replaced by a significant tension headache. He continued down the steep slope of the street. At its base, twenty yards away, in the entrance of another alley bathed in semi-darkness, a man had a woman pressed against a brick wall. His face, buried in her throat, her hand was pulling at his hair.

His heart began to pound once more as the hairs on his forearms stood to attention.

Fuck! Fuck! Fuck! You can do this Danny! You need to do this! You need to save the woman and question him about Aurelia. Just… just don't think about it.

He quickened his pace, as fast as his knee would allow, until he was just a few yards away. His body screamed to get away, but he continued towards his target.

You can do this!

He took a deep breath.

"GET THE FUCK AWAY FROM HER!"

He swung his cane hard. It connected with the jawline of the man who was turning around to face Danny.

"Oooof!" the man expelled as the cracking sound ricocheted up the steps of the alleyway.

The man hit the ground on his hands and knees.

"WHAT THE FUCK ARE YOU DOING?" the woman yelled. "Iain? Iain, are you OK, hun?" she asked as she stooped down and cradled him.

Iain grunted in return.

"I… I thought he was attacking you!" Danny protested.

"Are you daft? We were kissing! He's my boyfriend!"

"Ya fucking dick!" Iain said and then growled as he got to his feet.

"I'm sorry. I'm really sorry," Danny said.

Iain swung a punch which connected with Danny's cheekbone. The force staggered Danny and, as he took a step back, his knee buckled under him and he landed on his back. Iain rained fists down on him. For every blow which had very little force, there was one which hurt. A lot.

"Come on Iain, he's had enough!" the woman yelled and dragged him off Danny. Danny lay in the foetal position, his hands protecting his head.

Iain kicked him in the ribcage three times. Each one hurt more than the last.

The couple walked away, cursing. Danny's eye socket, both cheeks, and his lips were in pain. The bitter taste of copper filled his mouth. His lips pulsed hot and sore. His right ribs ached and made breathing a task. His knee ached more intensely than it had when he'd left hospital.

Dear God, please help! Please! I can't do this!

Mercy leaned on the flagpole at the centre of the tall, square bell tower of St John's Church on the western end of Princes Street as her untucked, long-sleeved denim shirt billowed slightly in the breeze. One of her favourite perches, the intricate carving of the bannisters and three spikes on each side allowed her to be hidden from view. This location allowed her to survey not only the entirety of the Princes Street Gardens, but also the Old Town leading up the hill to the historic Edinburgh Castle.

The yellow and white lights of the buildings still occupied, and the up-lighting of the many monuments and buildings of note, lent to a spectacularly illuminated nightscape, and the crowning focal point was the almost 1000-year-old Edinburgh Castle across the Princes Street Gardens.

Set atop jagged cliffs on three sides, the western defences of the castle complex were comprised of a number of outer perimeter defensive walls and attached bastions. Perfectly manicured lawns lay just within those western defensive walls at a staggered incline, offering a small, pleasant space in a dramatic edifice which had seen so much bloodshed throughout the centuries.

Mercy's smile disappeared as a small figure bounced along the castle's outermost perimeter wall 1000 feet away.

"Are you fucking kidding me?"

The figure, dressed in a pink tutu and black leather jacket danced along the lower wall of the castle's western defences. She pirouetted and jumped vertically another twenty feet to another bastion.

"Fucking halfwit!"

Mercy leapt onto the granite banister and, with a deep breath, she launched herself towards the figure, closing the distance in just a few seconds. Bracing herself for a crunching impact, she thrust her fists out in front of her.

A bone-cracking collision took place. Her target was sent sprawling backwards to the grassy hill and curled into a foetal position as she groaned.

Mercy landed on the wall her target had just been removed from, behind her was a steep and sudden cliff. She held her two badly broken hands in front of her face. Her wrists were misshapen and her fingers poked in unnatural directions.

"Fuck!" she whispered as she clamped her eyes shut and grimaced.

She forced her hands into fists once again. The bones popped and cracked back into position. She eased her fists as the bones knitted back together. The tension etched on her face eased and her breathing returned to normal. She jumped down from the wall, over the visitor handrail and onto the grass.

Lying in front of her, illuminated by the same lights which lit the grass and the castle, her target uncurled herself to show her ribs jutting at awkward angles. She grunted as she stretched her abdomen outwards. The ribs crunched back into place. She coughed, her breathing laboured.

"Rude much!" she shouted, then got to her feet.

"Hello Jessica," Mercy addressed her.

"Mercy, what the fuck was that for?"

"For your stupidity! What the hell do you think you are doing, jumping dozens of feet at a time and floating in the air?

And on the wall of the most heavily photographed landmark in the entire city! Any human could have seen you, and they all carry phones to record you doing it! It's asking to go viral!"

"What do you care?" Jessica asked.

"I care that we are not discovered by the humans! We've successfully kept ourselves within horror movies and airport novels because we *don't* pull stunts like that!"

"That's rich, coming from Edinburgh's *oldest* gargoyle! Tell me, what do you actually do on all those rooftops you kinky bitch?"

"I don't have time for your childish shite, Jessica. I have spent centuries practising how not to be seen anywhere I go. I wish you could say the same."

"Oh, for God's sake. Lighten up for once!" Jessica said with an exasperated expression.

"Look," Mercy said, closing her eyes and calming herself, "this isn't a playground for you to prance around in."

"That's exactly what it is! It's a playground where we can run, fly, and grab a bite to eat any time we want! You've just forgotten that," Jessica replied. "You've been living amongst the cattle for so long, you forgot that you are above them in every way. You should join me, Mercy. We could have so much fun in this city!"

"I'm not going to join another nest. Ever."

"No, I mean just us two! I know how you look at me," Jessica said with a smile and a wink.

"You can pack your fake flirty shite in. Just behave yourself, and don't go advertising us."

"And once again, Mercy decides to wallow in her lonesome, emo-goth phase. Seriously, doll, that look went with the death of Edgar Allan Poe. Start living a little!"

"You weren't even alive when Poe was going around. And I live just fine. But none of us will be living at all if our secret is revealed, and there are cameras *everywhere* these days," Mercy said. "One day you're going to get caught and there will be hell to pay for all of us."

Mercy stepped up onto the wall and turned around to face Jessica.

"Understand this: I don't care about you. I don't care about anyone. I only care about myself and what's good for *me*. If you fuck this up for me, you'll have me to deal with and you know how I treated rule-breakers."

A look of fear spread across Jessica's face.

"OK look," she said putting her palms up. "I know I wasn't here to see old-style 'angry Mercy', but just chill. You want me to stop prancing around, fine. Friends again?" Jessica asked with a hopeful smile.

"Just stop flouting your powers in public and stop targeting the poor and homeless. Try some rich people for a change. Or better yet, go on a fucking diet for a while," Mercy said, at which Jessica's smile disappeared.

Mercy shot into the air and was lost amongst the darkness.

CHAPTER 6

A week had passed since Danny had made his second mistake since leaving hospital and his face still displayed the marks of that mistake. He had darkened bruising around his left eye. His cheeks were tender to the touch and his bottom lip was still swollen. His ribs had thankfully improved and ached only mildly, and movement was still possible, knee allowing.

The sun had gone down and once more Danny was ready to leave the flat. He sat on the wooden chair next to the window, zipped up his jacket, and then proceeded to do what he had done every day of the last two months – stare out of the window at those passing below him on the Royal Mile and across to the entrance of Fleshmarket Close.

"Tonight I'll do it," he said. "Shat out of it these last few nights, but tonight I'll go out. How else am I going to find you?"

He rose from his seat, unsteady but with cane in hand, and left his flat. He slowly navigated the stairs down to the security door. He was light-headed. His dry lips smacked together as he took breath after breath. The tingling in his fingers competed with his sudden need to visit the bathroom.

Relax, Danny, relax. You can do this. It's all in your head. Just remember Aurelia. She's out there somewhere.

For hours, he walked up and down the length of the Royal Mile into the Cowgate area of the Old Town until his knee was in agony, his hip hurt, the muscles in his good leg were on fire from compensating for his bad knee, and the palm of his right hand ached from the constant pressure of taking his weight with each step.

He found himself in one of the many side streets just off the Royal Mile, passing another of the Old Town's discreet and foreboding alleyways, when the voice reached him.

"Come with me. I will drink you dry and your life will have served a purpose," the masculine and earthy voice echoed up the steps and into Danny's ears.

He turned to his left and followed the voice towards the close. His fear told him to run away but his determination and a strange, dislocated bravery spurred him on.

He poked his head around the corner of the building. Twenty yards away, a man with short blonde hair, a leather biker jacket and jeans held another man up against a wall by the throat. The victim stood still and did not fight back.

Right, be silent. Don't allow him to become aware of you until it's too late.

He crept towards them, lightening his stance, conscious of the subtle clacking of the cane off the pavement.

When he was a mere five feet away, the blonde man spoke once more without taking his eyes from the man pressed against the wall.

"Well, it seems we have a hero in our midst, and he is about to make the worst decision of his short little life."

Danny stepped forward and swung his cane. With a smack, it landed with ferocity on the blonde man's neck. The man did not move. He did not flinch, express pain or even the slightest discomfort. He merely released his victim. The victim did not run, show fear or emotion of any kind; he stood with a blank expression, staring back at his assailant.

The blonde man turned around to face Danny. He smiled warmly.

"Who am I to argue when an opportunity for a two-course meal presents itself?"

His smiled widened. His upper and lower canine teeth were noticeably longer than the others. With the exception of his dilated pupils, his eyes were pure white. Two black orbs set against marble white stared back at him.

"Fucking hell!" Danny said, his eyes wide, his mouth slack. He took a step back, and then another. "No! You can't be real! You can't be!"

With a swift movement faster than Danny's eyes could track, the vampire charged Danny. With one hand, the stranger pushed Danny with such force he tumbled through the air, hitting the wall seven feet away and crumpling onto the ground.

Danny scrambled for air, but his lungs would not allow it.

The vampire leaned over him, the smile still affixed to his demonic face.

"I respect your bravery but pity your foolishness. Now, relax. This will be over soon."

A strange, warm, fuzzy sensation pressed on Danny's mind. Oxygen filled his lungs and his limbs went limp. There was no fear or resistance, just absolute obedience to every word the man spoke.

He leaned into Danny's neck.

"Enough," a stern female voice announced itself from behind the blonde man. "Didn't your mother teach you manners?"

"I barely remembered my mother's lessons before I returned home and ate her," he replied and smiled once more.

He stood up and turned around.

"Hello Mercy," he addressed her.

"Malcolm," she replied.

"I don't mean to be rude, but you interrupted me right in the middle of dinner and I'm not really the type who shares his food."

Danny's calmness wore off and his anger and fear returned. His limbs began to gain strength.

"Not that one," Mercy said whilst still beyond Danny's peripheral vision. "I've been watching him for some time. When the time is right, I'll feast. Until then, he is off limits. Do not make the mistake of testing my resolve on this."

"Well, I wouldn't dare mess with the great Mercy the

Executioner. Fine," Malcolm replied with a tone of irritated resignation. "I don't really like lame ones anyway. They taste… off."

The man against the wall blinked and a look of terror spread across his face.

"Uhh! Uhhh!" he stammered. "Fuck! Fuck! HELP!" The man made to run but Malcolm had already returned to him and knocked him on the side of the head with a backhand. The man fell to the ground, unconscious.

"Perfect! Now I've lost my appetite entirely! You have become a party pooper in your old age, Mercy," Malcolm said, before he bent his knees and took to the air, disappearing over the roof of the nearby building.

"Jesus! He flew! He… he flew over the roof!" Danny stammered, his eyes fixed on the roof.

"Yeah," Mercy answered.

She stepped in front of Danny, then bent down until their faces were no more than a foot apart.

"It's you," Danny whispered.

"It's me," she replied.

Now Danny had a name for the woman who'd surveyed his helpless form when he lay in front of the taxi headlights – Mercy. Her eyes were also just two black orbs surrounded by the bone white of her eyeballs, matching the paleness of her skin. Her canines were also twice the length of her other teeth.

She looked at Danny with the same hunger that Malcolm had just seconds before.

"Where is Aurelia?" he asked.

Mercy leaned back with an expression of shock. Her canines retracted and her pupils shrunk back down to a normal size, revealing piercing light blue irises.

"What did you all do to her?"

"Jesus! Are you OK, hen?" a male voice called out.

Danny and Mercy slowly turned their heads in its direction.

A hipster-type in his early twenties stood next to the road, peering at them.

Mercy stood up and approached Malcolm's victim, who was slowly coming to on the ground.

"Come here, I need help," she replied.

The hipster trotted over to her.

"Help him up," she commanded.

"C'mere mate. You're alright," the hipster reassured Malcolm's victim and helped him to his feet.

Danny slowly and painfully got to his feet. He grabbed his cane and stumbled over to them.

Malcolm's victim rubbed his head and grimaced.

"OK, you two look at me," Mercy announced whilst facing both men, her back to Danny. "Both of you, count to twenty in your heads. When you reach twenty you will forget what you just experienced here. You will both go home, feeling warm and happy and you will sleep well tonight."

Mercy then walked away in the direction of North Bridge.

Both men continued to stand, staring directly ahead with vacant expressions.

"Wait up!" Danny said, and made after her.

"What do you want? Is saving your life not enough?" she asked.

"You're a vampire, aren't you?"

At that, Mercy stopped and turned to a breathless Danny.

"Don't tell me to go home. I want to know what happened to Aurelia," he said as she opened her mouth to speak.

Mercy sighed and continued walking with Danny in tow.

The hipster and Malcolm's uneaten meal began to blink. Their vacant expressions were replaced with ones of confusion. They exchanged awkward smiles, then walked off in separate directions, Malcolm's uneaten meal rubbing his head tenderly.

Danny and Mercy sat in plastic seats across from one other at a table in a late-night fried chicken fast food restaurant. After exchanging names, they had not spoken again.

Under the strip lighting of the restaurant Danny studied

Mercy's appearance for the first time. She was 5'10" tall but appeared taller with the one-inch heel on her leather ankle boots. She had a slender, almost athletic figure but had broader than average shoulders. She wore a light pink T-shirt with multicoloured butterfly prints on the front and a medium blue denim jacket with embroidered sequins across most of the back in a large daisy pattern.

Her skin wasn't quite as pale as it had been in the headlights of the car, however it still maintained a smooth alabaster hue, offset by her vibrant blood-red lipstick. Her long wavy brown hair was pulled into a loose, half-up half-down ponytail, and the rest of her free hair fell in natural waves over her shoulders and midway down her back.

Mercy casually nibbled at the fries in a greaseproof paper bag, whilst Danny toyed with his chicken burger. Finally, she spoke.

"I treated you to your meal. Are you not going to eat it?"

"Um, yeah, thanks. I'm just surprised that you can eat normal food."

"Of course I can eat normal food," she replied whilst chewing on another fry.

"I just figured that your kind only drank blood."

"We drink blood to survive. Our bodies need it, but we can eat and drink whatever we like for enjoyment."

"So is it only human blood you can drink, or…"

"This isn't a question-and-answer session, Cripple," she interrupted. "I bought you food to get your blood sugar up, but I'm not interested in telling you anything about us. You already know more than you should. The simple fact that you are aware that we exist is enough to get you killed. The only reason Malcolm allowed you to live is because I lied and claimed you for my own. Now don't push your luck or I *will* eat you."

Danny studied her face. It was impossible to tell whether she was bluffing.

"Fine, tell me what you know about what happened to Aurelia," he said.

Mercy stopped chewing and swallowed as she stared back at him.

"I know that you saw what happened. The man attacking her, deep down I knew what he was. He was a vampire. The way he bit into her neck. My rational mind doesn't allow for things like vampires, but when I saw him with her, and how he bit into her neck, I knew deep down what he was," he said.

Mercy smiled.

"I was right. It wasn't Dutch courage," she muttered.

"Sorry?" Danny asked.

"Never mind," she replied.

"Anyway," Danny continued. "In that instant, it all made sense, you know? The amount of people disappearing in the city. Him being able to disappear in the middle of a close. I mean, I didn't stop to think about it, I just ran to save Aurelia. But the taxi came from nowhere, hit me, and allowed him to escape with her. I just didn't understand how she was willing to leave with him, but given how both you and Malcolm were able to just talk to us and get us to do things, it makes sense now. Is it like hypnotism?"

Mercy studied him for a few seconds before sighing and rolling her eyes.

"Kind of," she replied. "Only it's much more powerful. Hypnotism is only suggestion when putting a human into such a vulnerable state. We can do it immediately and no one can fight it. Now enough questions about us and eat your food, human."

"Fine, was it a vampire who attacked Aurelia?"

"She was your, what... wife? Girlfriend?"

"Sister," Danny corrected her.

"Well, I hope you have other siblings because you're never going to see her again," she replied with a smile.

Danny screwed his face up in distaste.

"What?"

"Are you trying to be a cunt on purpose?" he asked.

"No, I just don't care what you think. I'm not trying to be

your friend. I couldn't care less whether you live or die, Cripple," she admitted and shrugged.

"That's a lie. If you truly didn't care, you wouldn't care about my blood sugar levels. Now, what was the vampire's name?" he asked.

"Who attacked your sister? Gabriel."

"Gabriel? Sounds like a twat," Danny said.

"Aye, he's a *colossal* twat. Look, I'm sorry about what happened to your sister, but you need to find a way of moving on."

"How can I move on when she's still out there?" he asked.

"She's *not* out there, Cripple. She's dead. You said it yourself; you knew it was a vampire. Sometimes they kill their prey right then and there, and sometimes they bite their victim to subdue them then fly them away to finish them off somewhere else. But the outcome is still the same. Her body is most likely weighted down, out there in the Firth of Forth. Or if Gabriel is being extra careful, he will have dumped her out in the North Sea, off the coast."

"I can't believe that. I have to believe that she is still alive."

Mercy shook her head and closed her eyes.

"Trust me, you'll just end up driving yourself mad. Let it go."

"No!" Danny replied, anger blazing in his eyes. "You didn't see the look in his eyes, Mercy! You didn't see her blood dripping out of his mouth as he smiled back at me. He walked away with her as I lay there helpless. She might still be alive, I just need to keep looking!"

"Cripple!" Mercy raised her voice, causing the four teens sitting at the table next to them to take interest in the conversation. "She's dead! That's the end of it. Move on!"

"Here mate, did you kill your bird?" one of them asked Danny whilst the others giggled.

"You'll either go insane, spending each night looking for a woman you'll never see again, or you might get unlucky and meet a vampire who kills you," Mercy said with her tone softer than usual.

"Wait, are you saying that there are vampires? Yous are a pair of freaks!" the teen added as he continued to eavesdrop on the conversation, much to the delight of his friends.

"Alright, look at me, all four of you," Mercy said as she leaned towards their table. Soon all four sets of eyes were locked on hers.

"You're going to sit there in absolute silence. You won't eat, you won't drink. You'll sit, staring ahead, like statues. When I leave, you'll forget you saw or spoke to us. Then you'll all shit yourselves."

All four teens sat rigid, looking directly ahead, like mannequins.

"Look," Mercy addressed Danny as she got out of her seat and checked the pockets of her jacket. "I'm sorry about what happened to her, and for what happened to you," she added, looking at his cane, "but the best thing you can do is just move on. Grieve. Hate the world for a while. Shag someone to take your mind off it. Speak to a doctor. Develop a drug habit. Whatever it takes for you to sort out your feelings."

She left the table.

Danny hurriedly grabbed his cane and followed her.

"Wait!" he called after her. He barged in front of her, blocking her path just outside the restaurant.

Inside, the teens unfroze, then scrambled in the direction of the public toilet.

"I'm going to find this Gabriel and when I do, I'm going to find out where Aurelia is, and I'm going to kill him."

Mercy snorted in derision at Danny's determination.

"Aye, good luck with that!"

"Don't mock me! I'm going to find him and I'm going to fucking kill him, and when I do, you'll regret ever doubting me!"

Danny stormed off. His knee screamed in pain. He was exhausted, but his mind was a riot. In addition to the realisation of the existence of vampires, he had a target, Gabriel, and Danny was going to hunt him down.

CHAPTER 7

Danny studied the carnage of the broken-down wooden chair in the corner of the living room, next to his disused crutches. He sat on his only other remaining intact wooden chair in his usual spot, looking onto the Royal Mile.

In one hand he held his kitchen knife. In the other, he held a sharpened twelve-inch section of chair leg. He thumbed the end of the stake and tutted.

"Not sharp enough," he muttered and continued whittling the end of the stake into a sharper point.

The chance meeting with Mercy the previous night had not left his mind since he awoke. Now, he was set on finding Gabriel with a sharpened portion of furniture and a fading memory of his face.

His stomach growled. It was 4pm, but he hadn't yet eaten. He limped over to the kitchen and peered inside the fridge.

Great. Ketchup and mouldy bread. Just bloody perfect.

He slammed the fridge door shut, fetched his trainers and bomber jacket. He slid the wooden stake into the inside pocket of the jacket. It fit snugly without bulging the lining of the jacket.

"Sandwich from the supermarket, then I may as well just stay out and scout the area before it gets dark in a couple of hours."

He grabbed his cane and left the flat.

When he stepped onto the Royal Mile, Mercy's voice sounded behind him.

"Hey, Cripple."

Danny turned to see her approaching.

"Are you stalking me?"

"Pal, I've been stalking you since that taxi tried to have sex with you."

Mercy was wearing her usual jacket, but her eyes were hidden behind thick oversized sunglasses, despite it being overcast. Her skin was clammy and her shoulders were slumped.

"What do you want?"

"I want to know if you were serious about what you said last night. About hunting and killing a vampire."

"Of course I was," he replied and hobbled closer to her.

Mercy continued to smile, but frowned as he approached her.

"Ease up, tiger. Are you trying to sell me drugs?"

Danny unzipped his jacket and showed her the tip of the wooden stake he had spent all day preparing.

Mercy lifted her sunglasses, exposing large dark, tired rings under her eyes. She peered inside his jacket.

"Awww, that's so precious!" Mercy said, mocking him as she lowered her sunglasses once more. "Yeah, I'm sure you'll kill vampires with that thing! *All* the vampires!"

"You don't have to be a total dick all the time!" Danny said.

"I know, but it's fun," she replied as she turned and walked away. "Come on Cripple, keep up."

"But I was going to go eat," Danny replied, pointing back at the supermarket entrance.

"Then go eat," Mercy replied, still walking at a brisk pace.

"Fuck!" he whispered and set off after her.

Keeping up with her was challenging and before long his knee and hip were aching and he was reliant on his cane with every step.

Without warning, she ducked into a small family cafe, selling all manner of cakes, sandwiches, and treats, with half a dozen tables and chairs

Soon they were sitting at the table furthest from the

counter, which offered the most privacy, with sandwiches, carrot cakes and two cappuccinos between them.

"Right," she started with a sigh. "Go ahead. Ask your questions," she added as she massaged her temples, before lifting a chicken salad sandwich and taking a bite.

"Umm, right. Jesus, where to start?" Danny said. "Umm, so how many vampires are there?"

"Not a lot. There's only me and one nest in Edinburgh. Eight of them, which is a fairly large nest. Let me get you started. There's not exactly a massive amount of us. And no, we don't rule the world. There's no cabal of vampires entrenched in government, not that I know of anyway. Most vampires are hedonistic arseholes. They're too busy indulging their pleasures to be planning world domination."

"And are you in the Edinburgh nest?" he asked, taking a mouthful of his BLT.

"No. I don't belong to any nests. I'm on my own. I like it that way."

"I take it you don't live under any bridges or in caves. So, how do you pay bills?"

"Seriously?" Mercy asked with a smile. "You have the chance to ask a real vampire absolutely anything and you ask her which electricity provider she's with? How hard did you hit your head on the cobble stones that night?"

"Ummm," he said, suddenly realising how silly the question was. "OK, some of the more basic questions. How many of the legends are true?"

"Most are nonsense and others have a grain of truth to them but have been massively overdramatized."

"I guess sunlight doesn't work on you?"

"Sunlight is an example of something with an element of truth becoming exaggerated. We can go out in daylight but it leaves us very weakened and drained, and our powers are gone. We're probably weaker than humans. Think of it like when you get the flu. That's how weak and ill we feel. I can just about manage to hypnotise humans but even that is a drain; the rest of my powers are gone. Only the oldest vampires can get our powers to work during the day."

"That's why you look like shit now," Danny added.

"Fucking charmer, you are. But yeah. That's why vampires only go out at night. It's when we are at our most powerful. Myth and legend has turned that truth into vampires bursting into fire in daylight."

"But you go out because?"

"All of my business is done with humans and so it is conducted during the day. Meetings and such. Like I said, I'm not like other vampires."

"So, what powers do vampires have?" he asked whilst sipping from his cup.

"Let's see," she replied. "Well, we are immortal. We don't age. We are much stronger and faster than any human. Oh, and we can fly. You saw that twat Malcolm fly last night."

"Yeah, my brain was exploding all last night."

"I'll bet. What else? We don't need to sleep in coffins, nor do we need human or animal familiars. We're invulnerable to garlic, silver, crosses, holy water, wooden stakes. Oh, and older vampires develop other powers."

"Such as?" he prompted her.

"Such as telepathy."

"You mean mind reading?"

"Yeah," she replied. "Also, a rudimentary clairvoyance, although only the most powerful vampires have that power. The older you get, the more powerful you become."

"I saw both you and Malcolm hypnotise people though," he said.

"Yeah, that is our main strength and our first natural weapon. We hypnotise people, easily and naturally. Like any predator, we don't like to work for our meal. We can lure our victims in, or we can make witnesses forget we were ever there."

"What about mir—" Danny began. Mercy had produced a pocket mirror and was reapplying her lipstick. She froze and looked up at him. "Never mind," he said.

They sat in silence as they ate and drank. Danny finished his sandwich while he processed what he'd discovered and Mercy allowed him to digest this new information.

"OK," Danny said, breaking the silence. "What about weaknesses? I need to know how to hunt and kill them."

"Now we're getting somewhere," she said with a smile.

"So, you need blood to survive. Is it only human blood?"

"I feed off animals," Mercy said, shuffling in her seat.

"So, it's a choice. The nest chooses to feed off people," Danny affirmed, nodding, but looking down at the table.

"We all have a choice in what and who we eat. Vampires are no different," Mercy said.

"What other weaknesses?" Danny asked.

"Well stakes to the heart work just fine, but it depends on what the stake is made of."

"That's why you laughed at the wooden stake," Danny replied, lamenting having needlessly ruined one of only two good chairs he had.

"Exactly."

"So, what does the stake need to be made of then?"

"Tiger's eye," Mercy replied, taking a sip of coffee.

"Tiger's what?" Danny asked, before producing his phone.

"Tiger's eye. It's a gem stone crystal," Mercy said and took another drink.

A cursory search on his phone produced a number of photos. Each of the shapes and sizes of tiger's eye displayed differed, but they all bore the same qualities: dark brown colouring with streaks of light brown or golden amber.

"Interesting," Danny said. "Pictures of unpolished tiger's eye looks like…"

"Wood," Mercy finished for him.

"Exactly. Sharpen it into a point and it would look like a wooden stake," he said.

"Any that's the whole point," she replied. "A grain of truth which gets distorted and exaggerated. And vampires are happy for such a distortion to continue, knowing that the most famous weapon against them, the wooden stake, is actually completely useless."

"So why does tiger's eye work?" he asked.

"I haven't a clue. Is it an allergy? With it being a crystal gem stone, is it something ethereal or mystical? Haven't a clue, and I don't think vampires know either," she said before taking another bite of her sandwich.

"What else do I need to know?" he asked.

"Vampires' biggest weakness is their arrogance. They are elitist snobs. They party with high society at night, but they ultimately view humans as cattle. They target and prey on the weakest in society, impoverished areas of the city or the homeless population. People who will go missing and the police won't even bother investigating."

"Bastards. Do they have no soul?"

"Oh, we have a soul, at least I think. However our longevity, our thirst, our being divorced from the human condition for so long, combined with our natural killer instinct, means that we very quickly lose our humanity. We become... cold and uncaring. It's hard to keep that part of you alive when your base instinct trains you to look at humans as food and nothing more," Mercy said with a pained look.

"So, they just target the very weakest in society? For all their power, they just sound like cowards. Parasites," he said, displaying naked contempt.

"You have to think of it like nature. When a lioness hunts, she doesn't choose the strongest member of the herd. She looks for the weakest. The one which is easiest to kill and will not fight back. It's like that with us. I'm not saying that it's right. Vampires don't live by human notions of right and wrong. It's just... smart."

"So how is their natural predator instinct, as well as their smartness, their biggest weakness then?"

"Because they always underestimate humans. Vampires may be super strong and super-fast, but it doesn't give them super-intelligence. They can be just as stupid as any human.

They are so elitist, so superior that they can be caught off guard by one willing and *able* to fight back. As a result, they toy with their victims. I've seen it countless times. They are used to humans being prey and nothing more. They are always in hunter mode. They are never in hunted mode."

"And that's where I come in," Danny said.

"Exactly, and you won't be completely alone. Speaking of which, a friend is here now," she replied.

There were six other people in the cafe, and no one was approaching them.

The door jangled open and a bedraggled man stepped inside. With well-worn clothing and an unkept appearance, others in the cafe stared at him. He spotted Mercy and took the seat next to Danny.

"Awright pal? I'm Franky," he said and held his hand out to shake.

"Danny," Danny replied and shook his hand.

The stench of stale, unwashed clothing and greasy hair wafted up Danny's nostrils.

Danny sat upright and shuffled slightly away from him.

"What do you have for me?" Mercy asked.

"Right. So, Thomas Briggs. Here's what I've got," Franky replied, producing from under his jacket a few crumpled sheets of paper and handing them to Mercy. Danny studied Franky; his fingers were discoloured and dirt was caked under his fingernails.

"Is this accurate? When was the last time this was updated?" she asked.

"Last night. I checked myself," Franky replied.

"Very good," she replied as she studied the papers. "Right. New task for you and your contacts," she said looking up from the papers and producing a small cardboard folder from her inside jacket pocket and handed it to Franky. "There's no perfect way of doing this, but we need an in to this nest."

Franky opened the folder and produced eight photos.

"This is who you're looking for, right here," she said,

pointing to one of the photos.

"He's a handsome devil," Franky said with a grin.

"His name is Gabriel. That's your primary target."

"*This* is Gabriel? *The* Gabriel?" Franky asked.

At the mention of Gabriel's name, a shiver ran up Danny's spine.

"Aye. But I suspect you will have trouble finding him," Mercy continued. "So I want you to study the other seven faces. Their names are written on the back of the photos. I have plenty of copies for your people if you need. If you see one of them, *any* of them, I want you to study them and report back."

"Fair enough," Franky said, studying each of the faces in turn.

"I want you to follow him and report. I want to know where he or she goes, who they visit, where they party. Everything you can. But tell your people not to go near any of them. Remember, they're all my kind, so *very* dangerous. Strictly observe and report. We're on a tight time scale here, so report back quick. I can start you off with Bohemia Bar across from Waverley Station. We last spotted Gabriel there. If you see Gabriel, then fantastic, but any of the others will do."

"Got it. Usual payment?" he asked.

"Triple," Mercy replied. "Like I said, this one involves a fair amount of risk, and speed is of the essence. Seriously, I need a report within the week. So triple pay. However, it is important that you tell them not to go near him under any circumstances."

"Aye, no problem. Right, see you soon then. Nice meeting you Danny," Franky stated with a smile as he got out of his seat and left the restaurant.

Danny smiled awkwardly, but remained silent.

"Why did you think that Franky might have problems with Gabriel? Why does he need to look for any others? Gabriel is the one we want," Danny said.

"Because the leaders keep themselves well hidden. Frankly it was a stroke of incredibly bad luck that you ran into him. The other vampires of a nest will often protect their leader, making the leader harder to get to. That's why we need an in. Any of the vampires will do, and Franky is the lad to find us that in."

"So, you have your own network of... what? Informants?" he asked.

"Informants, spies, workers, whatever you want to call them. And I have them in all sorts of places and in all sorts of professions. They find out information for me whenever I need it."

"What kind of information?"

"All kinds," she replied with a wry smile. "Look, I'm offering to train you to fight and kill vampires. Are you in?"

Danny pawed at his now-empty coffee cup.

Something's off here.

"Why don't *you* just kill them? You know how to do it. You have the strength that I don't. You have two working legs. And what did Malcolm call you? 'Mercy the Executioner'?"

"Because this is not my battle. You take care of your own. You bury your own. You avenge your own," she replied.

"No, that's not it. I'm not buying that," Danny replied.

"Fine, there's only one rule in the vampire world. The one that human stories get right: you never kill your own kind. It's the unforgivable crime. We just can't do it. Besides, do you really want someone else killing Gabriel for you? Or do you want to be the one who takes him out, and see the shock, fear, and regret in his eyes before he goes?"

"Yeah, you're right. I do," Danny admitted. "But why do you want to kill your own kind in the first place?"

"Because of the type of people they target. They are killing the network of informants and contacts I have spent years building. It's bad business for me. Plus, you've seen the newspaper headlines about the amount of people missing. If humans start to suspect that vampires are actually real, it will have profound implications for me. So it's best all round for everyone if Gabriel and his nest are dead. And you need Gabriel dead as retribution for killing your sister."

"Yeah, I do."

"Then forget hunting tonight. Meet me here next Tuesday," she said and slid a small card with an address on it across the table.

"Next Tuesday! That's over a week away! Why wait? I want to hunt Gabriel tonight!" Danny responded with a voice raised enough that the others looked over at him.

"Would you like to say that any louder?" she asked. "Nothing is going to happen before then. You must have patience. Look, you can be smart, have some patience, let some of my plans mature, then meet me at my business at 10pm next Tuesday. If you must go out to hunt tonight, just don't expect me to save your arse again. And you can leave the tooth pick at home, it won't do you any good," she stated with a smile before leaving the restaurant.

Danny stared at the card in front of him as he shook his head.

"A vampire with a business card," he said with a smile.

CHAPTER 8

Mercy scrolled through the offers for her latest piece. The most likely buyer was the Japanese government. They would almost certainly outbid even the richest of collectors. In Mercy's possession was a genuine Masamune katana sword circa 1300.

Japan's greatest ever swordsmith, Masamune's swords were renowned for their beauty, strength, and quality of workmanship. He rarely ever signed his swords, however the one in Mercy's collection was signed, and despite its age was in perfect condition. She'd submitted it to the Kyoto National Museum for appraisal and authentication and they confirmed it as a Masamune. Now the collecting world was ablaze.

Set for auction, the latest artefact was to be sold by Mercy to ensure that her business would be profitable for many years to come. The only one question left was exactly how many millions it would sell for. Rumours online had it set to sell for even more than Napoleon Bonaparte's sword.

Emails from collectors asking for her to name a price before it went to auction were landing in her inbox by the dozen. Her stock answer was '*Bid at the auction and stop bothering me, you chancer*'.

There were occasions when Mercy owned an artefact of great value, only to be contacted by a family member who could conclusively and irrefutably claim that it was a family heirloom. It was not uncommon for Mercy to have an uncharacteristic bout of sentimentality and gift it to a stunned, and forever grateful, descendent. But this sword was not such an occasion. Especially when it had been a gift for her.

Almost two centuries ago, she spent some time in Japan. By sheer chance, she stumbled upon a nobleman's family being attacked by a rival nobleman and intervened in a brutal and decisive manner. She had been there to save the nobleman's family and bloodline. As thanks, he gifted her his most prized possession: a Gorō Nyūdō Masamune katana sword and sheath.

She wheeled her chair backwards, to reveal a long, narrow metal flight box sitting on the floor at her feet. She placed the box on top of the desk. With a sigh she lifted the clasps and unlocked the box.

"One last look. For old time's sake."

She lifted the lid. Wedged in black protective foam, and wrapped in white silken fabric, was Masamune's katana, lying beside the scabbard.

She unwrapped the fabric and lifted the handle, laying the still razor-sharp blade flat on the palm of her hand. Truly a masterpiece. It bore a black handle with gold diamond-shaped ornamentation up to a golden guard. The curved blade itself was flawless, with no chips or indents. Silver in colour, it had a long black line running the length of the blade. The accompanying scabbard was black with silver detailing.

The Japanese government would deposit it in a museum and remove the handle to expose the base of the blade and Masamune's all too rare signature.

"This is probably the last time you'll be in one piece. Shame really."

Her fingers caressed the bumps and contours of the perfect wrapped handle.

In her mind, the rustling of leaves from the rows of cherry blossom trees set her at peace, the cherry blossoms coating the ground in a carpet of pink petals. The peacefulness of the forests through which she would travel. The pungent agarwood incense burning in the houses she would visit. The curious expressions from locals to see a white European girl travelling alone through their towns and villages. Learning the delicate beauty of Hanami, the tradition of admiring and loving the temporary beauty of short-flowering trees, and also the fragility of time; an alien concept to an immortal being.

"Good times," she whispered with a smile.

"Mercy?" Abigail announced herself as she entered the open door of the office.

"Hmm?" Mercy responded as she looked up from the sword.

"There's a woman here to see you. She said that she has an appointment. Her name is Margaret Duffy."

"Oh yeah, I told her that I would be here this afternoon so I told her to stop by. Bring her in," Mercy replied with a smile.

Abigail, the front desk secretary, smiled in response and disappeared.

Mercy rewrapped the sword, placed it back into its protective case and sat it on the floor once again.

A few moments later the familiar face of Margaret with her ruddy cheeks appeared.

"Hiya Mercy!" she said as she entered and sat on the chair across from Mercy.

"Hi Margaret, how are you doing?"

"I'm good thank you! I'm surprised that you asked me to come here. I've known you for a few years now and this is the first time I've ever seen your business!" Margaret said as she surveyed the bland features of the office.

"Well, I've been out of town for a few days and this was the best time for me to see you, because I have someone coming in later. How can I help you, Margaret?"

"Thanks for seeing me. It's just to discuss the amount of missing people in Edinburgh these days."

"I know, we've spoken about this before, Margaret," Mercy replied, drumming her long fingernails on her desk.

"I know we have, but it's just getting worse. More importantly, they all seem to be from the Pilton, Granton, and Muirhouse areas lately."

"So I've heard."

"I don't think it's any coincidence that these people all live in predominantly poor areas," Margaret said.

"It's not," Mercy replied. "These people are being targeted because they tend to keep their own issues in-house. Politicians don't care about them, and so why should they receive public spending? The police don't work quite as hard as they do in other, more affluent areas. It makes these people easy targets and the police aren't going to investigate their disappearances too hard."

"I service that area. I care about those people, Mercy."

"I know you do, Margaret," Mercy replied, looking down at the corner of her open laptop.

"I've spoken to the police, local councillors, and I keep hitting a brick wall. I don't even know where to start," Margaret continued. Her voice was becoming thready and the sound of her heartbeat was quickening in Mercy's ears.

"Margaret..." Mercy began.

"You've helped me out with things in the past. You've helped me with people the police wouldn't dare touch. I've never asked about your methods, and I don't want to know now..."

"Margaret."

"But this can't continue! I met a twenty-year-old mum by the name of Hannah yesterday. Her doctor referred her to Social Services and her file was sent to me."

"Margaret!" Mercy attempted to interrupt, this time with a raised voice, but it was no good.

"Her husband has gone missing. Hannah has been left to care for her one-year-old."

"And you don't think he just ran off?" Mercy asked.

"The police think that the husband took off, but Hannah knows that John wouldn't be the kind to do that. They were happy together."

"Did the police not think to link this case to all the other missing cases?" Mercy asked.

"No! They just don't care."

"They're not going to find him," Mercy said with little more than a mumble.

"You know something about this, don't you?" Margaret asked.

"Not directly, no. But all these missing people cases are connected," Mercy replied, looking at her laptop screen.

"Mercy, I need your help to sort this out. I honestly don't know the proper number of missing people because it's hard to know who has done a moonlight flit and who has actually gone missing. The numbers could be huge."

"I've heard the same thing from people in the homeless community," Mercy said as she clasped her hands in front of her mouth and closed her eyes and began to slowly swing left to right on her chair.

Gabriel, why won't you keep your animals in line?

"Like I said, I need you to find a way of stopping this. I had to do a lot of soul searching before we started working together because I know you do bad things."

"Would you shut the fuck up?" Mercy replied in a low tone.

Margaret immediately silenced herself, instead, choosing to sit meekly.

"I told you last time that I was on top of it. I am."

"I know that you know who is responsible," Margaret replied.

"I..." Mercy began to protest her innocence. However, Margaret carried on speaking.
"And for the life of me, I don't know why you don't just go to the police. But either way, you need to do something. Or I will."

Mercy's stare caused Margaret to shiver in her seat and clear her throat.

"Margaret, I do not like to be threatened. I don't know what you are thinking of doing but I strongly suggest you think again."

"Mercy, I'll go to the police. I'll tell them everything I know. The names I gave to you."

"Margaret, calm yourself."

"I don't even care that they'll lock me up. I thought it was all for the greater good, but—"

Mercy slammed the palm of her hand onto her table. Margaret recoiled, the shock silencing her.

"Margaret, I swear that those responsible for the missing people will be held to account. I've even recruited someone who I believe will be the answer to your prayers."

"Great, fantastic!" Margaret said.

"Although I don't yet know if he has the stomach or the motivation for it."

"Is there anything I can do to help?" Margaret asked.

"I can tell that your morals sometimes upset you. What gave you the motivation to come to me and ask the things you do?"

"Anger. Anger and frustration. You?" Margaret replied.

"The same. It was a long time ago now, but pretty much the same. Anger."

"Then perhaps that's your answer," Margaret said as she stood up and walked towards the door. "If you doubt this person, make them angry and see if their anger can be the motivation that they need." Margaret opened the door and went to close it behind her. "But let's hope that this works, because if people keep disappearing, I'll be going to the police and telling them everything."

She closed the door, leaving Mercy alone in the silent office one more.

Mercy stared straight ahead for a few seconds before throwing a pen at the door. It embedded itself in the door with a loud thud.

"Fuck!" she whispered and sprang out of her chair. She paced back and forth, along the short length of the cramped square office.

It would be so much easier just to hypnotise her into staying silent.

"Fuck me and my bloody morals. Gabriel would just get rid of her if she threatened him. I'm too bloody soft," she said as she continued to pace the length of the room.

What the fuck do I do? If I go up against Gabriel and his nest, I'm fucked. Even If I survive against them, the rest of the vampire community will never forgive me. I can't. I can only trust in Danny.

Memories of the time she came close to breaking the only rule vampires universally obeyed replayed in her mind. The old man's screams still resonated in her mind as acutely as the night she committed her crime. One of the many memories of her dark past which often flooded to the surface to remind her that she was not some reformed character; she was every bit as dark and terrible as every other wretched vampire walking the earth.

She checked her watch. Danny was due in a couple of hours. By the end of the night, Mercy would know if there was any hope left for Danny and, in return, any hope left for her.

CHAPTER 9

Danny stared at the modern two storey office block with warehouse attached, then down at the business card in his hand. The address matched. The business name matched: Perpetuity Antiques.

Is this really the correct address? 10pm, on the dot. Better ring. Find out if anyone is home, but if some random answers, I don't know what the hell I'm going to say.

He approached the visitor's entrance to the offices and rang the buzzer. He peered through the glass windows, but the lights were off and there was nothing more than the silhouettes of furniture and his own gormless expression staring back at him.

The glass doors unlocked and a surprisingly rejuvenated Mercy stepped outside.

"Hey, Cripple. Are you a peeping Tom too?" she asked with a wry smile.

"Aye, very good. What am I doing here?"

"You're here for training. Come in."

Mercy led him through a small office space with a handful of desks and office equipment.

"So, this is how you pay the bills? You work at an antique dealer?"

"I *am* the antique dealer."

"You *are* the antique," Danny quipped, at which Mercy smiled.

"I'm very rarely here. I do pretty much all of my work

online. The place is self-sufficient. I identify artefacts, buy and sell them. My employees really just arrange shipping, pay the company taxes and so on," she explained.

"Yeah, but 'Perpetuity Antiques'? A bit on the nose don't you think?"

"Everyone is a critic. I learned very early on that certain items will naturally accrue a certain value. So, I buy and store them. Anywhere between 100 to 300 years later, I'll put them up for sale. Some items I'll keep for much longer," she continued explaining as they went further into the building.

"Well, if there's one thing a vampire has plenty of, it's time," Danny said.

"Exactly. The main pain in the arse is keeping the artefacts at an ideal temperature and humidity to prevent them from degrading. It cost a bloody fortune to retrofit the warehouse."

Danny eventually found himself in a large room with no decoration and only two wooden chairs facing one another in the centre of the room. With no windows, the only source of lighting was strip lighting.

"We're here."

"I thought I was going to learn how to fight vampires," Danny said.

"You are. What were you expecting? A gym? A boxing ring? You're going to learn to defend yourself from vampires. If you want to learn how to fight, join an MMA club. You can't physically fight a vampire. They're far too strong and far too fast. Now take off your jacket and take a seat, then we'll begin."

Mercy sat on the seat opposite and studied her student. She shook her head.

"OK, the first thing you need to be able to do is defend yourself when a vampire tries to hypnotise you. It's a vampire's first and most important weapon, and so it needs to be your first line of defence."

"OK," he replied.

"Now," she said as she continued to stare at him.

A strange pressure began to weigh on him, similar to the

pressure Malcolm had forced onto him; a warm and penetrating influence which pressed against this mind. No physical pressure was applied, just a soft, intoxicating fuzziness.

"Pat yourself on the head," Mercy said.

He instinctively did as told.

"Right, stop. Fuck, I barely had to try. Now I want you to fight me. That feeling you have when I start to talk to you? Reject it. That's how we burrow into your head. You need to defend yourself. Now let's go again."

Danny repositioned himself on his seat, cleared his throat, and nodded.

You're not getting inside my head ever again! I am in control!

"Pat your head."

Danny patted his head again, bearing a vacant expression.

Mercy sighed and looked at the floor between them.

And so it began. Over and over, Mercy tested him in various ways, with a variety of instructions and, again and again, his defences failed.

Danny crumpled to the floor at least six feet from his chair. He screamed as electric shards of pain shot through his knee and up to an aching hip.

"WHAT THE FUCK?!"

"Yeah, you may as well come back to the seat," Mercy said.

"How did I get here? I was sitting on the seat just now!"

"Not really. You haven't been sitting on that seat for over thirty minutes."

"What? How?" he whined as he sat upright, clutching his knee.

"Well, I've had you barking like a dog, imagining that you are a mime artist, which was hilarious by the way! Then I decided to test your knee. You've been hopping on your bad knee for the last couple of minutes. I wanted to know if you really have a weakness in that knee, or whether it is psychosomatic. Unfortunately it is very fucked indeed. I was disappointed the first time you collapsed under it, but it actually began to look funny."

"You're a fucking arsehole!" he said with a grimace as Mercy continued smiling.

"At least I'm an arsehole willing to help you, and the only one, as I understand it. Let's take a break from the hypnotism and I'll teach you about some weapons you'll be using."

Mercy kicked Danny's cane over to him as she headed out the door.

"Is this even worth it?" Danny muttered under his breath.

"Of course it is," Mercy shouted from beyond the door.

He hobbled after her into the warehouse area. Stacks of wooden crates wrapped in plastic were positioned in different areas, all with labelling. Small wooden boxes sat on tables.

Danny approached one such box. The label read 'Circa 11th Century Oil Lamp, Constantinople. The Prince's Crusade.'

"Bloody hell," he whispered

That must be worth a bloody fortune! Are all these boxes and crates as valuable as this? Why doesn't she have better security?

"Are you keeping up?" Mercy asked over her shoulder.

"Um, yeah."

Danny found himself in another office next to the warehouse. This was markedly different. All manner of pictures of artefacts were pinned on walls and filing cabinets lined the far wall. A laptop attached to large monitors sat on the desk in the corner.

Mercy went to the opposite side of the room where there were a series of large safes, each differing in brand and model. She typed a code into one of them then pressed her palm against a scanner.

A series of clicks sounded before Mercy swung the heavy door open. She retrieved a couple of long, but narrow boxes and slammed the door shut.

"Take a seat," she said pointing towards a soft, light brown leather couch.

Danny gingerly sat and rested the cane against his thigh.

She pulled a chair across the floor and sat opposite him.

"These are your two best weapons," she said, before lifting

the latch of one box and opening the lid. She produced a long shard of tiger's eye crystal and passed it to him.

It was smooth, cold, and heavy.

"Huh, I expected it to be lighter. You just think 'crystal' and you think light."

"Yeah, but tiger's eye is solid, hard-wearing, and is heavier than most wooden stakes," Mercy explained.

"So, if I stab a vampire with this, will it hurt them?"

"As much as any other thing you choose to stab them with. However, it does not debilitate them and they heal within a few minutes. However, if you stab them in the heart it'll put them down for good."

"So how did you happen to have these? Isn't it dangerous for you to be near something that can kill you?" he asked.

"Why do humans own guns? These things remind me that no one is invulnerable."

"Can I keep this?" Danny asked.

"Sure, it'll do the job, plus I need to know that you *can* do the job before I give you anything more... specialist. Just remember, you did not get this from me. I'm already way out of line in helping you."

"OK," Danny said whilst studying the shard.

At twelve inches long, and with an uneven handle with one side rough, it had been sheared from a much larger piece. Most of the shard was dark brown, however there was a single vein of amber-gold running up its length. As he twisted it in his hand, the vein shone in the light.

"Remember, it's not fully sharpened, so when you plunge it into a vampire's heart you'll need to put every ounce of your power into it. It has to tear through clothing, pierce the skin, drive through the chest muscles, and shatter the sternum just to get to the heart," she said as she put on a pair of thick rubber gloves and opened the second, much smaller box.

"What's in there?" he asked.

"Something which vampires are extremely allergic to. Even the slightest touch sends waves of agony through our bodies *and* melts our skin."

"Bloody hell!" he replied. "Is it acid?"

"No. Something much worse," she replied, and then cautiously lifted a rough lump of silvery metal on a chain.

"Is that silver?" he asked.

"No, but it's the origin behind the myth that vampires are allergic to silver. It looks like silver when it's in its solid form. It's called galena."

"Galena?"

"It's a metal substance. I don't know why we have this reaction when it's mainly composed of lead, some sulphur, and a touch of silver, but we do."

She handed the galena over to him.

"Should I be wearing gloves too?" he asked with trepidation.

"No. It's harmless to humans, unless it's powdered. If it's inhaled as a powder it can cause lead poisoning."

Danny held it by the chain, then touched the galena with his other hand. Rough, but lighter than anticipated, it was cold and hard.

"Use this to incapacitate a vampire. The pain is beyond what you could imagine. Plus, it immediately weakens a vampire. That will allow you to stab them with the tiger's eye."

"So instead of wooden stakes and silver, it's actually tiger's eye and galena," he replied with a smirk.

"Yup, and vampires are quite happy to have you all believing in wooden stakes and silver. OK," she said, before taking a few deep breaths. She then slid her left glove off. "I want you to lay the galena on the back of my hand."

"What?" No!" he said.

"Trust me, you're not going to kill me, but you need to know what kind of reaction to expect and what kind of damage it can do. Now, do it," she said and held her hand out, palm down. She buried her face into her shoulder.

"Are you sure?"

"Mmmhmmm," she replied with a nod, before screwing her

eyes tight.

Still holding the chain, he slowly lowered the hanging galena down and onto the back of her hand.

She let out a squeak and buried her face deeper into her shoulder. Immediately there was a bubbling sound and a horrific burning smell which stung his nostrils.

She suddenly let out an ear-piercing scream and collapsed onto the floor.

Danny tried to pull the galena off her hand, but it was stuck to her melting skin. He yanked at it and tore it off.

She writhed on the ground in agony, clutching her hand. In one sweeping motion she lifted herself from the floor and pounced on Danny. Her irises had turned black. Her canines were protruding. She was panting, rage and hunger on her face.

"Please. Don't," Danny whispered.

The blood rage faded and her piercing light blue eyes appeared once more.

She rose and walked away, still grimacing in pain.

"Are you OK?" Danny asked as he grabbed his cane and hobbled after her.

"I'm fine!" she snapped. "I needed to show you what galena does to a vampire, and now you know. I'm fine."

"OK."

"Right. Now grab this," she said and threw something at Danny. He fumbled the object but eventually held on to it. It was a wooden stake. The same size as the tiger's eye shard.

Mercy's breathing was still fast and shallow.

"We're going to practice your technique on how to stab someone in the heart."

And so training continued.

Using herself as target practice, she allowed Danny to hack stab and slice at her, all to no effect.

"Jesus Christ, Cripple!" she yelled. "Is there anything you *can* do? Just take a seat, bloody hell!"

Danny slumped back into his chair, frustrated and dejected. His headache had progressed to migraine levels, his knee now buckled under the slightest weight, and he had failed in everything that Mercy had tested him with.

"Honestly," Mercy said as she sat down in the chair opposite him. "I had hoped for better. I mean, even as a cripple I thought you would have had more fight in you, but apparently not."

"Stop calling me that," Danny replied, a well of anger rising in him.

"Given how useless you are, I don't think a cripple like you has any right giving *anyone* any orders."

"Look, just give me a chance," he said.

"What the fuck do you think I have been doing all night?" she asked.

"I can do this. I just need to keep trying," Danny added.

"No, enough. I was looking for some slither of hope. Something to work with, but you're fucking useless."

"Ouch!" Danny replied, his eyebrows furrowed.

"The truth hurts. I was hoping that you would be the one. The one to turn the tide in this city, but you're not. And worst of all is that you're such a whiny fucking crybaby all the time."

"I'm not whiny," he whined.

"You forget that there are people who have it much worse than you. So you have a weakened leg and need a cane. But every day you'll see people who either have a more severe physical disability, a learning disability, or something even worse happening in their lives. But you can't get past yourself," she said.

"That's easy coming from an eternal being who has perfect health, is super-strong, and is super-fast. It's easy to preach when you don't have any problems yourself, so get off my back. I'm doing the best I can!"

"But that's it; it's not good enough. It's nowhere near good enough. I don't know what's holding you back, but it's not your fucking leg! I think it's fear," Mercy said.

"Of course I'm fucking scared. I'm fucking terrified. We're talking about me picking a fight with lethal supernatural beings with immense power, and fighting them to the death. Of course

I'm scared!" he shouted, slamming his fist onto his knee and immediately regretting it when the pain shot through him.

"I don't think that's what scares you though, Cripple."

"Stop calling me that."

"I think that you're afraid to really try in case you fail. You could excel in training and still shit yourself when it comes to confronting a vampire, but it's like you're not even willing to try to train. You're defeated before you start."

Danny lowered his head.

"You don't know me."

"Doesn't mean that I'm not still right. There's no room for whiny crybabies or cowards here."

"I'm not a coward!" he said in a quiet, growling tone, his fingers curling into fists.

"Your sister doesn't need a coward, she needs someone to grow a pair. But you're not willing to do that. You're not even willing to try. Not even for your own sister."

"SHUT THE FUCK UP, MERCY!"

"Oooo! Looks like the Cripple has fire in his belly after all! Now…" she began as she leaned forward, looking into his eyes.

Once again, the warm wave pressed against Danny's mind.

"Slap yourself in the face." Mercy commanded.

Danny's hand lifted a few inches, before his fist clenched, his nails cutting into his palm, and lowered onto his lap once more.

Mercy's eyebrows furrowed.

"I said, slap yourself in the face now!"

The pressure on his mind was now unbearable.

Noooo! Fuck you!

"Now!" Mercy shouted.

Danny's head was in a vice and, between the throbbing pain of his already existing headache and the pressure applied from Mercy, it was on the verge of exploding.

"NO!" Danny screamed.

He thrashed out of his chair and landed on the floor, aching, exhausted and in turmoil.

"Bloody hell!" Mercy said, her eyes wide. "That's the first time I've seen anyone reject a vampire! I mean the *very first time*. I had heard it could be done but I've never known anyone to resist it. But you did it!"

Danny lay panting on his back, looking at the ceiling, trying to block out all the pain.

"Come on. Let me help you up," Mercy said, and proceeded to lift Danny to his feet.

"Thanks."

"This is a huge accomplishment. I'm sorry for the things I said. They were shitty, but I needed to make you so angry it would focus your mind on a target and away from your doubts and fears. It seems that anger is what gives you the inner strength to fight back."

"Yeah. Some of what you said was right though. I've been half-hearted in searching for Aurelia because I've been afraid. I could have been getting out more, asking around more. But I haven't because I'm scared," he admitted. His eyes began to moisten and a lump swelled in his throat.

"Look, it's been a long night, and I can see you are exhausted. We've got a lot more training to do, but we've had a lot of success tonight. I'll call you a cab," she said as they slowly left the room.

Danny was slumped in the back of the black hackney cab as it headed towards his home in the Old Town. He was exhausted both physically and emotionally, racked with pain, but happy.

I can do this! After just one night of training I was able to reject her. I can do this! Nothing is going to stop me from finding Gabriel! That bastard is mine!

CHAPTER 10

Danny picked up the basket and ventured into the local supermarket, smiling at the others in the store. A residual pride still swirled inside from the night before. His knee was more painful than it had been in weeks, thanks to Mercy. But other than that, he was cheerier than he had been for a long time.

He smiled at an old lady who passed him in the aisle as he headed towards the milk and dairy section. Then Aurelia burst into his mind. The smile Gabriel gave over his shoulder. That she was still out there, needing him. A wave of shame consumed him for forgetting her.

The momentary wail of a siren snapped Danny into the present. He was in the middle of the road with two confused paramedics in an ambulance in front of him.

"Hey Cripple, fancy getting out of the way?" Mercy's voice called out.

Danny stepped onto the pavement. The NHS Scotland signpost a few yards from him pointed to various outpatient departments.

Why am I outside a hospital?

"But I was buying milk," he muttered, his expression of confusion maintained.

"Hey," Mercy said as she stood beside him. Her eyes were hidden behind her sunglasses, but she did manage a weak smile. Again, her skin was pasty and her scalp clammy.

"What did you do, Mercy?" he asked and closed his eyes.

"You know, just because you were able to resist me one time doesn't mean that you are immune. You need to have your guard raised at all times, because you never know when you are going to run into a vampire," she replied.

"Fine, fair enough. I'll be angry all the time. Being with you makes that easy, but you didn't need to hypnotise me and bring me all the way out here. Where *are* we anyway?"

"The Western General. Seem familiar?"

"Umm, yeah," he replied, looking around him.

"That's because you were taken here after that taxi made love to you. We're here to meet someone. There's been a problem and until it's dealt with we're not going to be able to get the intel we need on your vampire. Just follow my lead."

Mercy led Danny through the buildings on the hospital grounds, until they found themselves following a blue line down a long corridor.

"Why do you need intel on any of them? There are only a handful of vampires in this city. Don't you know where they live and where they have fun?"

"That's my fault," she replied. "I did originally keep tabs on them when they first arrived a year or so ago, but as they settled in without making waves, I lost interest. But now they've become bloodthirsty and relentless and all the info I did have on them is outdated. I don't know where they now live and where they frequent, not that I could do anything about it anyway, thanks to that golden rule of not killing our own. But now you are here," she said, and smiled at him.

"So all this fallout, all this blood and death and murder is a direct consequence of you not keeping a closer eye on them?" he asked.

"Exactly," she replied without a hint of offence having been taken. "OK, this set of stairs up to the third floor and we're there, I think."

They passed through a set of double doors to the left and began climbing the stairs. By the time they reached the second floor, Mercy was already panting and had slowed down.

"I thought *I* was the cripple. Do you want a hand?" Danny asked with a grin.

"Fuck off," she replied in between puffs.

They walked along a regular ward, until they found themselves outside a room, marked 'Room 13'.

"In here," she said.

To the far left end of the four-bed room lay a man with multiple dressings. As Danny neared him, the damage to his face became clearer. Two black eyes and a swollen lip couldn't disguise that it was Franky, the man he had met with Mercy recently.

"Franky, are you OK pal?" Danny asked.

"Just grand mate," Franky replied and cracked a pained smile.

"What have the doctors said?" Mercy asked.

"Two broken ribs. No organ damage and no internal bleeding so that's good. They're gonnae keep me in for a wee bit. They're sure that I'll be awright," Franky replied. His breathing was laboured and he took lengthy pauses in between sentences. "Got a knife held to my throat. Said that if I come back, he'll use it. I believe him. He's a reputation for stabbing people. Apparently the arsehole already killed a couple of guys. Everybody's too scared of him and his gang to talk."

"Who did it, Franky?" she asked.

"A guy called Thompson. Dunno his first name. Lives in Pilton. Dunno where, but I've been told his gang hang around Granton Church all the time. Ironic eh? He deals from there but the police don't bother. They could walk up to the cunt with drugs on him, but they don't. I think they're afraid of him. He's seriously bad news."

"Why were you attacked, Franky?" Danny asked.

"One of the pictures you gave me. One face is a regular at Bohemia. I haven't seen Gabriel yet. Turns out that one of them *does* go there: Cassius."

"Fucking Cassius, why does that not surprise me?" she said.

"I've been trailing the bastard ever since," Franky

continued. "See, Cassius likes to hunt in Granton, Muirhouse, and Pilton. I heard that Thompson identifies people in Pilton and Muirhouse who wouldnae be missed if they disappeared. I think Cassius is behind it. I was asking about Cassius and why he visits those areas. Thompson got wind of it and him and his mates paid me a visit."

"Thanks Franky. You rest up. I'll sort it out and make it up to you. After you are discharged you're coming to live at my home until you're fully recovered," Mercy said as she stood up.

"That's lovely doll, but—"

"It's settled," she interrupted. Without another word, Mercy left.

"Ummm," Danny added as he rose out of his chair and adjusted his grip on his cane.

"Relax, Danny. It's just Mercy being Mercy. You get used to it after a while," Franky said with a gracious smile.

"Cripple!" Mercy shouted from the corridor.

"Oi!" an elderly male voice yelled back from another part of the corridor.

"Yeah!" Danny shouted back at her. "Get well soon, Franky."

"Thanks, Danny mate. See you later."

"Your bedside manner leaves a lot to be desired, you know that?" Danny asked Mercy as they made their way out of the hospital.

"Wait here," she said, before heading into the hospital shop. A few minutes later, she emerged with a shopping bag.

"Right, I can't be arsed walking the whole way, so we're getting a bus," Mercy announced.

"Can we not get a taxi from the rank? There are a few just sitting there," Danny said as he pointed over at the parked taxis waiting for a fare. A wave of anxiety rose at the prospect of the bus.

"Nooo, definitely not," Mercy replied. "Trust me Danny, we don't want to get a taxi."

As they sat alone at the bus stop outside the hospital, a question which had been playing on Danny's mind finally escaped his lips.

"So, Franky knows pretty much everything about vampires?" he asked.

"No. He eventually figured out what I was, although he doesn't know about the nest other than there are other vampires in the city. We needed an entry to the nest and he has found it through Cassius. Franky never fails to surprise and impress me. So we'll target Cassius first and make our way to Gabriel through him."

"And is it solely homeless folk or is it others who know about vampires?"

"Only Franky knows about vampires, but I have all sorts of people as contacts, although they definitely don't know what I am and have no knowledge of the nest. I have police officers, social workers, charity workers. All sorts of people know all sorts of things independently of one another. There is one thing which ties them: they are very jaded with how the system fails innocent people. So they ask me for help. And I help them."

"In what ways?" Danny asked, his brows furrowing.

"All sorts of ways, but I'm not a charity. I usually want something in return, but if it keeps them happy then it works for both of us," she answered, looking down the road for a bus which hadn't appeared yet.

"I remember you and Franky mentioned 'payment as usual'. What does that involve?"

"Well aren't you a nosey wee bugger?" she asked with a smile. "Whatever they need. Some need money. Some need food. Some need a place to stay during cold spells."

"Do you not try to get them off the streets permanently?" he asked.

"I do if that's what they want, but it's not as simple as that. Some of them have serious mental health problems. Some can't cope with the demands everyday life places on them and they end up on the streets again. Others have difficulty adjusting and fall into bad ways again. If they want off the streets I give them all the practical support they need, including money and putting them in touch with those who specialise in such a thing. But if they just want money in exchange for a task, then money they get."

"And if they want to spend it on drugs and drink?"

"Don't be a judgemental prick, Cripple! Not all homeless people are junkies. You need to have a word with yourself and get that ignorant shite out of your head."

"Take it easy, Mercy!" Danny replied, holding his hands up in surrender.

"Easy? You know what's 'easy'? Walking past them in the street, pretending not to see them. I saw the way you looked at Franky the first time you met in that cafe. Judging him. Peering down your nose at him, After shaking his hand you looked like your wanted to cut your hand off with a rusty blade and have it burned. And you know what? Franky saw your reaction too," she said.

Mercy's expression was not one of offence or irritation. It was one of anger.

"There's no way he couldn't have," she continued. "But he didn't say anything because he has class. More class than you. Even now, when he's in the hospital, in severe pain and having had a trauma, he still greeted you as a friend. Let me ask you, when was the last time you *actually spoke* to a homeless person other than Franky? Have you ever said anything to one, other than 'sorry mate, I don't have any spare change'?"

Danny opened his mouth to reply, but no justification came to mind. The overpowering weight of shame settled on Danny's chest and shoulders, and he looked down at the pavement between them. Finally, he looked up.

"This is personal for you, isn't it?" he asked.

"What is?"

"You act like you're only interested in saving them because they are useful to you, but I think that you care for them deeply. I think you're lying to yourself to maintain an emotional distance," he said.

"Enough of your pop psychology shite. Just remember:

they're people. Decent people who got shat upon from a great height by life. And without *them*, you don't stand a chance of getting anywhere near Aurelia. Here we are," Mercy said as a bus appeared in the distance.

Before long, the local bus entered Pilton and both of them were disembarking.

"Why are we here?" Danny asked, though fearing the answer.

"We're going to have a wee chat with Thompson, and we're going to ask that he leaves people alone. Besides, we might get some useful information on Cassius while we are here," she said with a rare, wide smile.

It all sounded so innocent.

"OK, but I'm not sure if that's wise. You heard what Franky said about him being dangerous."

"Yeah, I know. We'll be super-careful not to get into any kind of argument. I promise," she reassured Danny with another smile.

Danny continued to frown.

Danny followed Mercy through the residential streets of Pilton.

"Wait up! It's not easy walking as fast as you with this cane!"

Mercy stopped in her tracks and turned to him.

"Fair enough. Now is as good a time as any. Here take this," she instructed and handing the hospital shopping bag to him.

He peered into the bag. Inside was a pair of two litre bottles of water, and bottle of high percentage alcohol-based hand sanitiser.

"And this," she added, taking off her denim jacket and handing it to Danny.

Mercy's pink top was inside out and back to front, the label resting just under her chin.

Danny suppressed a laugh.

"Shit! I forgot!" she said.

"What?" he asked.

She rummaged in the pockets of her jacket as Danny held it. She produced a small empty bottle, the kind normally used for urine samples.

"I always keep one just in case," she added with a smile as she slipped it into the pocket of her black jeans.

"What, in case you need a pee? How small is your bladder?" Danny asked with a smile.

"Smartarse," she replied, her increasingly infectious smile still in place. She removed her sunglasses and screwed her eyes up as she struggled to adjust to the sun which had broken through the clouds. She put her glasses in her jacket pocket.

Her face was grey, with dark rings under her eyes. Her scalp was sweating profusely. She closed her eyes and took a deep breath, then took something else from her jacket pocket. Danny only caught the briefest flash, but it was black and metallic.

"Right, are we ready? Try to keep up, OK? If we see him, and I'm sure we will, just stay back and let me do the talking," she said as she wiped sweat from her brow with the back of her hand.

"OK. But remember, please be nice and don't argue with him. You look really ill," he reminded her.

"You're a fucking charmer. Twat."

They approached the church; a small, one storey modern building, the kind built as a community centre which had been repurposed as a church.

As they reached the corner of the building, the voices reached Danny's ears.

"I kicked fuck out the cunt," the deep male voice said, as other male voices chuckled.

"Prick, so he is," another voice joined in.

Danny turned to ask Mercy a question.

"Shh," she said, pre-empting him. She scanned the windows of the nearby blocks of houses.

"Good," she whispered. She then produced what Danny had previously only caught a glimpse of.

Danny's eyes widened in shock as Mercy slipped spiked

knuckle dusters on each hand.

"Mercy! Bloody hell! They're illegal! And you said that you were only going to have a nice chat with them!" he whispered as loudly as he dared.

Mercy shoved each knuckle duster as far up her fingers as possible. She then clenched her fists. Four sharpened spikes, each half an inch long rested over each of her knuckles.

"Relax Danny," she whispered back. "These are only a back-up. I promise that I will not use them unless I *absolutely* have to. Now, how do my tits look? Perky?" she asked as she manhandled her chest so that her breasts sat slightly higher than they previously did.

"Errr. Ummm," Danny replied, with the sudden urge to stare at the grass beside them, his eyes wide.

"Extra-perky? Good, good," she replied, before clasping her hands behind her back. She hunched her shoulders together, accentuating her cleavage. She winked at Danny and blew him a flirty kiss, before turning the corner, her hands clasped behind her back.

Danny instinctively followed her.

Before them stood four burly men in their late twenties.

"Hey boys," Mercy said with a playful tone.

Each of the men immediately ceased their conversations and looked in Mercy's direction.

"I really need help. I'm looking for Thompson."

"That's me. What do you want?" Thompson asked. Whilst his gang were more interested in the flirty girl in her early twenties, Thompson was more reserved. More suspicious.

"I hear that you're the man to speak to who can get things done. I need a favour, and I think you're the only lad who can help me," Mercy said as she cocked her head to the side, her knuckle duster-clad hands still clasped behind her back.

Thompson's focus shifted to Danny. His ice-cold stare froze Danny in place. Thompson scanned him up and down. His eyes rested on the shopping bag in one hand then the cane in his other. He then returned his gaze to Mercy. He now sported an amused smile.

"Here mate, what's that walking stick for? Are you retarded?" one of Thompson's gang asked Danny, nodding towards Danny's cane as his friends laughed.

"My knee is fucked, mate. Got hit by a car when I was hammered," Danny replied with an unconvincingly tough demeanour.

"Daft bastard!" one of them said, the others chuckling.

"Aye, right enough," Danny replied with a smile.

"Aye, that's right doll," Thompson interrupted, answering Mercy's question. "I can get things done. What do you need?"

Mercy approached him and came within touching distance.

"I heard that you kicked the shit out of some homeless junky the other day for snooping on people. That was awesome!"

"Aye. That wee dick was asking dangerous questions about dangerous people. I had to make an example of him."

"Coooool! See, I have someone who I need to be dealt with like that. Could you help me? I'll make it worth your while," she said with a wink.

"Oh, aye?" Thompson asked, his smile now graduating into a full-blown grin.

"Aye," she replied.

"Who do you need done in?"

"You," Mercy replied.

"Eh?" Thompson asked, his expression of amusement quickly replaced by confusion.

Mercy swung her fist and it connected with Thompson's cheek with a loud crack.

When she withdrew her fist, his left cheek had been indented, with blood having sprayed across the face of one of his gang.

Danny, along with Thompson's entire gang, reacted with a collective "Ooft!"

Mercy struck another blow and the right side of Thompson's face was caved in.

Quicker than Danny could have prepared for, and with

more power than he would have expected, Mercy moved to the first gang member and landed a fist on his face, his nose immediately flattening, blood bursting from both nostrils.

Danny stood in shock as Mercy moved smoothly from one gang member to another, then to Thompson, then back to a gang member, expertly putting them down with careful and considerable strikes. Before Danny had processed what was happening, all four men were lying on the ground.

Mercy then grunted as she straddled Thompson's chest.

"How does Cassius contact you?" she shouted into Thompson's face.

"Fuck you!" he slurred.

She grabbed his short fringe with one hand and landed another strike, this time on his eye socket.

"HOW?!"

"I d-d-dunno!" he stuttered.

Another strike, this time to his other eye, her fists and knuckle dusters coated in blood.

"HOW?!"

"I meet him on Wednesdays! Outside Bohemia in the Old Town. I give him the name and address of some poor bastard. I dunno what happens. I don't want to know!" he yelled.

One of Thompson's gang stumbled to his feet. The flash of the sun shining on a blade caught Danny's attention.

"Mercy!" Danny shouted.

Instinctively, he swung his cane and smacked the knife out of the man's hand. The gang member focused his attention on Danny.

"Fuck!" Danny whispered.

The gang member drunkenly charged Danny. Danny held his cane out as a barrier and thrust it out at the attacker. It struck him on the bridge of his nose. Danny's momentum carried him forward and he crashed against the gang member. The attacker buckled backwards and Danny landed on him.

With his hands on each end of his cane, he repeatedly struck the man in the face, battering him into submission and near unconsciousness.

Danny panted, his eyes shot through with panic. His head was fuzzy and everything moved in slow motion as his adrenaline kicked in.

"If you go anywhere near that homeless guy again, or if I hear that you have attacked *anyone*, I'll come for you and I'll fucking kill you," Mercy said to Thompson with a cold, calm tone. "Then I'll find your family and I'll slit their throats. I'll kill everyone you care about. You family, your pets. Your aunts and uncles. Now look at me and listen."

Thompson whimpered and looked at her through tear-filled and rapidly welling eyes.

"I'll even kill the kids in your family. Even the kids. No one is off limits if you hurt anyone else again," she said in a quiet, ominous tone. "Now do you ever want to see me again?" she asked.

"No!" Thompson squeaked his response.

Grabbing his hair with one hand, she repeatedly punched his face. Over and over, until his face, hair and neck was entirely bright red, completely soaked in blood. His face was so destroyed, so caved in, that Danny had difficulty identifying a physical feature. She then opened his mouth. She repeatedly struck his mouth and with each punch, more teeth in Thompson's mouth vanished.

"So you'll remember me," Mercy then said with a smile. With a fingernail, she carved a large and deep 'M' into Thompson's forehead, and another large 'M' on each cheek, before letting go of his head.

"Mercy, you're gonna kill him!" Danny said.

Mercy whipped her head around to face Danny. Strands of hair were stuck to her sweating face. Her smile and the excitement in her eyes shocked him. She then looked at the thug Danny had subdued.

"Well look at you, Cripple!" she said and then chuckled. "You *can* crack heads when you need to!"

"You're going to kill him," Danny reminded her.

She looked down at the limp, helpless mess that was Thompson for a few seconds.

"He's fine. His heartbeat is strong, he's breathing fine. No major veins or arteries damaged. It's purely superficial. He'll live," she reassured Danny. "But you'll never look the same when you're healed, will you? You'll give little children nightmares and will be a cautionary tale to any other arsehole in this area who thinks that they can take your place. And worst of all, you'll see my mark in every mirror for the rest of your pathetic little life."

She produced the empty sample bottle and pressed it against the laceration on Thompson's cheek. The bottle began to fill with his blood.

She then surveyed the damage to Thompson's gang and offered a single sentence for each one.

"That one has a broken arm, moderate concussion, broken eye socket. That one has a few broken ribs, shattered jaw, broken nose, and damage to his left eye, most likely will be blind in that eye. The third one there has a broken kneecap, a couple of broken ribs, a shattered jaw, plus serious damage to his genitals thanks to the spiked knuckledusters, so there's a good chance he'll be infertile."

"Oh dear God," Danny murmured, fighting waves of nausea.

"Then there's the one you're sitting on," Mercy continued as she replaced the cap on the now full bottle and slipped it into her jeans. "You broke his nose, gave him a heavy concussion, and broke his cheekbone. See the misshapen left side of his face?"

"Oh God," he repeated.

"Come on," she said as she painfully got to her feet and walked away.

Danny struggled to his feet and limped after her, relying heavily on his cane.

"Remember my jacket and the shopping bag," she instructed.

"I've got them," he said.

After a minute of walking through streets, Mercy stopped at a corner with high, overgrown hedges on either side. She turned to Danny, her face and neck sprayed with blood. Her pink top was also sprayed. Her hands were bright red all the way to the wrists, with blood splashed up her forearms.

"Danny, get the water."

He dipped his hand into the bag and fumbled with the bottle. He shakily twisted the cap off.

"OK, pour the water out slowly. Into that drain."

Danny fought to keep his hands still as he poured a small amount of water out of the bottle onto the drain's grate at the side of the road. Mercy dipped her hands under the water and forcefully began to wash. When the blood was gone from her hands, arms, and knuckledusters, she splashed water on her face and wiped the splattered blood clean. By the time both water bottles were empty, the blood was gone from her skin.

She took off her top, revealing her bra.

"Keep your eyes to yourself perv!" she said with a chuckle.

Danny scanned the surrounding area for witnesses. The few windows with a view of the street were empty of people and no one else was on the street. Danny breathed a sigh of relief.

She flipped her top the correct way, swung her top around and put it back on the proper way around to reveal a large velvet love heart print on the front. The blood stains were now on the inside of her top, on her back.

"That's why you had it on inside out and back to front," Danny said.

"Yup."

"I thought you were just being a dizzy bitch!" he added.

"That too," she replied. She produced the hand sanitiser bottle and slathered a more than generous amount on her hands, forearms, and neck. "Seventy-five percent alcohol," she explained as she waited for it to dry in. "I don't like the smell of blood on me for longer than necessary."

Danny no longer cared. He just wanted far away from the crime he had just committed with a supposedly powerless vampire.

She donned her jacket and sunglasses once more. Her

appearance bore no evidence of the bloodbath she had engaged in just moments before.

"Right, let's go get a coffee. I'm buying," she announced, and walked off. "Don't put that bag or bottle in any bins near here."

Danny followed her in silence as they walked back in the direction they came, until they found themselves outside a large hotel which sported not only a gym, but also a restaurant and coffee chain outlet.

They sat in silence with their coffees and cakes in front of them, both untouched. With soft lighting and relaxing music being piped through speakers in the ceiling, it calmed Danny's jitters.

An ambulance screamed past the hotel, startling Danny. Then, a moment later, another and another, along with a police car which rushed by, lights on.

"Right, gimme that bag," she said as she slowly and painfully rose from her seat. Her forehead drenched in sweat, her skin deathly grey. He passed the incriminating evidence over to Mercy as she discreetly checked the vial of blood in her pocket.

"I'm off to the loo. Bursting for a pee," she announced and then left Danny alone.

Ten minutes passed. He scanned the faces in the cafe. None of the patrons paid the slightest bit of attention to him.

There was no blood on his hands but there was a noticeable tremble. He clenched them into fists and relaxed them multiple times.

"Hey," she announced as she came back and slumped herself into the seat next to him, the bag on the floor between her feet. She was less grey. She wasn't as clammy and her eyes were more alert.

"Hey," he replied, returning his gaze to the full coffee cup in front of him. "That really took it out of you, eh?"

"Yeah. But that little bottle of blood was just the pick-me-up I needed."

"I thought that vampires lost most of their powers during the day," he whispered.

"We do. It took all of my strength and focus just to catch you unaware in the supermarket and hypnotise you into getting into a taxi with me to the hospital."

"So how did you do... what... erm just happened... so easily?"

"That was just fighting skills that I have been forced to pick up. Centuries of having to fight to defend myself during the day. Being a single woman during the Middle Ages was a dangerous position to be in. I've spent multiple centuries in lots of different countries studying all kinds of hand-to-hand combat and martial arts. But those spiked knuckledusters did most of the work. You just need to know how to use them most effectively," she explained as she closed her eyes.

"Why couldn't you just, you know, hypnotise him to get what you wanted?"

"Because I didn't have it in me. I was running on empty. Besides, that was to send a message to Gabriel, through Cassius, but also to any arsehole who thinks it's OK to attack Franky or any of his contacts. They *have* to remember exactly what happened, otherwise it's pointless."

"But you hurt them so badly, Mercy," he complained.

"So?"

"Soooo, they're human beings. They're people. They might be horrible bastards. They might be absolute scum, but that's what the police are for. They're still human. I saw the enjoyment in your eyes."

Mercy however had slumped and was now leaning on him, her eyes still closed and her head resting on his shoulder.

"Do I get blood-joy, just like any other vampire? Yeah, I do," she said. "But I can control myself, and I was never going to kill any of them. But they needed to be hurt. Bad. Otherwise it wasn't a message. I left the fourth goon for you. And you didn't disappoint. I'm proud of you, Cripple," she said, and within seconds she was asleep, her quiet breathing falling into a regular rhythm.

"Fuck," he sighed and closed his eyes. "I don't want any of

this. I just want Aurelia back and I want to interrogate Cassius to find out where she is."

After a few half-hearted sips of coffee, he called a taxi, and bundled a drowsy Mercy into the back with her plastic bag and paid for the driver to take her home, wherever that was.

CHAPTER 11

"I'm ordering in. Want something?" Franky asked as he poked his head around the corner of Mercy's library. Mercy placed the photo of Gabriel on her lap and looked up.

"Where are you going?"

"I'm thinking Chinese. On your card, mind. I don't have a card."

"Get me chicken fried rice," she replied, and began studying the photo once more as Franky's head disappeared behind the door frame.

Three weeks had passed since Mercy had sent a message to both Cassius and Gabriel, via Thompson's face. Much had changed as a consequence. No more people had been reported missing from that area and, through Franky's contacts, Mercy had heard that the area of Pilton had become much quieter. Much more stable.

Peace returning to Pilton was not the only change. After a few days in hospital, Franky had been discharged and had moved into Mercy's Old Town home to continue his convalescence. The subject of how long Franky would choose to stay with her had not yet been addressed. Danny had continued training with Mercy every day at her home and had proven to be an excellent student in spite of his weakened knee.

The doorbell rang.

Shit, that order was fast, how long have I been looking at his photo?

Through the walls, the sounds of Franky opening the front door and Danny's voice echoed their way to Mercy's ears.

Danny appeared, looking more sullen than normal. He eased himself into the leather upholstered chair opposite Mercy and scanned the multiple bookshelves which lined three walls of the room. He unfolded a newspaper which had been tucked under his arm. He then passed it to Mercy.

Mercy frowned in confusion as she accepted the paper. She read the splash on the front page and immediately her confusion was gone.

VANISHED WITHOUT A TRACE.

45yr Old Thomas Briggs Becomes The Next Name Added to Edinburgh's Shameful Missing Persons Crisis.

The picture below the splash was the same picture that Mercy had given to Franky, that of a man with a portly face and shaver's rash. Short black hair, greying at the temples, and a slightly ruddy nose completed the more prominent features.

The seriousness of Danny's expression needed no explanation as he stared back at her.

"What am I looking for?" Mercy asked.

"I'd have thought that was obvious. Thomas Briggs. I remember that name being mentioned when I first met Franky in that cafe. He was handing over some kind of file or report to you. Any idea why he has gone missing?"

"No idea at all."

"Helluva coincidence, eh?" Danny asked.

"Yeah."

"So, who is he? Why did you have Franky report on him? What does he mean to you?" Danny continued grilling Mercy.

"Danny, he's nothing. It's just a coincidence. Now, are you ready for more training?"

Danny didn't answer, he just continued to stare at Mercy. Finally, he spoke.

"Sure," he said, before standing up and waiting for Mercy,

both hands leaning on his cane.

He followed Mercy as they made their way to the rooms which Mercy had converted into a makeshift training centre. They walked into a large room which was decked out with a number of crash mats, mannequins with replaceable centre plates, and various seats and chairs organised in specific patterns.

"Franky, in here! Bring your report on Cassius!" Mercy shouted and lifted a number of files all tied with a thick rubber band from a table in the corner.

A few moments later, Franky entered holding a crumpled file.

"Right, sit down you two," Mercy instructed. Danny and Franky both sat down next to one another. Mercy turned a plastic chair around and sat on it with her forearms resting on the back of the seat.

"Franky, you had your people finish your report into Cassius for you over the last week. What have they come up with?"

"Right," he replied as he opened his file, Danny peering over at it. "We started at Bohemia looking for Gabriel since that's where he ran into your sister, Danny. Turns out Cassius loves the place. We haven't seen Gabriel there though. But Cassius is there every week night. It's his favourite haunt. He lives in a huge town house in Moray Place in the New Town."

"Of course he does. I should have figured that he would live there. It's in the city centre in a really affluent street. You said it's massive?" Mercy asked.

"Aye, apparently it's more like two or three town houses built together," Franky said.

"Vampires like to live either together or very close to one another. It's for added protection. If this town house is as big as you say, it might house all of them," she said. Experience had taught her to never get excited over things which could go wrong, and yet the prospect of finding the location of the nest was tantalising.

"What else?" she asked.

"He leaves Bohemia at about 11pm. He wanders the old town for a wee bit, then either goes back to his house, or every other day he travels into Pilton, probably after receiving info from Thompson. By the way, Thompson got put in hospital, his face totally butchered. Hasn't been a peep out of him or his gang since. People there are enjoying the peace. Wouldnae know anything about that, would you, doll?"

"No idea," she said with a blank face.

"Anyhow, at the weekends he either entertains randoms at his home or goes to random places. House parties, night clubs. There's no pattern."

"Then we'll get him as he leaves Bohemia. We'll set you up near there to make sure he comes across you, Danny," she said. Danny nodded in silence. His nerves shone through his determination.

"Remember what we have rehearsed. You'll be homeless and will ask him for money."

"And if he ignores me, I'll get ballsy and follow him, pestering him."

"Exactly," she added. "Now, Franky, here is the rest of gang. I want you to include your whole network on this. All of them. The sooner we find out the whole nest's patterns, the sooner we can plan to take them all down. As soon as we make contact with Cassius, we'll be on a clock. Remember, Gabriel is the main target. You can start with the house in Moray Place and we'll see if my hunch about them living together is right. If it is, then it'll make scouting them much easier," she said as she handed the files to Franky.

Franky opened each of the files and scanned the information.

"There's a lot of people here. How did you manage to get a picture of each of them when you know so little about them?" Franky asked.

"When they arrived in the city, they contacted me. Wanted me to join their nest. I told them I had no interest. I made a point of scouting out who they were, what they looked like, and some basic info. They settled down and I didn't hear any rumours of any kills, so I figured that they were only hunting for survival. After a while I stopped spying on them. By the time they started killing on such a regular basis, all of my info on them was outdated. Even where they lived."

If only I had kept a regular eye on them rather than trying to ignore them, we wouldn't be in this situation, and all these people wouldn't be dying.

"Awright, I'm going to make a couple of calls to get the ball rolling while we wait for the takeaway coming. I'll need to go and see most of my people tomorrow morning first thing, because most of them don't have a phone. At least we can get started with that big house on Moray Place. See yous in a bit," Franky said as he walked towards the door. "Oh and Danny, I didnae know what kind of Chinese you liked, so I just got you chicken fried rice, same as Mercy. Is that OK?"

"Aye, that's lovely. Appreciate it," Danny replied.

Mercy and her student sat in silence for a moment, until he spoke.

"Mercy, quick question."

"Hmm?"

"Vampires can fly, so why do they walk anywhere? What's the point of tailing these vampires? Won't they just fly from place to place?"

"Most don't. Just because flying is a fascination to you humans, doesn't mean it's like that for us. For us it's as dull as dirt. Vampires actually enjoy walking with humans, walking amongst them, even on public transport. It's because they like to tease themselves I guess, plus they're always in hunter mode, looking out for the next victim or next potential one night stand."

"And what about you?"

"I like mingling with humans because I live with them. I do business with them. They're not food to me. Vampires mock me for living like a human, but the truth of it is they just like to window shop and feel the vivaciousness of life surrounding them on the streets. Anyway, ready to get started?" Mercy asked.

"Of course, so what first? Striking? Fighting off hypnotism?"

"Neither," Mercy replied. "First, some information to prepare you for what's going to happen when you kill a vampire."

"Go on," Danny replied.

"Remember when I asked you to bring a sports holdall a couple of weeks ago?"

"Yeah, I left it in the corner there," Danny replied, nodding towards the corner of the room behind Mercy. "I was hoping that we'd get to that."

"If you succeed in killing a vampire, what happens to their body is… unusual."

"Go on," Danny prompted.

"The body undergoes a rapid change. Within a few seconds the body turns into a white crumbly, dust-like substance, barely held together. I can only describe it as being similar to a formation of loose, fragile chalk. A decent breeze will blow the body into dust."

"Jesus! So if there was no wind at all, the dead vampire would look like a chalk statue?" Danny asked.

"Yeah. It's very handy that it can be crumbled away to dust so easily because it means that there won't be a body left for people to find, only mounds of white ashy, chalky powder. It's just a tremendous shock to the system, seeing it happen to someone. You can't prepare for it, you can only expect it to happen. But that's where the bag comes in."

"Oh God! Don't tell me that you expect me to shovel the ash into the bag! That's too grim!" Danny protest with an expression of sheer distaste.

"Relax," Mercy said with a smile. "The remains will be dispersed with a breeze. Remember, there's always some kind of wind or breeze in this city. Or the dust will be dissolved the next time it rains. No, but what will be left is the vampire's clothes."

"Clothes? Oh."

"Well, the shirt and trousers aren't made of vampire!" Mercy said. "The clothes and jewellery are left behind. You need to quickly stuff them into your bag."

"I guess that makes sense. Any advice for me?"

"Aye. Make sure you shake out the socks," she replied with a wicked grin.

"So, what should I do with the belongings?" he asked.

"Just hand them in to me. I'll make sure to dispose of them properly."

Danny nodded before speaking. "Tell me more about vampires," he said.

"What do you want to know?"

"Anything," he replied. "What else kills them?"

"Nothing."

"What about beheading?" he asked, his eyes narrowed in suspicion.

"No," she said.

"No? They have no fucking heads! It's not connected to their hearts!" he exclaimed.

"Just tiger's eye in the heart, Nothing else that I know of works."

"What, do they grow a new head or a new body?" he joked.

"Neither, I don't think," she said. "You still exist, but in the worst of ways. It's the ultimate punishment vampires force upon one another, left for only the most serious crime; killing one of our own kind."

"Tell me more about this punishment," he said.

"Your body is buried separate from your head. You have no control over your body, but for some reason you can still feel what it feels."

"So if you tickled it with a feather..."

"You'd still be able to feel it."

"That's fucked up," Danny said with a bemused smile.

"That's not all. Your head is buried in a small box, whilst your body is wrapped in a shawl lined with galena dust."

"But I though galena…"

"Exactly," she said. "The galena is not thick enough to melt through the body. It burns the body at the same rate that the body regenerates nerve and pain receptors. The result is that you have total visual and auditory sensory deprivation, i.e., you can't see or hear anything. Remember, your lungs are separated from your throat and voice box, so you couldn't speak even if you wanted to."

"Fucking hell!"

"You can only remain silent in the silent dark, screaming a silent scream, feeling the constant agony of the galena burning your entire body for eternity. All you know is the pain, until your mind breaks. Even then, the pain never, ever stops. There has to be a deterrent from vampires killing their own kind. Besides, nature tells us not to."

"What do you mean?"

"It's hard to explain. I can only describe it as a feeling deep inside you telling you that killing another vampire is wrong, trying to stop you from doing it. But even if you manage to ignore that intense feeling, you have the punishment of an eternity of excruciating pain to think about."

"How do you know all this?" Danny asked.

"Because I was the one the elder vampires turned to, to either hunt human vampire hunters or to hunt my kind who had broken that one sacred rule."

"When we first met, Malcolm called you 'Mercy the Executioner'," Danny said.

"It's what they called me. And I was very good at it," Mercy replied looking at the floor between them.

"And now you've gone from killing vampire hunters to training one," he stated with a smile.

"Life *is* strange."

"So what else? What happens when you die and turn into a vampire? Does it hurt when you die? What's it like to lose your soul?" he asked.

"You don't die and you still have a soul. At least I think," she said.

"Oh, I just figured that when you turn into a vampire your body dies."

"It's not like the movies or TV shows. Your body doesn't die, and you don't lose your soul, if such a thing even exists," she explained.

"So how can vampires be so cruel to their victims?" he asked.

"You talk of vampire cruelty. There is no animal crueller than humans, and they have a soul," she replied, to which he nodded.

"It's a number of things," she continued. "Never underestimate the power of the hunger. Plus being increasingly removed from humans for an increasing amount of time removes you from the human condition. When you add to that the fact that the hunter in you only sees humans as food, it makes vampires gradually more and more inhumane. As a result, they become increasingly cruel as they look for their kicks. After all, they're only playing with their food."

"So that's it then, there's no other possible way for a vampire to die?" he asked.

"Well, technically they can die without even being touched," she said.

I was hoping not to tell him, but I can't lie to the boy. For fuck's sake!

"What does that mean?"

"You can kill a vampire's sire. If you kill the sire, you kill not only that vampire, but also the vampires he created."

"Wow, but how?" he asked.

"Basically, they are intrinsically linked. When the sire dies, the other vampires become human and return to the chronological age they should be. So if a vampire was thirty when they were sired, and they have been a vampire for 300 years, they will return to being human with the body of a 330 year old, which is an abnormal age for a human, so they turn to dust. There's no escaping time."

"But if a vampire has only been a vampire for a few months…" Danny began.

"Then they will return to being human, only a few months older," Mercy confirmed.

"Wow, with Gabriel dead, we could take out the entire nest in one go," Danny said, his eyebrows raised in excitement.

"Exactly. Gabriel will be very difficult for you to get to, though. We'll need to draw him out. As a rule, vampires always protect their sire, because if the dies, they die. That's why we are targeting the rest of his nest. But it's a fine line, because we don't want him asking for help," she said.

"So that was your plan? Sounds like a solid plan," he conceded.

"Thanks," she replied.

"Anyway Mercy, I forgot to tell you. I ordered a lump of unpolished tiger's eye and a lump of galena. They arrived a couple of days ago. I spent ages trying to sharpen the tiger's eye as finely as I could, but it was bloody difficult!"

"I can imagine. Tiger's eye is tough to carve by hand," she said.

"I've got them here. I'd like you to take a look and check that they… uh…"

"Are genuine? That you aren't going to attack an ancient, lethal, predator many times faster and more powerful than you with a lump of plastic?" she asked, her smile returning.

"Something like that," he said. The uneven and splintered shard he produced bore the appearance of genuine tiger's eye.

"Gimme," Mercy said and accepted the shard from him. It was uneven, unstable and had cracked in a number of places. The point was still quite dull and was off-centre from the core of the shard. But still, it was unmistakably tiger's eye, and it would still do the job.

"Yeah, this is the real deal, but did you run it over in a fucking tractor? It'll do the job, but you'll need to put your full force into it, to get it through their clothes, past their skin and bones, into their heart."

"Thanks for filling me with confidence," Danny replied, rolling his eyes. "Anyway, here's the galena."

"That's good," Mercy replied.

"Well?

"Well what?"

"I need to check that it's real galena," he said.

"And you can check with Cassius."

"Mercy! Come on! I need to test it!"

"Not on my skin you don't! You saw how it affects us! It's like me tasing you in the nuts, only, like a hundred times worse!"

Danny's crestfallen and pouting expression was reminiscent of a toddler whose favourite toy had been taken away.

"Fine!" she snapped, to which Danny immediately grinned. "Right, hold it out in the palm of your hand, but do not move your hand!"

Danny held it in front of her at chest height.

Fuck!

She stuck her left pinkie out as her hand hovered over his. She slowly lowered the tip of her pinkie onto the cold, rough surface of the galena.

The searing pain travelled up her arm, spread throughout her body, and hit her brain as her fingertip began to melt. Even though she lifted her hand away, the waves of pain pulsed through her body, taking her energy from her.

She recoiled, grasping her finger and its melted tip.

"Mercy! Are you OK?" Danny asked as he crouched over her.

The anger in her rose. Her eyesight became vibrant and clear. Her hearing became acute. Her canines pressed against her tongue. His heartbeat sang to her, and her stomach growled.

She took a couple of breaths and the anger subsided. Her vision and hearing returned to normal as her fangs retracted.

"How do you think I feel, ya bawbag! Next time you ask me to test your galena, I'll shove it up your fucking arse sideways!"

"It's real galena then? Good, good," Danny replied calmly.

"Cheeky wee prick," she muttered.

"It's astonishing the immediate effect that it has on vampires. It's beyond just an extreme allergy. It's like... it's supernatural," he said.

"Of course it's supernatural. What part of tiger's eye, galena or eternal super-strong beings seems natural to you?"

"OK, you don't have to be a salty bitch, hen," he said, sitting with a powerful posture and a confident smile, bordering on cocky.

Good, kid. You'll need that confidence.

A smile turned into a giggle, which led to Mercy bursting into laughter, which soon became infectious as Danny followed suit.

"Alright, what training are we doing first?"

"No training tonight. The three of us are going to have Chinese, and we're going to watch some vampire movies so I can mock them and tell you and Franky how wrong they are."

"No training tonight?" Danny asked. His eyebrows were raised in genuine surprise.

"No more training. You're ready."

"Really?"

"Really," she assured him. "Tomorrow night, you're going to kill Cassius and nothing will ever be the same."

CHAPTER 12

"Shut the fuck up, Cripple!" Mercy shouted, as Danny continued to scream.

The biting wind caught at the back of Danny's throat as, mouth gaping open, they continued to soar high above the streets of Edinburgh.

"HELP!"

"Shut your fucking mouth!" she scolded him. "The whole point of flying at night is to be silent and unseen. Emphasis on *silent!*"

Danny stopped looking down and instead screwed his eyes shut tight and readjusted his failing grip around Mercy's waist as she flew parallel with the ground far below.

"My God, stop being a wimp!" she said.

"I'm gonna fall!" he squeaked, followed by a few whimpers.

His grip around her neck continued to loosen

"Fuck! Fine!" Mercy snapped, and flipped around so she was flying with her back to the ground, facing up at the sky. Danny was now lying directly on top of her.

"Thank God!" Danny shouted.

"What, did you think that flying with a vampire would be like Lois Lane flying with Superman? It doesn't give *you* the ability to fly!" she said.

Danny straddled her, wrapping his legs around her thighs, the pain in his knee a very distant concern. He lay flat on her, his head buried in her cleavage and his arms wrapped around her back.

Mercy continued to fly, stiff as a plank of wood, looking awkwardly at the stars above her.

"Hey, hey! Not so tight on the legs and get your face out of my tits! We're not on a date!" she said, but Danny wasn't listening.

"I swear to God, Danny, if I feel you get a hard-on, I'll drop you from here!"

"Don't flatter yourself!" he replied in a panicked tone.

Mercy looked over her shoulder down at the ground as they approached the heart of the Old Town

"Right, I can't see where I'm flying. You're going to have to guide me down. Look for a place which is dark, there won't be CCTV, and there are no cars or locals walking around. Try one of the smaller closes," she said.

Danny opened his eyes and scanned the streets below them. They approached an alleyway which matched Mercy's requirements. He gradually and awkwardly guided her down until Mercy flipped over six feet from the ground and unceremoniously dumped him, before gracefully rotating upright and landing feet first.

Danny painfully got to his feet and checked his belongings, still clutching his cane. The compact holdall was still wrapped around his shoulders. He rummaged in the unfamiliar inside pockets of the borrowed jacket and touched both his tiger's eye stake and the fist sized lump of galena.

He then started fussing with his clothes. Dull unidentifiable stains littered the jacket and the jeans. They were frayed at the seams and were worn thin at the joints. The heavy mustiness and residual body odour smell assaulted his senses, adding to his uneasiness. The musk of greasy hair on the collar caused a queasiness, exacerbated by nerves.

"Did I have to wear a homeless person's clothes?" he asked.

"Oh, I'm sorry, is His Highness dissatisfied with his attire this evening?" she mocked him. "Yeah, it's a cold night and you're bloody freezing in those clothes. What part of being homeless do you think is all snug and warm? I told you, Cripple, you need to get rid of that arrogance. They're no worse than you. You're just pretending to be homeless, in the hope that Cassius is tempted by you. You need to look the part. Just be grateful to be as pampered as you've been in your life to this point. You get to go back to a nice warm home after this."

They stepped out of the close and onto one of the side streets; it was quiet with no traffic or people in sight.

"Remember, he'll almost certainly be in Bohemia right now but will probably be leaving soon. You're setting yourself up at the bottom of Fleshmarket Close. There's a chance he'll run into you. Now what do you do?"

"I... um ask him for spare change?"

"And if he ignores you?"

"Press him, follow him?"

"Right, but don't get aggressive. If he's not in the mood to eat, he'll just tell you to step out in front of traffic, and you'll have to either expose yourself as immune to vampire hypnotism, or actually get run over again."

"So what then?" he asked.

"Butter him up. They're all narcissists, so say a few things about how good he looks. Hell, flirt with him if you can. Lots of vampires will shag anything with a pulse if it turns them on."

"OK," Danny replied and took a few deep breaths.

"Good luck. Don't get eaten, and I'll stop in on you later," she said, and walked back down the close.

"Wait, what if..." he said as he went back onto the close, but she was already in the air and gone.

The walk to Fleshmarket Close was torturous and fraught with fears and doubts. Like a foot soldier marching toward a battlefield, he began to question everything Mercy had told him about how he had to be the one to do the fighting.

His doubts reached a crescendo when he stepped onto the Royal Mile and passed his home. In that moment, he wanted to go home, have a shower, and go to bed with a hot cup of tea and a slice of toast. He wanted to reject this mad world of vampires and bloodshed. But Aurelia was on his mind every second of every day. He had to find her, and doing this was the only way.

He stepped on to the top of Fleshmarket Close and followed it down, past where he first met Tom, towards where Gabriel attacked Aurelia. He stepped onto the cobble stone road where the taxi had hit him. A flash of headlights, shining off the stones and the shop windows, made him flinch backwards.

His mind screamed memories into his conscious, of the tyre squeal, hitting the front, grill and landing on the bonnet of the car, before rolling off.

His vision blurred slightly and his heart began to thump its way through his chest. He couldn't get enough air. The world began to swim in front of him. He stumbled away from the road and leaned against a shop window.

Oh God! I'm having a heart attack or something! God, please help me!

Tears began to run down his face as he slumped his back against the glass and curled into the foetal position. After a few minutes, the symptoms eased.

Come on Danny, Aurelia needs you! You can do this!

He got back to his feet with great help from his cane. With rubber band legs, he crossed the road and continued his journey down Fleshmarket Close.

Come on Danny you dick, be brave!

He gruffly sniffed and wiped the tears from his face with the sleeve of his jacket.

He reached the agreed place to set himself up as locals passed him by, making their way up the close.

This is way too busy and public! How am I going to be able to kill this vampire with people coming and going like this?

He sat on the cold stone ground, just a few yards from a small flight of stone steps next to the arched entrance of Fleshmarket Close. Through the arch and to the right was Bohemia and, inside, his target. Or not. Perhaps Cassius had deviated from his pattern; this could all be a waste of time.

He moved his lump of galena from his inside pocket to

his left outside jacket pocket. He then slid his home-sharpened stake up his right sleeve.

All the techniques she trained me on, but she never told me the best place to hide my stake! Fuck, I'm going to die tonight, aren't I?

A sudden seriousness struck him.

Actually, I AM going to die tonight. There's no way I'll be able to kill an eternal creature stronger than a hundred men, faster than the eye, and who can actually fly. It won't matter if I surprise him.

"Christ, what am I doing?" he whispered and ran his hands through his hair.

Just go, while you can. You can lie to Mercy that you didn't see him.

Still, he continued to sit cross legged, occasionally straightening his right leg to try to ease the aching. Another twenty minutes passed and he brought both knees up to his chest with much grimacing. A whirlwind of everything and nothing entered and left his mind as he waited.

He asked the few people who passed him for change and they all ignored him. Some pretended not to see him and others put their heads down and increased their pace.

You saw me, you pair of sly bastards! Does it hurt to give me some coppers? Putting your heads down and slinking away. Probably think that their money will be wasted on drink or drugs when all I'd use it for is a coffee or a sandwich out of a shop.

That's when it hit him.

Holy fuck. That's me. They're me. I'm the arsehole who puts his head down and walks on. I'm always thinking that if I give them any money, it'll be just to pay for their next hit.

Danny sat in his shame.

Oh Danny, you are a complete arsehole, aren't you?

Another twenty minutes passed.

It's got to be after 11pm now. I don't think that he's coming after all. Thank God!

He exhaled a long and shaky breath and smiled as a beautiful woman appeared through the stone archway entrance to Fleshmarket Close, climbed the dozen or so steps, and passed him.

His eyes followed her as she walked up the gradient of the close, away from him, her alluring perfume still in his nose. Wearing a fitted leather biker's jacket and cream-coloured skirt, her pixie cut hair was a dark auburn under the street lighting.

Anyway, right, home.

He released a relieved toothy grin.

Turns out Cassius didn't show up after all, so I don't need to lie to Mercy. Thank Christ!

He was still smiling at the entrance when a familiar face appeared through the archway. Danny had studied a picture of that face for hours at Mercy's home. It was the face of his first target, Cassius. Cassius, however, had his eyes on the woman he was following.

Tall, with long straight black hair and black eyes, he climbed the steps and passed Danny. His stroll was effortless, his gait perfect. He wore a perfectly tailored white shirt, black waistcoat, and trousers.

Fuck! I've missed my chance!

Danny stumbled to his feet and as he reached over for his cane, his tiger's eye stake slid out of his sleeve and clattered onto the ground, the sound echoing up the close before rolling down towards the steps.

"Fuck!" he whispered as he clumsily stamped on the stake to prevent it rolling any farther. He clutched both it and the cane and looked back up at Cassius.

Stuffing his stake in his jeans pocket with one third jutting out at an awkward angle, Danny shuffled after his prey, just as Cassius stalked his.

He was a few feet away when Danny spoke.

"Spare change please?"

"No," came the answer in a deep and confident voice.

"Aww come on, just a pound mate!" Danny insisted.

"No!" Cassius snapped without looking back.

Cassius was striding up the slope of the close and the distance between them was growing.

"Come on to fuck, mate! Don't be stingy, ya Anne Rice-looking prick!" Danny shouted, his anger showing.

Cassius stopped mid-stride.

Oops.

Cassius turned to look at Danny. Danny's heart didn't drop to his stomach, it fell out of his arse and rolled down the close.

"Umm, spare change please?"

Cassius looked irritated and completely focused on Danny.

"Anne Rice-looking prick, am I?"

"Well, um... it *was* a compliment," Danny said with a weak smile as Cassius drew closer to him.

"Stand still," Cassius said.

That same warm fuzzy pressure entered Danny's mind.

I'm gonna kill you, you bastard.

As Danny's ire rose, the fuzzy pressure faded.

"Well look at you, my poor unfortunate soul," Cassius said with a smile as he surveyed Danny. "Your heart is hammering!" he added and licked his lips.

"That's because I'm talking with someone so handsome and... sexy?" Danny replied, his tone dripping with uncertainty.

"I was going to enjoy a rich steak and fine wine at home tonight," Cassius said as he looked Danny up and down once more. "But I guess a cheap and nasty takeaway on the street will do. Now..." Cassius continued.

Danny found himself fighting a fresh wave of that fuzzy pressure.

"Come with me," Cassius instructed.

Danny followed in silence.

After a couple of minutes walking, Danny found himself being led down a set of stairs into an alleyway off the Royal Mile.

"This'll do," Cassius said as he stopped walking.

Danny grasped the stake jutting out of his jeans and slipped it behind his back.

"What happened to Aurelia?" he asked.

"What?" Cassius asked as he turned to face Danny.

"Is Aurelia still alive?"

Cassius's eyes narrowed as he put his hands on his hips. His unbuttoned waistcoat parted, exposing more of his shirt.

"You said you wanted a steak," Danny said as he readjusted his grip on the stake.

"Eh?" Cassius asked.

"I have one for you!" Danny said as he summoned every ounce of grit, determination, and strength.

All the love, anger, fury, joy, pain, and heartbreak welled into a ball of energy in his hand. Danny zeroed in on Cassius's heart and, with everything he had, Danny thrust the stake towards his target.

He didn't know what it would feel like to plunge something sharp into someone's chest, but he *was* surprised when the stake landed hard on his chest with a metallic *ching* and didn't move past creating a small hole in Cassius's shirt.

Both sporting a frown, Danny and Cassius briefly stared at one another.

Cassius pushed Danny away with such force that Danny slammed against the stone wall of the alley, expelling all the air from his lungs. As he landed on the ground, the stake broke free and rolled to the feet of Cassius.

Cassius chuckled.

"I should have known when I heard you mention Anne Rice, but I didn't twig."

Cassius kicked Danny in the ribs, but through luck, Danny's shoulder was in the way, leaving Danny with a dead right arm.

"Oh God!" Danny wheezed as he struggled on all fours. Cassius stood over him, his expression dripping contempt.

"Lucky me," Cassius said and burst the top few buttons off his shirt, exposing a smooth chest and a silver circular medallion on a chain over his heart. "Still, sorry to be the bearer of bad news, but wooden stakes don't work, boy!" he said and picked up the stake.

Danny got to his feet but was still bent over, sucking for breath, with his right knee giving way periodically.

Cassius's smile faded as he continued to look at the stake.

"Tiger's eye," Cassius whispered. "Where did you get this? Did you hear me? *Who* told you about tiger's eye?" Cassius demanded in a loud, booming voice.

"Your mum," Danny replied as he gradually straightened up.

"Do you think this is a joke?" Cassius asked. His eyes were black and his canines hung low. "Who told you about us? Who told you about tiger's eye?" he asked as he grabbed Danny by the throat, but did not squeeze.

"What did he do to her?" Danny asked. "What did Gabriel do to Aurelia?"

"How do you know Gabriel or Aurelia?" Cassius said, before it began to dawn on him. "Wait, are you Aurelia's brother?" A smile appeared on his demonic face.

"What happened to her?"

"Oh boy, just wait until I tell her what has happened to you. But now, time for a snack."

Danny fished for the galena in his jacket pocket.

As Cassius leaned in, Danny grabbed the back of Cassius's head and pressed the lump of galena into the side of his face.

There was a second or two before the screaming began.

Danny wrestled the stake out of Cassius's hand and, as Cassius scratched at the hand pressing the galena to his face, Danny pressed the tip of the stake to Cassius's heart. With all the strength he had left, he charged at Cassius. Both men landed hard against the opposing stone wall, and the stake drove its way deep inside the vampire's chest. From the wound, white-grey chalk spread out in all directions. The screaming stopped and Cassius visage was replaced with a chalk edifice of a tortured scream, frozen in place. Danny's hand easily slid through the head and the body crumbled to dust as he fell through the husk of the vampire.

Danny's knee buckled and he landed on his rear. Around him was a chalk white dust and empty clothes. In a small mound of the dust a dented silver medallion on a chain shone back at him.

"Fucking hell!" a male voice came from the opening of the alley. The torch from a phone shone down the stairs onto a coughing and gagging Danny, who squinted against its glare.

"Never mind, it's just some headcase junky," the voice trailed off in volume and the shining light disappeared.

Danny hurriedly stuffed all of the clothes, the shoes, and the jewellery into the sports holdall, pausing only to look at a silver ring with a lion decoration on the face. He pocketed it and, cane in hand, painfully and tenderly shuffled home.

CHAPTER 13

Mercy rung the buzzer and waited at the security door. She scanned the dark of the courtyard as she waited.

I can't believe he actually did it. He killed a vampire. He had the guts and resolve to see it through. Maybe the cripple really IS the one to solve all our problems.

Eventually the door buzzed and she pushed it open. By the time she reached his front door, Danny was already waiting with his door open, a can of beer in his hand.

"Cripple," she addressed him.

"Mercy," he replied with a smile.

"How are you holding up?" she asked.

"Fine, fine I guess," he replied, though not convincingly, then stepped aside, leaving the door open for her.

"Well, are you going to let me in? I feel our conversation should be out of earshot of the neighbours."

"So, it's true that you need to be invited in?"

Mercy nodded.

"Then come in please," he replied.

Mercy stepped over the threshold of his home and into the red carpeted hallway.

"Normally it's not an issue, as we would just hypnotise people into letting us in, but you're immune to that now," she added as she wandered into the living room.

Cheap yet tasteful furniture sat on a dark cream carpet with magnolia wallpaper decorating the room. The smell of dust hung heavy in the air as it layered most of the ornaments.

"I love what you've done with the place," she said.

"What? Oh, yeah. Aurelia decided decorations, colour schemes, and stuff," Danny said as he shuffled in. "Want a beer?" he asked as he disappeared into the kitchen. His gait was slower and much more pained than usual.

Cassius obviously fought back more than Danny described in his phone call. His voice was jittery then. The adrenaline was still flowing when he called, but he seems calmer now.

Mercy sat on the couch, crossing her legs as she surveyed the rest of the room. In the corner sat two crutches and the remains of a broken chair. Musty, stale air filled the room. A sharpened wooden stake lay next to the other three chair legs.

"Waste of a good chair," she muttered with a smile.

Danny returned with Mercy's beer. As he stretched his hand out to hand her the beer, the sleeve of his top slid up his arm, exposing a large patch of dark blue and purple skin.

That's a fucker of a bruise. There was definitely a fight. He's lucky to be alive.

Danny slumped next to her on the couch.

Mercy cracked the can open, took a gulp, and sat it next to two still-sealed packs of co-codamol 30/500mg which themselves bore a layer of dust.

"So, how did it go? Still shaky? Adrenaline still high?" she asked.

"Fine. Yeah, still a bit wobbly, hence the beer. It went OK, I think. I mean, I was a bit all over the place but I got the job done."

"You seem a bit more... tender than usual. What happened?

"Well, I pretended to be hypnotised like we planned and he took me into an alleyway. I took my stake out and stabbed him in the heart as hard as I could, but I hit this," he said, then produced a sizeable silver medallion on a chain with a prominent dent in the centre.

Mercy burst out laughing.

Danny's initial frown gave way to chuckles.

"Oh, for fuck's sake, Cripple! Trust you! Trust your first time to be a vampire wearing that big ugly thing!"

"Yeah, you didn't think to teach me about vampire bulletproof vests!"

His words sparked a fresh round of guffawing and when it naturally died down, he continued.

"Anyway, he gave me a hefty shove. Knocked the air out of me and I think my chest will be bruised tomorrow. He tried to kick me in the ribs but my arm got in the way. So I had a dead arm, although given the force, I'm lucky he didn't break my arm. But the problem is when he saw that my stake was tiger's eye and not wood, well he wasn't happy. Still, thank God for that galena. Mashed it right into his face," he said.

Mercy winced.

"And when he was preoccupied with the pain, I drove the stake into him. That vampire dust gets everywhere! I had to have a shower when I got home to wash the vampire out of my hair!"

"Yeah, it does! It really does," she replied.

"Someone arrived after I killed Cassius and shone their phone torch on me, but Cassius had crumbled, so they only saw me sitting on my arse covered in dust with a few clothes scattered. They thought I was mental and left me to it, so that's good," he said and took another gulp of beer.

"It's convenient that vampire bodies can easily crumble to nothing. A lot handier than having to dispose of a corpse with fangs. As long as there are no witnesses to the stake going in, you're pretty much away scot-free. Listen Cripple, we've started down a path and there's no going back now. You realise that, don't you?"

"Aye, I know," he admitted.

"Good. It begins. We'll need to speed things up substantially now. Franky will report back in the next few days with info on the rest of the nest. It took weeks to get Cassius's report ready and now we need another seven, so the reports won't be as detailed, even with his entire list of sources. We should have enough to work with and hopefully some useful info on Gabriel. We'll move soon after. But first..." Mercy said. Danny leaned forward in his seat waiting for her to finish. "Can I use your toilet?" she asked.

"Oh, you... um..."

"Pee? Yes, vampires pee."

"Oh, good to know. Anyway, second on your left," he instructed.

It was as Mercy was returning from the toilet when the scent reached her. She had smelled it before, just as a vampire had once smelled it from her. She followed it through the open bedroom door. It was faint, but unmistakable. It led her to the wardrobe containing a collection of women's jumpers, jackets, and coats.

She took a thick wool jumper from the hanger and sat on the bed. She held it to her face and breathed in deeply.

A few moments later, she was interrupted by Danny when he loudly and deliberately cleared his throat at the door.

"Oh," she said as she snapped out of her trance. She had been lying on the bed, holding the jumper to her face. "Um," she mumbled as she sat up in bed.

"After you had been gone for over forty minutes, I thought I'd check on you. You didn't pee in here, did you?"

"I was here that long?" she asked. "Sorry."

"I get the feeling that an explanation as to why you happen to be in my sister's bedroom, on her bed, isn't out of the question here," he stated before returning to the living room followed by Mercy, still clutching the jumper.

After a few moments' silence, where Mercy sat on the couch like a schoolgirl being chastised by the headmistress, she began speaking.

"I think that there is a chance that Aurelia is alive," she said as she looked up at Danny.

"I know."

"You do? How?"

"I was holding out hope that she is still out there somewhere, although that hope was waning pretty fast. It was starting to become more about revenge in my mind. But after meeting Cassius, I realised that she may be alive. But more on that later. First, carry on with why you think that she is alive all of a sudden."

"It's how humans get chosen to be sired, that is, turned into a vampire. They smell a certain way. It's… indescribable, but it's very strong and it calls out to a vampire. I mean, anyone can be turned, but someone with that natural scent…"

"Wait, so you choose who to sire because of a smell? Really?" he asked, his scepticism clear to see.

"You don't understand. It's like catnip to us. It's overwhelming. It's like, a human who smells like that can survive the siring."

"What do you mean can survive the siring?" he asked.

"A vampire can attempt to sire any human, but the vast majority of regular humans don't survive it. Some normal humans can, especially if the sire knows how to do it well, but most humans can't handle vampire blood in their system. It's toxic and usually fatal. But for people with that scent, they handle it much easier. Not all survive, but a far greater percentage of them do. It's like an advert that nature is calling out for them to be turned into vampires."

"And Aurelia smells like that? Why can't I smell it?"

"Normal humans can't, but vampires can. I dunno. Maybe it's a different kind of pheromone or something. A pheromone that only a tiny number of humans have. I dunno why it would make their systems more able to cope with vampire blood. Maybe it's not biological at all, and something more…"

"Supernatural?" Danny suggested.

"Yeah. Fact is, if you have that pheromone or scent, if you have that thing which calls out to us, you're likely going to survive the siring."

"Do you think that Gabriel sired Aurelia?"

"Almost certainly. We call them 'the chosen'. It just means that someone, or something, nature maybe, *chose* them to be naturally eligible to become vampires. It's more than likely Gabriel tried to sire her."

"That makes sense," he said. "While Cassius thought he had the upper hand, he said 'wait until I tell her what has happened to you'. I couldn't be sure that he wasn't just fucking with my head to be cruel but now that you've told me about these possible pheromone things, it definitely sounds as though she is still alive."

"That's fantastic news, Cripple!"

"I know. We can get Aurelia back. Back and human," he said with a surprising calmness.

"If you kill Gabriel, you kill everyone *and* get your Aurelia back. Two birds, one vampire. You're taking this news surprisingly well. I'd have thought your mind would be exploding!" she joked.

"It is. I'm just a bit overwhelmed. I've spent the last hour in the shower, washing vampire off me, realising that Aurelia is definitely alive. I mean, I've been increasingly aware that she is dead. Then tonight I find out that she is definitely alive, but she's now a vampire. I honestly don't know how to act. My mind is a fucking riot right now," he admitted.

They sat in silence for a moment. Finally, Danny spoke again.

"So, tell me all about this siring process."

"I don't know if that's..." Mercy began.

"I want to know what Aurelia has been through," Danny interrupted. His tone was not one of anger, merely resolution.

"Very well," Mercy replied.

Danny stared through the carpet.

"Well, even though you are a vampire, that's not the end of it. You see, a new vampire is completely feral and cannot be trusted to control their instincts. They have to be kept away from humans as the sire trains them how to control their thirst and the effects of blood-joy. The whole process can take months."

"Right now she'll be completely feral. She'd attack me even if she saw me?" he asked. He then placed his head in his hands.

"Look, I wish I had more reassuring advice but I don't. What I can absolutely say for certain is that the remaining vampires in the nest are still out there and will continue killing."

"I'll kill every one of those bastards," he said in a low, growling tone.

"That's it," Mercy replied. "Keep that anger. It'll sustain you."

"I hate to think of Aurelia out there, feral. Giving in to this 'blood-joy'. What is blood-joy anyway. I've heard you mention it before."

"Humans call it 'blood lust', but it's not lust. When we taste blood, it's like a release. Think of it like an orgasm, only a thousand times more intense. It's absolute euphoria, only unlike anything you may have experienced. The taste of the warm blood as it fills your mouth. You can feel it inside your chest when you swallow. Then warmth and purest energy radiates from your core, along with absolute euphoria. That's why we call it blood-joy."

Danny nodded, and they both sat in silence for a few moments.

"So, what's next?" Danny asked, still looking down.

"Well, I should have more information on the pattern and movements of the remaining nest members, and then we'll go hunting again. This time, we'll need to be much faster. Right now they'll be sleeping, but when they wake up this evening they'll wonder where Cassius has gone. It won't be long before they realise something is wrong. When that happens they'll be much more careful and harder to trick, so we need to kill as many of them as fast as possible."

"Bring it on," Danny said.

The night continued with both sitting on the couch. One beer became three, and they began to chat about non-vampire related topics. Mercy found herself genuinely enjoying the company of another for the first time in centuries.

"Surely you weren't this much of an arsehole when you were human?" Danny said with a smile.

Mercy smiled.

"Cripple, I've always been an arsehole."

"How old were you when you were sired?" he asked.

"Twenty-three. Never mind that. Tell me about you and Aurelia. Why did your parents call her 'Aurelia'? Nowadays it's a very uncommon name."

"She was called Aurelia because it has been a family tradition forever to call the women in the family Aurelia. Our Mum was called Aurelia, and one of our aunts, all down throughout our family tree."

"For exactly how long?" she asked.

"God knows," he replied. "Aurelia is my very best pal. It's thanks to her I'm not a gibbering fucking wreck today."

"What do you mean?" Mercy asked.

"Oh, it's a long story."

"I'm a timeless nocturnal creature. I've got plenty of time. Now give me the abridged version."

"Fair enough," he replied and took a deep breath. "I should start with the accident which changed our lives. Our mum died when I was seven and Aurelia was nine. We were walking down the street and a car mounted the pavement. It ploughed into us. Drunk driver apparently. Mum shoved me away and I hit my head. Aurelia broke her leg, but Mum took the full brunt of it. It hit her directly and pinned her against the stone wall behind her. I still remember looking up from the ground. Under the car I saw Mum's feet and shins. I thought she was fine. But then I saw the blood begin to run down her shins. Then I heard Aurelia scream."

Mercy nodded and listened without comment. A presence announced itself inside her chest. Something which had been dormant for a long time awoke.

"I still have nightmares every now and again," he continued. "I remember me and Aurelia hugging Mum, crying. She was crying too as she was folded over the bonnet of the car. She was telling us that she loved us. We were hugging her, but she didn't have the strength to move. She asked Aurelia to take care of her little brother and she said that I would make her very proud when I was a grown up."

"And with what we're doing, I'm sure she's very proud. You're facing death each time you face a vampire and the forces of evil to save your big sister. If that's not a reason to be immensely proud, I don't know what is."

"Cheers," he replied, looking at his lap. "Soon afterwards, I started having panic attacks and not wanting to go outside. Dad had to pick up the pieces, including his wife dying, his son panicking whenever outside, and his daughter going quiet and sullen. Perhaps he should have guided me through it, but he was so overwhelmed that he just caved and let me stay in. It affected Dad worst of all. He became really insecure and paranoid about our safety. He wanted us to stop going outside. It got worse, to the point where we were being home-schooled. We didn't have friends. The three of us were insular, and Aurelia and me, we became increasingly isolated."

"Must have been tough on you both," she said, to which Danny shrugged.

"It was just life for us. He died just last year. Heart attack. As far as we knew he didn't have any heart problems. He just keeled over one day. That was us left alone. We had to find our way together. She applied for a job here and when she got it, we moved from our home town of Glasgow to here. She got me a job in her work, so we both work there. We live together to share bills, otherwise we wouldn't be able to afford to pay rent in this city. As a matter of fact, I'm getting into deep shit with my landlord because I haven't been back at work. Dunno if I even have a job," he continued with a smile which quickly faded.

Danny rubbed at the can of beer in between his hands as he stared at the top.

"I've always been nervous when going out. I had full-blown panic attacks, but thanks to Aurelia supporting me, I've improved a lot. But it's just the two of us together. I guess I've never been able to make friends, and Aurelia had chosen to forego friends and boyfriends. All for me. And I took her for granted all this time. She put me ahead of herself all her life and that's what got her into this trouble."

"What do you mean?" Mercy asked.

"Well, on the night Gabriel took her, we were leaving Bohemia. We left early because I had a migraine and was starting to feel quite panicky. I asked to go to a newsagents. She was going to go straight home. She was encouraging me to go myself while I felt anxious. I guess she thought that it would be good for me. But I pestered her into coming with me. When she was vaping outside, that's when Gabriel grabbed her. If only I wasn't such a mental fuck up or a coward, she would have got home safely and none of this would be happening."

"No, no," Mercy replied. "Look, that smell called out to Gabriel. If you had gone alone, he would have just followed her and taken her anyway. If you had both gone home, then he would have hypnotised you into letting him in. He would have killed you and taken Aurelia anyway. This isn't your guilt to carry, trust me."

"I just feel that her baby brother has been a millstone around her neck," Danny said.

"What age are you both anyway?" Mercy asked.

"Aurelia is twenty-one. It was my nineteenth birthday last week."

"Oh. Shit birthday. Well happy belated birthday."

"Thanks," he replied with a half-hearted smile.

"I'm sure your dad would be proud of both of you," she said.

"Well, Aurelia judges Dad really harshly. She thinks that he stifled us too much. She didn't have a normal upbringing. We didn't have proper life experiences or friends. She blames him for that."

"And do you feel the same?"

"No," he admitted. "I mean, Aurelia is right, but I'm a bit more forgiving. Dad did his best. Sure, it wasn't healthy, but he was insecure and he didn't have any support or advice. He made poor choices and decisions, but his heart was in the right place."

Mercy nodded.

Should I give him a hug? That's what people do, isn't it?

"Annnyway," Danny said with a smile and a sigh. Enough

about me. So how old are you?"

"Does it matter?"

"To me it does. Stop this 'every man is an island' pish. I already know that you're pure dead mysterious," he said, to which Mercy laughed. "So just tell me," he prompted.

"I was born in the year of our Lord 1453."

"Wow, you *are* old! But you don't look a day over 500."

"Smartarse!" she replied, her smile widening.

"I didn't know that the name 'Mercy' was as old as that," he said.

"It isn't, I don't think. I was actually born with another name and, before you ask, it's a name I don't like to be reminded of," she replied.

"Fair enough," he said, holding his hands up. "So, how were you sired? How did you come into contact with a vampire?"

"It's a long story," Mercy replied.

"I've got time."

"Well, I was twenty and I had already been married off. I didn't love my husband, but what the woman did and didn't want was of no consequence then. See, I've never *liked* men, but imagine trying to tell people that you are gay in the 1400's. You'd either be packed off to a convent if you were lucky, and if unlucky, you'd be burned as a witch."

"Jesus!" he said.

"Still, Robert was nice. He was a good man and he was nice to me. I did love him in a way, but I could never tell him the truth. Then when he went off to battle at the lord of the land's request, I soon found myself a widow. I still mourn him. He took care of me, and though he didn't know that I was living a lie, he still wouldn't have judged. He was gentle and I still miss him to this day."

"I'm sorry. I mean for being married off to a man where you had to keep yourself closeted for your safety, and then to be left alone. I can only imagine how hard it must have been for you."

"That was life back then," she said with a shrug. "There was this girl though. She herself was married and had a son, John, whom she worshipped. But I could tell when she looked at me. Even in medieval times there was such a thing as a gaydar," she said, to which Danny laughed.

"We got close, and even though we were just friends, I could tell that we both wanted much more. Every time I saw her though, there was a fresh bruise on her body. Her husband was a bully and an abusive arsehole. I wanted her to get help, but what could we do? Back then a wife was the husband's property. Besides, he was highly respected in town. So we had to just put up with it, with me salving her wounds, helpless to help her."

"It must have been infuriating as well as frustrating," he said.

"One day she came to my door. She was panicked and covered in blood. He'd hit her once too often. She grabbed a knife and stabbed him in the chest. Looking back, by the amount of blood on her, I'd say she struck the heart or an artery. There were witnesses though and she had to run. They scooped John up before she could get to him, and so she ran on her own."

Mercy's shoulders were slumped and she was picking at her nails.

"We had to make a split decision. I was young and impetuous and she was in shock at having murdered her abuser. We decided to run together. It meant leaving her little boy behind, something which shattered her. She never got over it. You don't just switch off being a mum."

Danny nodded in silence.

"We moved to a different part of the country and set up home in an abandoned cottage in a forest with a nearby town. With us both pitching in, the cottage was soon beautiful and we even tended a small garden. We made blankets and mended clothes to make money from the local townspeople. We told everyone we were sisters. In truth we could finally be married, if not officially. But she never got over losing John. The number of times I would wake up to hear her weeping in the dark..." she said and shook her head.

"Did you ever try to go back for John?" he asked.

"We were finalising plans to, but we never got the chance. One night a vampire came calling. His name was Claude. He saw a small cottage outside of town as an easy target. I opened the door to him and invited him in after he told me to. Claude bit me first and drained me so I'd be weak. Helpless. Then he killed her. I saw the look of terror in her eyes as I lay on the floor. He dropped her dead body like it was nothing. Like it was a sack of filthy old clothes. We looked in one another's eyes. Me in hers, and her vacant stare right through mine. I wanted to die by her side, but he picked me up and took me off."

"I'm sorry, Mercy. I'm so sorry," Danny said.

"To this day, if only I had done what she said and just ignored the door, I would have had a happy normal life with her. Anyway, Claude told me that I was one of the chosen. He sired me. I remember every part of it to this day. The bitter taste of his blood in my mouth. The nausea I felt from his blood in my stomach. The fevers, the vomiting as my body tried to fight his blood, before it gave up. I still remember the torment of losing myself as the animal took over. The feral stage, forgetting who I was, and only thirsting for blood, and the never-ending unquenchable thirst."

"Christ," Danny whispered.

"Then when I was able to get out and to control myself around humans, I was fully integrated into the small and close-knit vampire community. I learned all about us. What killed us, the different ways we could die, and also the punishment for killing one of our own. I enjoyed the power being a vampire gave me. I loved it. And I was a faithful servant. But I never forgot her. I never forgot what Claude did to her. What he did to my Aurelia," she said, remembering her true love's smile and tender touch.

"Aurelia? You mean your wife was also called..." his voice trailed off. After a moment he spoke again. "So that's why you reacted like that when we first met. You looked like you were about to kill me after seeing off Malcolm. I mentioned *my* Aurelia and you looked so weirded out."

"Well, it's an exceptionally rare name these days. It's been a long time since I heard someone speak that name, so yeah it took me aback."

"Well," Danny said raising his can. "To our Aurelias."

Mercy touched her can to his and they took a drink.

"Right, I've got some business to attend to and you need to get some sleep after the night you've had," she said as she stood up, grabbed Danny's holdall, and took it with her.

Danny accompanied her to the front door.

"I'll be in touch when Franky has reported back. Then we'll hunt again."

"And by then I should have a new toy to show you," Danny hinted with a smile.

"I dread to think," Mercy replied. "You're one of the good ones, Cripple. You had the courage of your convictions to see it through and kill Cassius. You knew that there was a better than average likelihood of you being killed, yet you were still brave enough to do what's right. We'll get Aurelia back. We'll find a way of getting her back to you, somehow. Both your parents would be very proud of you."

"Well look at this. Mercy has a human side after all."

"Fuck off, Cripple," she replied, her smile still present.

With that, she opened the door and left.

Let him have this moment. After so much preparation, so much insecurity and so much fear, he deserves this victory. If we don't work fast, I'll have to tell him about the consequences of what he has done.

Mercy let out a long sigh and took to the skies in an instant.

CHAPTER 14

How am I going to interrogate him without alerting him?

The overpoweringly musky stench of cologne stung Danny's nostrils as he walked up Chambers Street, side by side with the second vampire on Mercy's hit list: Douglas.

Where the hell is he taking me?

The faux-hypnotised Danny continued to stare ahead as his victim took the lead.

At well over six-feet tall with short blonde hair, he wore a white Henley shirt and faded jeans. With a heavily muscular build and pronounced jawline, Danny would hate to have to take on a human of such size, never mind a vampire.

A week had passed since they had dispatched Cassius and things had become increasingly tense in Mercy's home. Finally, they received Franky's report on the entire nest. Actions, movements, patterns, and times were laid out in neat detail. All except Gabriel. Mercy had been frustrated to hear that details on the nest leader were disturbingly sparse. With no identifiable habit or predictable movements, he rarely left the house, and when he did, he would disappear after a few moments. Mercy had decided that in lieu of their priority target Gabriel, Douglas should be the next to be hunted, and so Danny walked in silence by his side.

Approaching Douglas and suckering him into hypnotising Danny had been easy enough. The difficult part was coming up: how to find out about Aurelia without Douglas freaking and killing Danny, or flying away and alerting the rest of the nest that a vampire hunter was in town.

This is like walking a bloody tightrope! At least I have time to think of a strategy while he leads me to his ambush place. Plus, he hasn't even seen my toys.

Mercy had been delighted when Danny showed off his toys: a pair of black leather SAP gloves, the fingers cut off at the middle knuckle. The SAP gloves contained an inner layer of steel shot on the back of the hands and the fingers. This added weight and kinetic force with every punch would serve to deal extra damage to the recipient of each punch, as well as protecting the knuckles of the sender. Best of all, because they were classed as defensive clothes, they were legal.

Danny had modified these SAP gloves. A healthy dollop of superglue running from each knuckle down to the end of the cut-off fingers and pressed into powdered galena meant that every strike would pack a vampire-thumping punch. The biggest secret however was on the palms. A small flat lump of solid galena had been stitched into each palm, meaning that all he had to do to overpower a vampire was literally get his hands on them.

He initially tested their subtlety by asking to shake hands with Mercy, only for Mercy to offer her hand before he stopped her. The pride in Mercy's smile shone through.

They passed the National Museum of Scotland and its iconic circular building on the corner of Chambers Street and George IV Bridge, and Douglas' destination and intended ambush site became clear.

Really, well that's a little on the nose.

Across the road sat the Greyfriar's Bobby statue, the monument erected in honour of the world-famous diminutive Skye Terrier for his commitment and loyalty to his deceased owner. The life-sized statue whose nose had been rubbed to a brassy shine by romantic tourists was a totem symbolising the very best of Edinburgh and its people: loyalty, love, dedication, and hope. Bobby's statue stood watch outside the black wrought iron gates of Greyfriar's Kirkyard, and the ominous darkness beyond.

Set between an art shop and a pub lay the gates to the Kirkyard, widely considered the most haunted cemetery in the world. The gates lay forever open, always welcoming both new visitors and new residents alike.

Fuck's sake.

"In here," Douglas said without emotion, and they entered the world famous Greyfriars Kirkyard, headed up a short but steep cobble stone incline, and passed the headstone of Greyfriars Bobby.

I always dared Aurelia to come here with me at night, and she always told me 'not a fucking chance'. Ironic that I get to visit the place at night with a vampire intent on murdering me.

"Over 100,000 humans are buried here, although the true number might be as high as half a million. Most cemeteries are places of peace and calm. This is a place of sorrow and punishment," Douglas continued.

Should I reply? Would a hypnotised person talk or would they remain silent? Shit, what do I do?

They walked the length of the gothic Baroque style church at the centre of the cemetery. It was brightly up-lit like most other notable buildings in the city, but beyond it, the gravestones and tombs lay in gunky blackness

Danny followed Douglas as they passed a number of wrought-iron mortsafes on the left of the path before making a sharp left hand turn and walking up another slope. This path, lined by trees, was not cemented, and tree roots jutted out of the uneven dirt. In near-blackness, Danny's toe found one of the roots and he stumbled and collapsed.

Fuck! I can't see where the fuck I'm going! I can't take out my phone. A hypnotised person wouldn't think to do that. Where the fuck is he taking me?

"Get up, moron," Douglas said without turning around.

They came to a stop at the rear wall of the cemetery. Collapsed and overgrown crypts gave way to a pair of black iron gates which were chained and padlocked together. Beyond lay a long narrow strip of the cemetery with crypts lining both sides as far as the light would allow the eye to see.

Why would a section of the cemetery be closed? Is it structurally unsound? There isn't any roofing, so it doesn't look any more unsafe than any other part of this fucked up place.

"I lived here once," Douglas said as he gently placed a hand on the iron bars of the gate. His tone was no longer affirmative. It was now ponderous, sad even.

Is this an ambush or a fucking tour?

"I mean, I was a prisoner here. This is the Covenanter's Prison, the world's first ever concentration camp."

What the fuck?

"Back in 1638 my father was present as a young man to witness the signing of the National Covenant, an oath that we Presbyterians would protect our religion from interference from the Crown, and its attempts to impose Episcopalian practices on us. My father didn't live to see us being defeated at Bothwell Brig four decades later, and the interment of 1,300 of us here."

Douglas' fingers tightened around the bars of the gate as he spoke.

"In 1679, for nearly four months my kin and I were held prisoner over there, beyond that wall. We were kept out in the open air, exposed to the elements. Many died of exposure or starvation. Others were tortured to death by sadistic guards. My kin were buried on this stretch of land right here."

Danny readjusted his gloves behind his back.

"A few managed to escape. Some promised to take the king's peace and were freed. 250 were sentenced for deportation, but the ship sank off Orkney and over 200 drowned. But those who wanted to fight for our covenant paid the highest price. They were tortured and executed here. I saw it all happen and, day by day, I lost all hope," Douglas said. His voice was barely a whisper.

Should I just jump him now? No, I need to ask about Aurelia. Shit, what do I do?

"Hundreds of us were murdered at the instruction of this man," Douglas continued after clearing his throat, his voice loud and assertive once more. "Follow me," he instructed.

A fresh wave of pressure flooded Danny's mind. However, he kept it at bay.

They turned to their left and walked past a number of open-air crypts lining the boundary wall before they arrived at a large circular granite mausoleum surrounded by decorative pillars and a domed roof. Weeds sprouted out of the dome in all directions between the gaps in the stone. A few steps led up to two tall narrow wooden doors. Bolted shut, each door had a square missing panel allowing a small glimpse into the blackness of the tomb inside. A blast of ice-cold air stabbed at Danny's skin and was gone a few seconds later.

The fuck? Danny rubbed the goosebumps on his forearms. *What the fuck was that?*

The high-pitched barking of a small dog, unseen in the darkness, sounded behind them, causing Danny to jump. It turned into angry growls, and then silence.

The atmosphere of this place is fucking stifling.

"This is the mausoleum of George 'Bloody' MacKenzie, the psychopath tasked with breaking and slaughtering us. Covenanters became a persecuted minority. It was known as 'The Killing Time'. When Bloody MacKenzie died, the sick fuck was buried here, right next to the prison, so he'd always be looking over those he tortured and murdered."

Danny shuffled.

"Gabriel found me when I was in the prison. He could tell that I was one of the chosen. He took me away and gave me a new life, but I never forgot the lesson I learned here – that humans are animals. Humans have no saving graces. No redeeming features. There is no God, no plan, and no value to life. Humans should be treated as they treat others, like cattle."

Danny's heart continued to pound. He closed his eyes briefly and took a few deep breaths before opening them once more.

"Every time I hunt, I bring my prey here. I explain why I brought them here, and then I bite them right in front of Bloody MacKenzie, so he can see that what he did. I can torture him every single fucking time, and there's nothing he can do about me desecrating both his grave and his memory every fucking time. Now come here," Douglas instructed Danny, without taking his eyes off the mausoleum.

"This is a good place for it, I guess," Danny said, nodding and scanning the surrounding area.

"Eh?" Douglas said, turning to Danny.

"No witnesses. Even in this part of the graveyard there is unlikely to be any homeless people looking for a place to sleep. A graveyard though? A bit on the nose don't you think?"

"I... what?" Douglas said with an expression of profound confusion.

"Relax," Danny said, approaching his quarry with a relaxed smile, belying the barely-controlled panic underneath. "Relax. I'm a good friend of Cassius. He taught me about the hypnosis and how to block it. He's in mainland Europe right now. Had to leave on short notice," Danny said.

"I was wondering what had happened to him," Douglas said.

"Yeah, he's fine. But he always worried about introducing me to you, but for now I'm off the menu. He asked me to take care of his affairs for him while he was away."

"He shouldn't be telling *any* human about us. When he comes back there will be hell to pay," Douglas said with a thread of anger in his voice.

"I'll leave you to sort that all out when he returns," Danny said with an air of dismissiveness. "I'm sorry that you and yours were treated like this, but it's a little sad to hear that you are still so bitter even after all this time. I'd heard about the Covenanter's Prison. Just another of the stories about this cemetery. The plague pits, the alleged hauntings. You've only been back in Edinburgh a year or so. Did you hear about what happened to MacKenzie's body?" Danny asked.

"No," Douglas replied, his expression of perturbed confusion clear, even in the moonlight.

"I read about this place when I moved to Edinburgh a few months back, but didn't have the chance to visit," Danny said. "About a decade or so back, two youths broke into this mausoleum. They found his body. Allegedly they desecrated the grave and the police found them playing football in the graveyard with a skull. Before that though, a homeless man broke into the mausoleum looking for shelter from the rain. He fell through the rotten floorboards and landed on the coffins, and below that, a mound of bones from an old plague pit. Since then hundreds of people have been attacked, bitten, and scratched by unseen forces."

"I'm not surprised. The masochistic cunt was probably rejected by Hell and now exists only to forever overlook those he tortured and brutalised as they lie just yards from here. But now he looks on in horror when I bite my victims in front of him. That way, it's he who is being tortured, as I desecrate the steps of his burial place with the blood of my victims."

"Do you actually see him? Can vampires see ghosts?" Danny asked, his eyes widening.

"If only you knew what else was out there, human," Douglas said with a knowing smile.

Come on Danny, stick to the point. Just bring Aurelia up. I don't know how long this charade will last before he gets suspicious.

"Anyway, I was told by Cassius to help Gabriel take care of Aurelia. She'll still be feral, and Gabriel doesn't want all his hard work in siring her to be for nothing," Danny said.

"I wouldn't go near her right now. She's a feisty one for sure, but she's coming around," Douglas replied.

She's definitely alive! Thank God!

Douglas chuckled as he looked into the distance and placed his hands on his hips, before closing his eyes and shaking his head.

"You know, you're good but you made some mistakes," Douglas said, looking back at Danny. In the strong moonlight,

Douglas' smile was easily visible.

"What do you mean?" Danny asked.

"No human would be left to look after a feral vampire. No human would survive it. Cassius would know that. Plus, one sire, one newborn vampire. You don't get multiple vampires looking after one feral vampire. It's more personal than that. But there is one bigger thing which has given you away." Douglas grabbed Danny by the throat, hoisting him six inches off the ground.

Fuck.

"Your heartbeat. Your voice is calm and relaxed, but your heart is going like a hummingbird. I should have seen it from the beginning. Now, where is Cassius?" he asked. His eyes turned black, the whites of his extended canine teeth growing brighter in the moonlight.

"I'll take you to him," Danny replied in a croaking voice with his windpipe on the verge of collapsing.

Danny placed his gloved hand on that of Douglas. Douglas immediately let go of Danny's throat and Danny landed on the path. His knee buckled under him, but the other knee held out.

Danny forced his hand over Douglas' mouth. With Douglas screaming into Danny's hand, and clawing at the glove, Danny produced his stake. He swept the feet from under Douglas. As Douglas fell backwards, Danny went over on top of him, stake pointing down, using his weight to drive the stake into Douglas' heart.

Douglas' scream was silenced. He turned his head to face Bloody MacKenzie's mausoleum and he smiled as he turned to chalk. Danny's weight caused Douglas' body to immediately crumble into dust.

Danny sat up, coughing as he got air back into his lungs as plumes of dust drifted into the night air. He gently rubbed at his throat and took a few breaths.

Job done! I'm getting good at this!

Danny chuckled to himself as he bagged up Douglas' belongings from the piles of dust. He stopped momentarily to pick up a silver ring. The ring was identical to the ring Cassius wore. He put it in the pocket of his jeans.

A whoosh and earthy thump on the grass behind Danny announced the arrival of Mercy.

"Well done," she replied

"And did you like the gloves? I got the idea from your knuckledusters."

"Yeah, I like it. What the fuck were you talking about? I was watching you both but couldn't hear. You spoke for ages but he didn't attack you, even when he realised that you weren't hypnotised."

"Local history. He would have been an interesting guy to go for a pint with if it wasn't for all the blood drinking and murder. Mercy, can vampires see ghosts? Douglas said if only I knew what else was out there. What did he mean? Or was he just fucking with me?"

"Focus, Cripple!" she said with a clap of her hands. "It's great that you killed another vampire, but you need to kill them much quicker. You got lucky this time."

"What do you mean 'lucky'? I had it all in hand," Danny dismissed her.

"Because he made the mistake of grabbing you by the throat and talking. Other vampires would have just snapped your neck that very second, and all the galena in the world wouldn't have saved you."

"Relax, Mercy!" Danny said with a smug grin. "Like I said, I had it all in hand."

"Don't get cocky, Cripple. I know that you are enjoying this newfound confidence, but don't get arrogant. It'll get you killed. Now," she continued looking at her watch, "it's probably too late to get any of the other targets tonight, given their patterns. Bugger! We'll need to be faster at this."

"What's the rush anyway? We know that Aurelia is alive and is still semi-feral. We have time," Danny said as he zipped the holdall closed and straightened up.

"Not everything is about Aurelia. I'm trying to get the nest dealt with, because every day that goes by more homeless people go missing. More people in poor areas disappear, and the authorities don't give a shit. It's on *us* to help them. Keep an eye on the bigger picture. These bastards live in luxury, enjoying all the spoils that life has to offer and in order to keep living, they suck the poor dry and discard them! They're fucking vermin! They're parasites! They leech off the lowest masses of humanity and they do it with a fucking swagger." The anger in Mercy's voice was naked. It was raw.

"I thought that you were just doing this so that your network of helpers and informants wouldn't be decimated. I thought you were just doing this for you," Danny said.

"I am, but it doesn't make what I said any less true. Besides, I told you earlier, as soon as you killed your first vampire, the clock started ticking. We don't have much time left. So go home, get some rest and we'll try to hunt multiple targets tomorrow."

"Yeah but you didn't say *why* a clock was ticking. I feel you're still hiding things from me. Besides, what's all this 'we 'stuff? If you want to get more targets why don't you lift a finger and try killing one of them yourself?"

"We've been through this," Mercy said, before Danny continued.

"Yeah, yeah. The whole 'one rule we never break' pish, but it doesn't wash with me, Mercy. I'm risking my neck here and I'm all alone. You'd think that you would be willing to pitch in, given how strong and accomplished you are. We could get it done so much quicker. Besides, we're alone. You could kill them and no one would ever know. I don't know what it is that's holding you back, but from here it looks like cowardice."

Mercy slowly stepped towards him.

"Be careful with your words, Cripple."

"Why? Does the truth hurt? I'm the one who is doing all this. What are you doing?" he asked, squaring up to her.

"What am I doing? Who was the one who told you how to kill them? Who told you about tiger's eye and galena? Who did hand-to-hand combat training with you? Who trained you to do what no other human alive can, resist their hypnosis?

Who collected all the information you need to target your prey? Who gave you all the information on the nest? Without me, you would be wandering around the town at night, picking fights with drunks and getting your arse kicked."

A swell of anger rose above his punctured pride.

"Look, just gimme your file on the nest," he instructed her, holding out his hand.

"Sorry?" she asked.

"I know that you keep it on you whenever we are doing something nest-related. Let me see it."

With her eyes narrowed in suspicion, she produced a halved folder from the inside pocket of her denim jacket and handed it to him.

"You want me to do all the killing? Consider it done. I don't want to see you again. As far as I'm concerned, if you're not going to get your hands dirty and actually *help* me, then we're done."

"Are you kidding me?" she asked.

"I said we're done!" Danny said as he walked away.

Two down, six to go. I'll read the report tonight and tomorrow, and I'll take them all down myself.

He turned around to glare at Mercy, but she was gone.

CHAPTER 15

Mercy sat with her glass and glared at the wooden target board.

Arsehole!

She picked up another knife and threw it at the eighteen-inch target hanging on the back of the kitchen door. It lodged in the outermost ring with a thud.

Arrogant arsehole!

She sipped the blood in her wine glass. It was cold and bitter to the taste.

Arrogant, ungrateful arsehole!

She picked up another knife and threw it at the target. It landed handle-first and bounced off the board, clattering onto the tiled floor.

He takes MY file and pisses off with it. He kills two vampires and now he thinks he's Van Helsing. Even the real Van Helsing didn't think he was Van Helsing. He's going to get himself killed, and it's going to be my fault.

She picked up another knife and threw it at the target. Franky popped his head around the door. The knife missed the target and landed on the door, three inches from his face.

"Fucking hell, Mercy! Are you trying to kill me?" he asked as he stepped inside the kitchen.

"If I wanted to kill you, you'd be dead," Mercy said and took another gulp of blood.

Franky surveyed the chaotic spread of knives on the target and door, as well as the collection of knives lying on the floor.

"Aye, you're definitely on top of your game tonight, doll."

Mercy drained the blood from the glass.

"What do you want Franky?"

"I'm off to bed. I'm knackered and it's late. Just wanted to check whether you're still brooding from the other night. Aye, I see. It's affecting your aim as much as your attitude."

"What do you expect me to do?"

"Talk to the boy."

"There's no reasoning with stupidity," she dismissed him.

"He's no stupid. Aye, he's reckless, but he's no stupid. But he's killed two vampires after months of feeling powerless. Cut the lad a wee bit of slack."

"I don't need your advice," she said and threw her final knife. It landed flat on the target board and clattered onto the knives on the kitchen tiles.

"Maybe you do," Franky replied.

"He was arrogant! He was implying that I've been no help. Going on this self-righteous path, he's going to get himself killed." She leaned forward in her seat towards him. "He called me a coward, Franky!"

"Aye, OK, that's a wee bit uncalled for," Franky conceded.

"A wee bit?" Mercy said with a look of bemusement at such an understatement.

"OK, a big bit. But you have to look at things from his angle. He doesnae understand why he cannae actually get help when trying to kill them. You gave him the tools he needed. You gave him the information he needed and trained him as well. But when he's out there risking his neck, he's all alone, and I'll bet he feels it."

"I can't help that Franky. I've told you about our one rule."

"I know, but chances are when they find out that vampires are being offed, they'll figure you're involved *anyway*. Besides, you're still loading a gun and pointing it at them. You *are* responsible for them being offed. Just because you arenae the one who stakes them, that excuse willnae wash with them."

Mercy continued to glare at the target.

"Speak to him, Mercy. Even if you just check on him and make sure he's still alive."

The doorbell rang from the other end of the house.

"Sake, man! I'll get it, then I'm off to my bed for the night," Franky said and left the kitchen.

Maybe I should check in on him. I still have a responsibility for the arrogant wee shite.

Mercy closed her eyes and listened through the numerous walls.

"Hello," the voice at the door greeted Franky.

Mercy's eyes burst open.

"Awright mate, how can I help?"

"I want you to invite," the voice replied as Mercy rose from her chair, "me in."

Mercy was already behind Franky and covering his mouth with her palm as the man finished his instruction. She turned Franky by the shoulders and stared directly into his eyes.

"Franky, stay silent and go to the kitchen. Clear up the knives. Stay there until I say otherwise."

Franky walked away from both Mercy and the visitor in silence.

"Nice try, Gabriel," Mercy said.

In front of her was the familiar visage of Gabriel, leader of the Edinburgh nest. Conventionally handsome, but with a cocky grin which always set her on edge, he wore his light blonde, shoulder length hair swept back. He held both sides of the outside brickwork and his broad shoulders covered most of the door frame.

Want to manspread any more, you repulsive twat?

"Where is the trust?" Gabriel asked, his smile remaining.

"What do you want?"

"Simply to have a pleasant chat with my old friend."

"Bollocks. What are you here for, Gabriel?"

"Mercy, o ye of little faith."

Arrogant, smug prick.

Mercy stood in the doorway in silence.

"Very well. Two members of my family seem to have disappeared these last few days. For them to leave unannounced at the same time, has me... concerned."

"Oh. Who has gone?" she asked.

Gabriel remained silent as he studied her.

Mercy blinked and drummed her nails on the wooden door frame.

"It was Cassius and Douglas."

"Oh," she replied.

"Do you know what happened?"

"No," Mercy replied.

"Hmmm, that's surprising," he replied.

"How so?"

"Come now, Mercy. It's abundantly known that you always research enemies and allies alike. As a matter of fact, I know that you put one of Cassius's human contacts in a hospital a while ago. In addition, Jessica informed me that you had exchanged tense words recently."

"That's because she was prancing around like a six-year-old ballet dancer on the walls of Edinburgh Castle. You don't want any of your nest disclosing the secret of our existence. There would be dire consequences for both you and your nest."

Gabriel winced twice at the word 'nest', before smiling once again.

"You prove my point, Mercy. The idea that you *haven't* been keeping a constant eye on my family and I, well, it is insulting."

"So I'm best known for being a nosey neighbour am I?" she asked with a smile.

"No, you are best known for being the most brutal and savage hunter that the vampire world has even known. You were a living legend. Then suddenly you turn your back on your kind. No reason given, no consideration allowed, simply goodbye. And now you live the life of a hermit amongst the cattle."

"My reasons are my own, Gabriel. Now, I don't know what happened to your arsehole nest members..."

"I despise that word," he said with a calm, even tone, but

with his eyes screwed tight.

"But it has nothing to do with me," Mercy continued. "And while you're here, do you mind slowing the body count down? The number of missing persons in this city is ridiculous."

"Like you said, it has nothing to do with you. As for my missing family members, if I didn't know better I would swear there was a vampire hunter in the city. If there was, I'm sure you wouldn't mind coming out of retirement to help your brethren."

Mercy stood still, focusing on keeping her mind thought-free.

"If you refused, I would have to send up a flare, and I would hate to think of the body count amongst your precious cattle when all vampires in the surrounding area overwhelm the city."

"I'd rather that didn't happen," she said.

"Then I shall be in touch and, who knows," he said as he reached out through the doorway, only for his hand to press against something solid and invisible, "perhaps you will trust me enough to invite me in for a cup of tea... or a bite to eat," he finished with a wide, menacing grin.

He turned and went down the eight steps and onto the pavement, scanning the street for humans and the windows for faces.

"I'm meeting Ewan and Jessica shortly. We're having a soirée later. You are most welcome. After all, in the past you partied harder than any of us. Tell me, when was the last time you filled a bathtub with blood? I remember you often indulging in that little vice," he said as he looked back at her. "It's funny. The only way a vampire hunter could be successful is if a vampire told him our secrets. There would surely be hell to pay for her. Even if she didn't kill a vampire by her own hand, she would still be culpable. But perhaps Samuel can decide. After all, Samuel is one of the few elders even *you* were wary of. Oh, and I am *not* a 'smug prick'."

With that, he stormed into the sky and out of sight.

She breathed out a shaky breath.

"Fuck," she whispered, and closed the door.

She walked back to the kitchen, where Franky stood beside a neat bundle of knives on the worktop.

Does he know? No, he can't. Not yet, but he's suspicious. If another vampire goes missing, he'll definitely send out a distress signal, then we're all fucked. We've been too slow after all. I need to get to Danny before he goes out hunting again. He doesn't know what's happened.

"Relax, Franky. I'm off to Danny's house."

"Um, OK. Wait, you hypnotised me, didn't you? You promised me that you would never do that. Not to me. You gave me your word," he said, but Mercy wasn't listening. She was already donning her jacket.

"Mercy!"

"I'm sorry!" she shouted back. "I know I promised but it was literally to save your life. Now keep calling Danny. I'm going to his house. If you get through to him, ask him where he is and report back. And for fuck's sake, tell him not to hunt again!"

CHAPTER 16

Danny coughed as he waited, his stomach gurgling and cramping with nerves. Charlotte Lane was an unassuming little road, just off a much busier Queensferry Street. In the evening, it was frequented by locals going to and from various bars. After 1 am the lane became much quieter, the type of lane where dealings could be done, which otherwise would not be done earlier in the day.

Franky's report on Ewan had him using Charlotte Lane on the way back to the nest in Moray Place, just a few streets away, and so Charlotte Lane was the perfect place to ambush him. Danny walked past two competing pizza restaurants and continued until he reached the lane which ran down the side of West Register House.

Built in the early 1800's, it housed the national archives. It was, however, having major restoration and conservation work being done to the edifice. As a result, scaffolding and green netting covered all four sides of the building, with only the large green dome at the centre, topped by a golden bell at its peak, still visible.

Maybe I should speak to Mercy. I acted like an arrogant arse in the cemetery, and that's not me. It's thanks to her I got here. Then again, I'm still right about not getting any help while hunting, and if she's not going to help me, using her special vampire powers, then sod her.

"Fuck!" he whispered and shook his head. "You're better

than this Danny."

It's not right that I should expect her to put her life on the line for me and Aurelia. She already risked herself by training me.

He produced his phone and lowered the screen brightness in the darkened alleyway. He selected 'Mercy', and his thumb hovered over the call icon. The battery icon at the top read '2%'.

Bugger! You forgot to charge it Danny, you idiot. Fuck it, never mind. I'm hunting anyway. I'll call her tomorrow. Maybe.

He switched the phone off and slipped it back into his pocket. He touched the tiger's eye stake up his sleeve, its sharp tip pressing against his finger. He stepped back onto Charlotte Lane, puffing his cheeks as he did so.

I hope he comes soon because my knee and hip are killing me.

He readjusted his grip on his cane and leaned on it heavier than before. Stalking this small road back and forth for three hours was now taking its toll.

Danny froze mid-yawn as two figures turned onto Charlotte Lane, heading in his direction. As they grew closer, their voices reached Danny, the woman's first.

"I'm so excited, Ewan. This party will be fantastic! From what Gabriel told me earlier, a lot of people have been invited. It will be quite the feast!"

"Mmmm, I hope there are some cute lads there. All these stinking homeless. They taste as foul as they smell. Why can't we have some prey with class and breeding? Is it too much to ask?" he asked

"Ask Gabriel. He should have met us already. I bet he's back at the house having fun," she replied.

Danny scanned their faces. Even in the semidarkness in between the street lighting, it was clearly Ewan.

There are two! I never expected this. Is the woman a vampire? Shit! I can't take two at once! What do I do?

Just a few yards away, the woman's face and identity became clear from one of Mercy's photos.

Evie! That's Evie! I hadn't even thought about her yet! What do I do? Do I let them go? Aye, just let them pass. Be smart, smile politely

if they look at you, then put your head down and let them go.

Danny stepped out directly in front of them, his quarry just a couple of feet away.

They stopped in their tracks, both advertising their confusion at Danny's behaviour.

"Wow!" Danny said.

What are you doing, you halfwit? You were going to let them pass! Let them pass!

"Just wow! You two are gorgeous! Absolutely gorgeous! I'm sorry for being so rude and overly familiar, but I just had to say it! I'm just taken aback by how beautiful you both are!"

"Why, thank you sweetie! Isn't he a cutie, Ewan?" she asked, beaming.

"He has his, umm… forceful charms," Ewan replied, scanning Danny up and down again. "What is your name, lad?"

"It's Danny, handsome," he replied with a coy smile, staring at Ewan's crotch, then back at his face.

"Are you thinking what I'm thinking, dear?" Evie asked.

"Hmmm, nah, Quality, not quantity," Ewan said.

"Oh, come on, there's quality there, besides, the more the merrier, and this one isn't homeless. Didn't you just say you wanted some breeding? But I'm first on him. You can have my leftovers," Evie said, biting her lip.

Danny smiled coyly at her.

Evie approached him and placed her hand on his shoulder.

"Such broad shoulders!" she said with excitement dripping from her lips.

That familiar warm, fuzzy pressure entered his head once more. This was stronger thank both Cassius's and Douglas' powers. More forceful. More alluring.

Aurelia's suffering entered Danny's conscious mind. His anger stirred once more and his mind cleared. Evie's attempts faded away.

"Follow us, cutie pie. You're going to have the night of your life," she said.

Danny's smile faded, replaced with a well-rehearsed blank

expression.

They walked further down the lane.

"I have a secret," Danny said.

"Oh, yes?" Ewan replied.

"I know what you are. I've spoken to Gabriel already. I want to join you. Even though I'm not one of the chosen, I want to join you. Gabriel told me of the risks, but is willing to let me try. Tonight, the siring process is going to begin on me," Danny said, at which point both Ewan and Evie stopped walking. In the streetlights, their confused expressions told Danny all he needed to know.

"Is it?" Ewan asked.

"He seems to know everything," Evie interjected. "He must be telling the truth."

"Gabriel wants to increase your numbers after the siring of a girl named Aurelia. He wants me to try. An experiment as a non-chosen."

"Why wouldn't he tell us? And why is he trying to sire two humans at the same time?" Ewan asked Evie.

"I dunno, hun, but Gabriel has been a bit off since Cassius and Douglas left with no word."

"You *are* aware of the likelihood of it not working, I take it?" Ewan said, turning to Danny.

"I know, and as I told Gabriel, I'm willing to take the risk," Danny replied.

"Very well," Ewan said, and all three continued walking.

"May I ask a question?" Danny said.

"Of course," Ewan said, an expression of uncertainty mixed with confusion still on his face.

"How did the siring process go for this Aurelia? Did she survive? Is she enjoying her new life as a vampire?"

"Don't worry about her, just worry about your chances," Ewan replied.

"Ewan, stop it!" Evie said, her confused expression now replaced with one of happy intrigue. "Aurelia is just fine, sweetie. She's still a little… wild, a little untamed, but she's doing well, and I'm sure a man as brave and willing as you will survive the siring process no problem," she said and kissed Danny on the cheek.

Danny smiled and touched his cheek where her cold lips had been.

The scoffing sound from Ewan was caught by Danny. The stake slipped out of Danny's jacket sleeve, into his hand. Without a word, he turned to Ewan and slammed it into his chest as Ewan wasn't looking.

As Ewan's face turned into a silent scream of agony, Danny reached his gloved hand out to Evie's cheek. The galena pressed into her skin and the melting began. She opened her mouth wide to scream, but Danny thrust the stake into her chest. She quickly turned into a chalk shell.

Danny took a deep breath.

It worked! It bloody worked! Awesome! I'm unstoppable!

On Ewan's finger was an identical ring to the other vampires Danny had dispatched. As he grabbed the ring, Ewan's hand crumbled away, leaving Danny holding the ring and some dust. Ewan's corpse continued to crumble to nothing. Danny took Evie's ring and her body followed suit. Within a few seconds, Danny was left with piles of chalk-white dust and some clothes in the middle of the lane. He pocketed the rings.

Scanning his surroundings, Queensferry Street was empty.

He shuffled his holdall from around his back when a figure at the other end of Charlotte Lane caught his attention. Standing there was a man with light blonde hair, swept back, watching Danny.

Fuck! Fucking, fucking, fuck! A witness!

The man took a step towards Danny. Danny stumbled to his feet, turned on his heels and made for Queensferry Street.

Within two steps, a hand grabbed Danny's shoulder, the talon-like nails piercing his skin and burrowing in, before whipping him around. Danny's soul iced over. The face was all too familiar. Blackened pupils, elongated canines and claw-shaped fingers did not disguise that Danny was face-to-face with

Gabriel, the leader of the Edinburgh nest.

"You caused this! All of this is *your* fault!" Danny said.

Danny fumbled with his stake, but Gabriel batted it out of his hand upwards. It flew over the roof of a nearby building.

"You will suffer like no other before you!" Gabriel said with a distinct animalistic growl in his voice. A voice no human could make.

Danny swung a fist at Gabriel's face. He connected with force and left four knuckle burns on the left side of Gabriel's face.

Gabriel winced in pain and his excruciating grip on Danny's shoulder loosened.

Danny let go of his cane and swung his right hand, once again finding Gabriel's face. He grabbed Gabriel's head. The two lumps of galena stitched into the palms of his gloves pressed hard against Gabriel's cheeks.

Gabriel shrieked and clutched Danny's hands. He prized Danny's hands off his face, exposing two large, melted portions of his face. Under the holes in his skin, white cheekbones and, below, rows of perfect molar teeth smiled back at him.

How the fuck can he withstand the galena?

Gabriel let go of Danny's hands and fell backwards, clutching his face.

No stake!

Danny stumbled and limped towards Queensferry Street, as fast as his knee would allow. Everything became slow motion. He tried to run faster, but both legs were slow and heavy, like wading through syrup. He expected claws to dig into his back at any second. He neared the adjoining street and allowed himself a glimpse over his shoulder.

Gabriel was on his knees, kneeling over the ash remains of Ewan and Evie. He unleashed a pained scream, a broken-hearted scream, filled with equal parts agony and rage.

Danny's heart hammered. His breathing was fast and shallow. He mumbled incoherent nonsense.

His head whipped in all directions. There were no other humans.

Safety! Must find safety!

A bus turned the corner from Princes Street, into Queensferry Street. Across the road from him was a bus stop. His situation was simple: either hail that bus, or die.

Gabriel was now on his feet and staring at Danny.

Danny hobbled onto the road. Just a few feet away from the stop, his knees buckled and gave out. He fell onto the road with the bus bearing down on him. He got to his feet and stumbled onto the pavement. He waved the bus down. It stopped, the doors opened and a worried driver stared at him.

Thank Christ!

Danny hobbled on to the bus, put a £5 note into the fare machine, took his ticket and sat on the nearest seat. He stared back in Gabriel's direction. Above Charlotte Lane, standing on the stone balcony surrounding the up-lit dome of West Register House, Gabriel stared down on him.

Danny shuffled to the rear of the bus as it made off, with him looking out of the rear window. The bus pulled away, but Gabriel stayed on his perch.

I barely escaped with my life! I've lost my cane and my stake. Gabriel knows my face now and he'll be warning the others, so hunting the rest of them just became damn near impossible. There's going to be hell to pay. I am so fucked!

The bus sent Danny off to the wrong part of the city, in the opposite direction of home, but he was alive. For now. There was no telling how much longer that was going to be the case.

CHAPTER 17

Danny sat on the chair next to the window of his living room, staring down at the passers-by. A young couple were taking selfies together in front of the sign at the opening of Fleshmarket Close. The woman was pretending to scream up at the sign, a smile affixed to her face.

Danny smiled.

What I would give to have her back. She's out there somewhere, being tortured. A gentle soul trapped in the body and mind of a rabid animal. What I would give to trade places with her, to spare her from that agony.

His mind wandered once more to times where he'd taken her for granted. The silly arguments which, in the heat of the moment, were so important but now meant nothing.

"All the times I was such a spoilt, lazy bastard," he muttered as his thought's escaped his lips. "I'll find you, Aurelia, and I'll never take you for granted ever again."

He tore his eyes away from the window and he instead studied his new cane.

"Lucky timing," he said with a wry smile.

Ordered a week before, it was intended to replace the old brown wooden one he'd abandoned when fleeing from a wrathful Gabriel. He had let out a joyous laugh in front of a confused courier who had delivered it earlier in the morning. A sleek black polished metal cane, its handle was silver in appearance and was in the shape of an intricately carved eagle.

He smiled as he pressed a discreet button near his thumb and slid it to the left. The cane clicked and the top third sprang loose from the bottom, revealing a nine-inch blade inside, jutting out of the underside of the handle.

He bent down, pulling a mid-sized brown cardboard box over to his feet. He opened the flaps and rooted around. Inside the box lay a selection of fragments of tiger's eye. Each one was pointed, some sharper than others, but all could, in a pinch, be used as a stake. He surveyed the diameter of each one, comparing it by eye to the diameter of the inside of the cane.

The buzzer sounded, indicating a visitor. He closed his cane and made his way to the front door, stopping only to buzz the visitor in.

When he opened the door, Mercy was staring at him. She didn't look happy to see him, or angry. Just awkward.

"Come in," he said and walked away from her.

She followed him into the living room and slumped onto the seat. Her eyes were sunken and dark, her complexion was grey.

"Does sun tan lotion not help?" he asked.

"No it doesn't, smartarse," she parried, devoid of her usual sarcastic tone.

Danny sat back on his seat without offering her a drink.

"So how have you been?" she asked.

"Fine, fine. Hunting, eating, sleeping. Repeat."

"Tell me you haven't had any success," she said and closed her eyes.

"I thought you'd be happy," he replied.

"Normally I would be, but there have been some developments. Gabriel came to see me last night."

"How did he look?" Danny asked.

"Um, his usual smug, dickhead self as always," she replied.

"So, he wasn't upset or anything?"

"No," she said. "Why? And why can I smell blood?"

Because Gabriel sunk his nails into my shoulder blade. I hope the twat doesn't have vampire rabies.

"Well, I was out hunting last night."

"And?" she prompted him.

"And I had some success," he said and smiled.

Mercy closed her eyes, as though he had just informed her that he had fallen in with the vampires.

"Tell me about it then," she said.

"I went hunting Ewan. I chose my spot, Charlotte Lane. I waited forever but finally he arrived. But the thing is, he wasn't alone."

"What do you mean?" she asked.

"Evie was with him."

"Fuck! So you ran. You did the smart thing. But what success are you talking about?"

"I confronted them with all the information on the nest. I told them that Gabriel was wanting to experiment with me. That he wanted to increase the numbers and was willing to try to sire an unchosen. And they fell for it. Just long enough for me to stake both the bastards within a couple of seconds of each other. Took them both by surprise," he finished with a wry smile.

"You killed two vampires at the same time?" she asked as she looked up at him, her eyebrows raised and a hint of a smile at the corners of her mouth. "Fucking hell! Well done! That's *very* impressive!" she said, though her smile gradually faded and morphed into a concerned frown. "Although there will be consequences now. Consequences I was desperate to avoid," she said.

"Thanks, but what consequences?" Danny asked.

"Gabriel paid me a visit. Fucker even tried to hypnotise Franky into inviting him in. He was questioning me about Cassius and Douglas. Asking if I knew anything about their disappearance. Of course I said no, but he doesn't believe me. He suspects that a vampire hunter is in town. That's why I wanted us to work as fast as possible, because it was only a matter of time after the first vampire went missing that he would begin to suspect the truth."

"Shit," Danny said under his breath.

"Exactly. He threatened to send up a flare. In other words, inform the entire Scottish vampire community to descend on the city."

"Shit," he whispered once more.

"Yup. And with you killing more, even though it was two at a time, he will know now. That flare will be sent up very soon when he realises that another two vampires have disappeared."

Danny closed his eyes.

"Bugger. There is no 'when' about it. He already knows," he admitted.

"What? How? How do you know?"

"Well, after I staked Ewan and Evie, I was collecting their belongings as normal. That's when I saw him at the end of Charlotte Lane, watching me. Gabriel. He attacked me. Dug his claws deep into my shoulder blade, which is why you can smell blood. He batted my stake away, so now I dunno where the hell it is, and it's the only one I had sharpened."

"Focus, Danny. What happened after that?" she asked.

"He was going to kill me, but I pressed my galena gloves into his face. Melted his skin. But he was still strong enough to actually prize my hands off him, but thankfully he was in enough pain that I was able to escape by getting onto Queensferry Street and grabbing a random passing bus. But he knows that there is a vampire hunter in town. I thought he'd just chase me from the air, but he didn't."

"Fuck!" Mercy said as she stared blankly at him. "Fuck! Fuck, fuck, fuck, FUCK!"

She put her head in her hands for a moment before standing up and pacing the length of the living room, back and forth.

"Right, did he mention meeting you before? Did he mention that he knew who you were?"

"No, just that he was going to make me suffer," he said.

"Good, so there's at least a good chance that he didn't recognise you, and that your identity is safe."

"But so what if he brings more vampires to the city? That's

just more to kill. In the end we'll be doing an even better job," he said with a half-hearted smile.

"It doesn't work that way, Cripple," she replied. "When vampires realise there is someone hunting them, they call on other nests for help. Even worse, there is an elder in our area. The vampires will then swarm on the area and search until they find him or her. Now they'll be coming for you. About thirty-six hours from now, dozens of vampires will be hunting you, and they won't stop until they find you. That's why there are *no* vampire hunters. After they kill a couple of vampires, word spreads, and their days are numbered soon after."

A sinking weight dragged his stomach downwards as a wave of panic rose.

"OK, I'll be much more careful in future," he said.

"It's not just that though," she replied. "Whilst dozens of vampires are in the city searching for you, who do you think they will be feeding from? The homeless in the city, as well as impoverished areas, are about to be slaughtered. It'll make the recent disappearances look like a picnic. Our actions have now put others in extreme danger. We have a responsibility to them," she said.

"Is this the same 'I'm a loner and don't care about anyone else' Mercy I know? I'm proud of you, girl," he said with a smile.

"Fuck off, Cripple. I'm serious," she retorted.

"Tell me you have a backup plan then," he said.

"I've got a couple, including my nuclear option. First choice is to get you out of here and lead the vampires away."

"How are you going to do that?"

"When they arrive, they are almost certainly going to ask me to lead the hunt for you. I was the one they came to when it needed to be done in the past, so the idea that they would leave me alone when I'm in the same city is fanciful."

"But you're not going to actually come after me though," he said, gulping louder and harder than he would have liked.

"Don't tempt me," she replied. "I'll put you in touch with someone I know who will get some excellent fake identity documents for you, then I'll get you out of the country using them. In the meantime, I'll pretend to search for a few days, then I'll lead them south to another city. Perhaps somewhere in England before giving up. Still, they will remain in Edinburgh, killing left, right and centre for those couple of days while I'm pretending to look for you."

"No," he replied.

"What do you mean 'no'? I'm trying to save your life here, Cripple."

"I'm not leaving without Aurelia."

Mercy sighed and closed her eyes.

"Besides, what you said was right; our actions have had consequences, and you will just be dooming the homeless population down south. My conscience can't allow that," he explained, looking at the wearing in the carpet.

"Look, now is not the time to be a hero," Mercy said.

"Well... what if you kill me?" he suggested. "If we kill Gabriel first, Aurelia turns human again. Then you can kill me and take my body to any other vampires in the city. You blame Gabriel's death and the death of the others on me. It means that they will be satisfied and will all disband again. And they won't look for revenge on you."

"Are you really willing to sacrifice yourself like that?"

He nodded, his face filled with fear and doubt.

"Aye," he said with a weak smile.

"That's noble, Cripple, but it won't actually solve anything."

Suddenly a wave of brilliance hit him.

"Wait, I have an idea. I think it could work."

Mercy frowned and eyed him sceptically.

"Go on. Tell me your master plan."

"You said that I have thirty-six hours?" he asked.

"Aye. The other nests won't arrive for a day, as they will need to order their affairs before travelling. Then they'll need to get caught up and they'll have a welcoming party. That means we have perhaps thirty-six hours, if we're lucky, before things become impossible for us."

"Then we kill the entire Edinburgh nest before the other nests arrive. If we can take the remaining four members out, we can get Aurelia back. When the others arrive and ask you to join them, you can convince them that the vampire hunter will have moved to another city because the nest the hunter was targeting is already dead. With the job done, the hunter will have left the city already"

"I dunno man, that's thin. That's really thin," she said, shaking her head. "Plus, they'll still continue to look for you in other cities.

"We don't have much of a choice, do we?" he asked.

"Well, killing the remaining four will be damn near impossible. They know that they are being hunted. Their guard will be up," she said.

"We have to try. You said that vampires are arrogant. They are always in hunter mode. Possibly they won't take this seriously and will continue to hunt."

"Nah, it's too risky," Mercy replied. "That's a big leap of faith that you're taking here."

"It's possible though. Right. Look here," he said as he opened the folder which was sitting on the coffee table. He took out each file on the remaining nest members and spread them across the table.

"Alright, what are you getting at here?" Mercy asked.

"Today is Thursday," he explained. "Each of the remaining members have set patterns on a Thursday night. Even Gabriel has been spotted out on a Thursday."

"Yeah he has been seen out, but there is no pattern of movements for him, so that's useless."

"No, it's not," Danny argued. "We can take out the other three and then lie in wait for him returning to the nest in Moray Place. Sure it would be ideal if we got Gabriel first, but since he doesn't have a reliable pattern. At least we can be sure that we will be facing him when he's alone."

Mercy opened her mouth to speak but no words came out.

"Mercy, if it doesn't work, we'll go back to your plan."

"Fuck, that is the least thought out, most half-baked plan I've ever heard," she said.

"Well, your plan wasn't too good either," he retorted.

"Lay off. I never claimed to be a mastermind, and I've never gone to war with my own kind before," she said.

"Neither have I. We're doing the best we can, but we're in the dark here. Has anyone succeeded in taking out an entire nest?" he asked.

"Just once that I know of. I always killed them before they became that successful," she said.

"That's ironic," he said with a bitter smile. "Look, we've got Jessica, Malcolm, Hannah and Gabriel left."

"I know that," Mercy said flatly.

"Let me finish. At 10pm Jessica will leave Fountain Park and will be arriving at Bar One in Festival Square, across from The Usher Hall. She'll be looking to flirt with guys and pick one up for God knows what. At 11pm, Malcolm is always up at the Old Town, on his way to The Bridges nightclub. At midnight, Hannah will be on Lothian Road heading towards Princes Street. If we find places to set up, I can intercept each one of them in turn. When I've killed them, I'll park up at Moray Place and wait for Gabriel to arrive. I can take them all out in one night."

"And how are you going to get to each place so fast?" Mercy asked.

"You are going to be my taxi. When I'm done, you are going to pick me up, and fly me to the next spot, and so on. I'll be the one staking them, but you can help me get from place to place within a few minutes."

"Sounds perfect, but you know that they won't be there at those exact times. No one is that robotic when having fun on the town. Not even vampires."

"Speaking of which, why are these vampires so bloody boring with their same old routines?" he asked. "I mean, it just seems too weird to go to the same place at the same time on a certain day every week. It's just weird."

"Having an enjoyable routine helps with the passage of

time. When you are alive for centuries, time has no meaning any more. Day to day life, week to week living is what keeps you sane. It seems boring to humans, but that's only because humans have a finite amount of time in which to have adventures and experiences before they wither and die. Vampires are creatures of habit and such a routine provides them with security. You'll find that there are days where they wing it and do something else at random."

"So why do you not have strict routines like them?" he asked

"Because in rejecting the vampire life, I had to reject everything about that life. Other than needing blood to survive, I fought to get myself out of that life, mentally as well as physically. I still feel my vampire nature calling on me to create more structure in my life, but if I'm going to be closer to humans, I need to live as close to them as I can. Speaking of routines and your master plan, no vampire has a routine quite as rigid as you are making out they have."

"I realise that, and it may take a lot of waiting around tonight and plenty of improvisation, but it *can* be done. It has to be done," he reassured her.

"And what if they double up for safety?"

"Well I just killed two at a time last night. I can do it again. If any vampire is a no-show, then we'll move on to the next location," he said.

"And if they are all just bunkering down until help arrives?" she asked.

"Then the whole night will be write-off, but at least we can then go with your backup plan."

A few seconds of silence passed.

"Mercy, we need to try. We can't just sit on our arses waiting for a horde of vampires to descend on the city. If this does work, then when the other vampires contact you, you can tell them that they were too late and that they should try another city."

"The chances of us pulling this off is—"

"I'd rather not think about our chances," Danny interrupted

her.

"Fair enough. Now sit on your chair and get your top off," she said.

Danny frowned.

"Ummm, Mercy... I," Danny began.

"What was it you once said? 'Don't flatter yourself'," she replied with a mischievous smile. "You're still bleeding. You obviously didn't dress your wound properly and I can't have you walking around smelling like a barbecue to any vampire who gets close to you."

Danny pulled his chair over, took his top off, and allowed Mercy to inspect his wound.

"Oooft, I'll bet that hurt," she said.

"It did. It's like his nails were spikes, they dug into the skin."

"Well, you're lucky these cuts weren't deeper. One more question; what did you think about when you were with him?"

"Umm, just shitting myself that there had been a witness. Um... then when I realised who he was, and then when he fought me off and I knew that I was in trouble without a stake, I was only preoccupied with getting away. Why?"

"Because Gabriel can hear people's thoughts. You have to make sure that you quieten your mind when you are in his presence because he will be listening."

"Fuck, he's that old?"

"Aye," she said. "Your wound has done a pretty good job of clotting. It's already healing, just weeping slightly. I'll clean and dress it properly. How is your movement and dexterity?"

"Not good. Lifting my left arm is very sore and bending over hurts," he said.

"Bugger. Well, you're going to have to work with your right arm and walk with your cane on your left."

"Great, like things aren't bad enough. I have a knackered right knee and left arm, meaning it's only good to hold my cane, which will be on my wrong side to support my knackered knee. On top of that, I'll be walking around smelling like a buffet to any passing vampire. At least it can't get any worse," he said, wincing at Mercy's less than delicate touch.

"Don't jinx us, Cripple."

Before long, Mercy had cleaned his wound and, using Danny's first aid kit, had dressed the four claw-shaped wounds.

"Right. Get some rest then meet me at my house at 8pm and we'll walk through the particulars of the plan to take them all out," Mercy said.

"We'll do this, Mercy," Danny said as she headed towards his front door. "By hook or by crook, we'll kill all of them."

Mercy smiled briefly before leaving in silence.

CHAPTER 18

The clock on Danny's phone read 9.55pm. The wooden benches furnishing Festival Square were causing Danny's hip to ache more than usual. The rustling of the tree branches above him in the gentle breeze helped his mind to settle.

This is going to work. This is going to work. Christ, please let this work.

His stomach had been cramping for almost two hours now and he had visited the toilet an embarrassing number of times before Mercy had flown him to a discreet area just off Lothian Road.

His queasiness had just subsided from the less-than-comfortable flying of Mercy, which was reminiscent of a hawk flying with an unsuspecting rabbit in its talons.

The tree-lined Festival Square was busy with revellers going to and from various bars and events; not the kind of place for staking a vampire. He stared at the public art installation in front of him. A number of granite balls of varying sizes sat in a disorganised manner. He scanned the entirety of the square. The sun had set and the area was well-lit, offering no shadowy locations to ambush Jessica.

I'll need to make contact with her first, then hope that she leads me somewhere quiet.

He stood up, turned around, and walked over to the tables outside the trendy Bar One. It was a favourite place of Aurelia's. He shook memories of them drinking and laughing from his mind.

Focus, Danny.

He faced the small section of the square which wasn't obscured by trees, benches, and features in the direction of Lothian Road; the direction in which Jessica would most likely appear. He produced the photograph of her. A beautiful girl in her early twenties with a troublesome smile and platinum blonde hair, Jessica had the features to get her way without needing to hypnotise unsuspecting humans.

He tucked the photo into the inside pocket of his jacket, readjusted his fingerless galena gloves, and leaned on his cane once more.

"Hey there, gorgeous," the female voice said behind him.

Danny startled and spun around, his heart wedged behind his tonsils. His knee gave way as he did so, and he hit the concrete paving, bottom-first. Jessica stood over him, a curious smile on her face.

"Oh, sorry," he said with an embarrassed smile.

"That's quite alright," she said with a smile sweet enough to affect Danny's blood sugar levels.

"Umm," he said as he struggled to his feet with his cane.

"Are you waiting for someone?" she asked.

How did she know to target me? Is this a trap? Is it just luck that she chose me? Shit, what do I do?

"What? Um, no I was just wondering what to do with my night. I'm bored and in the mood for a little adventure."

"Funny, I'm feeling the same way," she replied. "How about we spend some time together?" she asked.

That warm fuzzy feeling pressed against his mind as her light green eyes peered into his'.

Thoughts of Aurelia's plight focused his mind and the pressure eased.

"Follow me, gorgeous," Jessica instructed and walked away. Danny looked her up and down as her back was turned. At 5'2" and wearing a white lace cardigan and short white pleated skirt which billowed out slightly, she presented herself as the innocent flower type which would be catnip for most men.

He followed with a faux-vacant expression.

Right, where is she leading me from here?

She led him past a set of stairs going under an arch, across from the bar.

This is still too public, where the fuck are we going?

She approached a winding set of cement stairs which led to a sublevel car park with the open sky directly above and a pedestrian walkway running along the length of the car park on the right.

She took him off to the right, under the walkway, into a more secluded part of the car park, before turning back to him.

"Just stand there, gorgeous," she instructed, to which Danny complied, his vacant expression still on display.

Why isn't she doing anything? Should I break and talk to her, throw her off and stake her? Why is she just staring at me?

A whoosh and thump behind Danny startled him.

He spun once more.

She stood in front of him with a twisted smile. The smile of a hunter who has trapped her prey.

"Aurelia?" Danny said.

His sister stood before him. Her irises were jet black, her canines protruding. Her eyes bulged with excitement. Her tongue licked at the tip of one of her canines.

"Aurelia? It's Danny. Do you remember me? It's Danny. I love you."

Faster than his eyes could track, Aurelia pounced on him, pinning him to the ground. She leaned over him, her canines pressed into Danny's neck.

"Aurelia, please. I'm your baby bro. Don't," Danny whispered.

The pressure of the teeth on his neck lessened.

"Uh-uh, Aurelia, honey," Jessica said, restraining her by the shoulders.

Danny squirmed out from under her and scrambled to his feet. He turned towards the stairway. In front of him stood the familiar forms of Gabriel, Malcolm, and the familiar face Danny recognised from Mercy's photos as Hannah.

"You have been a lot of trouble to us, human. Who could have known that my Aurelia's own brother would be the one to take so many of my family from me?"

"Aurelia is not yours. She's not anyone's," Danny said, his anger rising.

"You are most impressive, Daniel," Gabriel continued, "but now your adventure is over, and I must make an example of you."

"Spare me!" Danny spat.

"I *will* spare you. You see, a few friends will be arriving in town tonight, and they will all want to meet you, though you may not want to meet them."

"Tough talk from a bully with his gang behind him. Tell you what – just me and you. Let's settle this one-on-one. If I win, I walk free, so does Aurelia. If I don't win then you can torture me all you like," Danny suggested.

"That is not much of a bet. I already have you. You have to be holding at least some cards."

Fuck, what do I do?

"There's no one coming to help you. You may as well comply and I may end your suffering sooner. Now tell me, who trained you? Who told you about galena and tiger's eye? How is it you can block our hypnotism?"

Don't. Empty your mind, Danny. Just empty your mind.

"I don't know. I just can."

"Liar!" Gabriel shouted. "I have been courteous until now, but trying my patience is not recommended."

Where are you?

"Mercy isn't here," Gabriel replied. Danny stood slack-jawed with furrowed brows.

Gabriel smiled and looked down at his feet.

"And so it is. I have my answer."

Fuck!

Danny closed his eyes and grimaced.

"Do you think Mercy will help you? She is nothing more than a liar who has been manipulating you! She does not care about humans, and she certainly does not care if you live or die. Why are you protecting her?"

"I'm not! And at least she doesn't eat humans! She lives on animal blood. Something you could choose to do, but you are all murderers."

They all laughed. All except Aurelia, who was still being restrained.

Danny walked around them and backed away, towards the stairs.

"Is that what she told you? Here is a little truth: only human blood sustains us. Animal blood is as useful to our basic survival as a cup of tea. She kills humans just like we do. She is a hypocrite and a liar."

"No, that's not true. She cares about humans. I've seen it with my own eyes," Danny argued back.

"You've seen her manipulate people. She wants us all dead so she can begin her own group. Her own 'nest', as you call it. Only they won't be family like we are. They'll just be pawns like you, for she is incapable of loving like we do. She values only what benefits her. I've known her for centuries, Daniel. She manipulated you into doing the killing for her," Gabriel said as he began to follow him.

"Where do you think you are going?" Malcolm asked Danny with an amused smile.

"I'm just playing the odds," Danny replied. He looked back at Aurelia. "I'm sorry, sis. I'm so sorry."

"HELP! SOMEONE PLEASE HELP! PLEASE! SOMEONE HELP ME!" Danny screamed as he slowly backed away from them.

A number of people from Bar One ran to the edge of the walkway and peered over the side, down at Danny and the vampires.

"Hey! Get the fuck away from him!" one of the viewers shouted.

"Leave him alone!" another woman shouted. One by one,

they produced their phones and aimed them down at the scene in the car park.

"Get to fuck!" another man shouted.

Danny ran as fast as his knee would allow. He got to the steps, He craned around. Gabriel was following him, whereas the others were still standing in their places. With his knee on fire, and giving way with every other step, he made is way up the stairs and began to limp in the direction of Festival Square. He had reached the archway to his right when he was caught by Gabriel, who spun him by the shoulders.

"Sucks when you have to run at human speed, eh?" Danny said with a smile. "Leave me alone!" he shouted.

"Here, mate. Are you awright? Get the fuck away from him!" a man shouted as he approached Gabriel.

"You," Gabriel said to the man. "Run to Lothian Road as fast as you can. Then run in front of the first fast moving bus you see."

The man left Gabriel and ran past Danny.

"No!" Danny shouted and tried to clutch the man. He was too strong for Danny and shrugged him off.

"You can't rely on your humans to save you every time, Danny. And you cannot trust Mercy either. You cannot trust anyone, not even the humans, because you won't know which ones have been sent by me. You are alone in this. Completely alone, and I'll be hunting you. We *all* will," Gabriel said, and smiled.

In the distance behind Danny, the air brakes of a bus screeched, and multiple screams briefly filled the air.

"Even Aurelia will be hunting you, and let me tell you, she is an outstanding hunter. She was born to be a vampire," Gabriel continued, his smile widening. "Never mind the rest of them, they…" he continued and looked back down the stairs, in the direction of the remnants of his nest.

With a violent jerk Danny found himself flying through the streets of Edinburgh, rising steeply into the evening sky. His head swam with dizziness before he momentarily blacked out with the blood rushing away from his brain.

When he came to seconds later, he was in the arms of Mercy as she flew.

She stared ahead, flying in silence.

He wasn't grateful for the save. He was suspicious.

CHAPTER 19

Danny sat on the plush leather chair facing the fireplace, trying to ignore his headache. Mercy sat in the accompanying chair, a few feet from him. She was staring at the fire. They had not spoken for thirty minutes.

Can I trust her? Was Gabriel just fucking with my head? If I can trust her, then why is she so fucking secretive all the time? What is her second name? Christ, what is her real FIRST name? They may be vampires, but I'm killing for her and I don't even know her real fucking name!

He stared at her, studying her profile intensely.

Does she only eat animals? Gabriel and his nest laughed when I told him. That was spontaneous laughter. They seemed genuinely amused by the prospect of her eating animals. I haven't actually seen her eat anything other than sandwiches and fucking coffee.

His hands were trembling. It was ever so slight, but it was definite. He sighed.

There's no doubt that she's charismatic, and she can wrap people around her little finger without relying on hypnotism. Just how much has she wrapped me around her finger and how much of this has been my own doing?

Meanwhile, Mercy was biting her nails as she stared into the flames. Not in a nonchalant manner. She looked worried.

Still, there are differences. Gabriel made that poor guy run in front of a bus just because he got in his way. Mercy hypnotises people so that they forget they ever met her. She could be as cold-blooded as

Gabriel when dealing with irritating humans, but she has never told a human to kill himself. She genuinely seems to care for them. So maybe Gabriel really was fucking with me.

She still did not turn in his direction, even though she would occasionally look at him out of the corner of her eye before staring back at the flames.

Maybe I can trust her. Maybe I can't. This is fucking torture. What was it Gabriel said? That I can't trust any people in case he has sent them. That means any random person I pass in the street might try to kill me. I can't allow anyone to get close to me. Then again, that wouldn't be the case if he wanted me to suffer. I can't imagine he would let some random human kill me when he seems to want to torture and kill me himself. Does that mean he was lying about not trusting other humans? Was he bluffing? Was it a double bluff? Was he bluffing about all of this? Fuck's sake.

He massaged his temples in slow circular movements with his forefingers and closed his eyes.

And Aurelia. She was a different person entirely. Wild. She was going to kill me. Mercy told me that new vampires are feral, but I kinda thought that Aurelia would be different. But she wasn't. She didn't recognise me. She just wanted to feed. Gabriel didn't have to bring her. He had me walking into his trap regardless. But he brought her to be cruel. He wanted me to see her like that. He wanted me to know that she is lost to me. It was cruel.

I thought that if only I could see Aurelia again, regardless of what state she was in, there would be a little bit of my sister still in there. A piece of her that recognises me. A little piece of her that I can reason with, but there's nothing left there. The vampire has taken her completely.

Tears rolled down his cheeks as he silently stared into the flames.

Now my grand plan is in ruins. I genuinely thought it would work, but I should have known better that it would be transparent. Mercy tried to warn me, but I was so convinced that it would be successful I didn't want to listen. I've killed four vampires relatively easily, I just thought that the plan would go just as well. Fucking idiot. Dozens, maybe hundreds of vampires are about to flood the city. They'll be feeding while they search for me. All those lives will be lost, and their blood will be on my hands. My fault.

He sniffed and looked back at Mercy. She still stared into the fire. He hurriedly wiped away his tears.

I'm so out of my fucking depth here. There's no hope left, no chance we can win this. It's purely about saving lives now. There's only one thing left to do: go to the nest in Moray Place and surrender myself to Gabriel. Whatever they do to me, hopefully the other nests will leave immediately, and at least I will have saved the lives of those who would have been prey to the new nests. At least I did something worthwhile.

His focus returned to Mercy. She was smiling into the fire with her fists clenched.

Mercy stared into and through the flames.

Well, fuck. That was a fucking horror show. I should have left the stupid bastard back with Gabriel. Now I'm fucked. I've thrown my lot in with the human and there's no going back. Not even if I kill him and present the body to Gabriel.

The stares from Danny bore into her as he sat in the chair next to her, in her lounge. The lights were dimmed and the historical objects cast long shadows on the walls.

Why did I let him talk me into that fucking plan? I could tell that it was half-baked. It's no surprise. I should have overruled him with my own plan. Now my plan is fucked too. Still, my Plan A wasn't very good either. We went far too slow and allowed time for Gabriel to grow suspicious of members of his nest going missing, so I can't really lecture the Cripple on his shitty plan.

She began to bite her nails as she stared into the flames.

I'm fucking dead. I'm a dead woman walking. As strong as I am, there's no way I can defend myself against the number of nests which are going to descend on Edinburgh now. Until now, I could always plead ignorance of the Cripple's actions. Even if they charged me with killing vampires, I could always claim that I hadn't lifted a finger. It was a bloody thin argument and more of a technicality, but it could have stuck. Maybe. But tonight, I fucked myself. With me saving him, I've shown myself to be actively helping the human. Now I'm destined to end up in a couple of galena coffins. Fuck.

Through her peripheral vision, she saw him continue to look at her.

There's no way out of this. They'll torture him for years, and when his human body fails, they'll probably try to turn him into a vampire. If he survives the transformation, then they can torture him over and over with galena. That's his future. Mine is to be decapitated and wrapped in a galena shroud.

Mercy allowed herself the briefest of smiles before her stony-faced expression returned.

Ironic that I'm destined for the same agonising fate that I have placed on others. Poetic justice if there ever was any. Don't know if there is an afterlife, but I always thought that if I ever died I would get to see her again. I would run into the arms of my Aurelia. But now I'll never see her. I'll be staring into the dark forever while my body melts over and over in a separate box. Oh God, I'm never going to see her again. I'll never see her again.

Her eyes moistened. In her peripheral vision, Danny wiped tears from his eyes.

No. Fuck that. I don't care that there's no hope for us. I've never backed down from a fight, and I'm going to go out fighting. Besides, there's my Plan X. My nuclear option. It was the one I hoped I wouldn't need, but it'll shake the vampire world to its very fucking core. I'll put the plan in place now and wait while the cogs move. I owe it to every single one of Franky's people and all of Edinburgh to go down swinging at as many of the pointy-toothed fuckers as I can. Getting Cripple out of the country safely, then taking Gabriel down with me is all that matters now.

Mercy clenched her fists and smiled a menacing smile. A smile laced with ill intent.

CHAPTER 20

The ringing of Mercy's mobile phone broke the silence in the room.

Mercy cleared her throat as the fire crackled and Danny sniffed long and deep.

"Yeah?" Mercy answered. "Aye. Aye, that's fine," she continued, still staring into the fire.

"Tell them they don't have a choice. After tomorrow night, there will be dozens, maybe even hundreds of vampires, depending on how far they've come from. They'll all be looking to feed."

Danny strained to hear anything through the speaker pressed to Mercy's ear but it was useless

"Well at least try. Also, when you are done, I want you back here as soon as possible. I'm sending up a flare of my own."

Danny furrowed his brows.

"Alright, bye," Mercy said and pressed the disconnect button.

"Was that Franky?" Danny asked. Mercy nodded.

"Look, Mercy. I've been doing some thinking. I'm going to the nest and handing myself in. I need to take responsibility, and if surrendering means that the other nests don't come, it'll be the right thing to do," Danny said and took a deep breath.

"That's very noble, Cripple, but it won't make any difference. Not anymore," she replied, shaking her head. For the first time, she tore her eyes from the fire and looked at him.

"What do you mean?" he asked.

"The other nests are on their way. They'll be arriving in a few hours and when they get here, they will spend some time in the city being entertained. It's very rare that one nest visits another, and so when it happens there is a banquet and the hosts treat their guests for days, sometimes weeks," she explained.

"Oh," Danny said, his face etched with worry.

"It's like when multiple mobster families congregate, it's a very big deal. The vampires talk business, vampire politics, and their future. During which the hosts go all-out to entertain them. It doesn't matter what the guests are into, the hosts provide it and a lot of it. So dozens of vampires will be congregating on Edinburgh and will be fed off a small army of people. Like I told you before, your death won't fix anything. They'll just have some celebratory banquets with lots of locals on the menu."

"Fuck's sake. What can we do?"

"Well, I've sent Franky off to tell all of his contacts and their people that they must stay off the streets at night until further notice. It's going to be a fucking buffet for the vampires if they don't. It doesn't matter where they go, it just needs to be off the streets."

"Do you think it will work?" he asked.

"I dunno. For some, aye, but for others, they have nowhere they *can* go. No halfway houses, no homeless shelters which can take them in. Plus, others may just refuse and take their chances."

"Shit," Danny whispered. His heart sinking at the prospect of a whirlwind of death targeting Edinburgh's most vulnerable.

"It's not just that though," Mercy continued. "They'll still look for others. The areas we've spoken about, the areas that the authorities don't give a shit about, they're in trouble too. A lot of good people who happen to live in a poor or deprived area are going to be targeted. Areas like Muirhouse, Pilton, and the rest. They're packed with good people and they're in trouble."

"How so?" he asked.

"Remember what I told you? They choose houses and families who won't be missed. They hypnotise one member of the household into inviting them in and then they're done for. Only now, they won't do any kind of research. Literally anyone is a target."

"No, we need to stop this," he said shaking his head with a disbelieving smile. "I honestly dunno how, but we need to come up with something. Please tell me you have something up your sleeve!"

"Maybe. Something I've been planning if all else failed. My nuclear option. We need to let them arrive first. Even then, I need to figure some stuff out, because everything else we've done has led to this situation. We're genuinely at our lowest point here, and we can't afford to fuck up again."

"I know," he said.

They sat staring into the fire for another few moments. Finally, Mercy broke the silence.

"Why have you been looking at me weirdly?"

"What do you mean?" he asked.

"Ever since I picked you up and flew you out of that ambush, you've been staring at me with a wonky look on your mug. You've been... off with me. What's going on?"

"Nothing."

"Cripple, don't bullshit me. I have an outstanding bullshit detector."

"It's nothing," Danny reaffirmed in an increasingly half-hearted manner.

Mercy stared at him.

The daggers burrowing into him caused Danny to look back at her. Her expression was accusatory.

"Talk to me," she said.

Fuck it.

"What do you eat?"

"What?"

"Do you eat humans? Do you drink their blood just like all other vampires?"

"I told you," she said. Her face was a vision of alarmed confusion.

"Yeah, you said that you eat animals. Thing is, I'm not sure I believe that anymore. Gabriel told me that vampires need human blood to survive. That animal blood won't work, and given his reaction when I tried to defend you, I... I believe him. So tell me the truth. If you want us to keep working together, tell me the truth now," he said and waited for a response.

Let's see how good my bullshit detector is.

Mercy sat for a few seconds. Her clenched jaw betrayed her stillness.

"Come with me," she said, rose from her seat, and walked out of the room. "Cripple!" she shouted, prompting Danny to get out of his chair and scurry out of the room after her.

Mercy led him to a new part of her house. A part he had never seen before. They went down three flights of stairs and into the basement containing the training equipment Danny had seen before and an extensive collection of wine racks he hadn't. They went through another two locked doors and arrived in a dingy cellar room with minimal lighting. The stale mustiness of damp coated Danny's nostrils as he peered through the gloom. In the centre of the cellar were three large dog cages.

In each cage there was a bundle of clothing and a blanket, beneath one of which emanated a faint whimpering. In the corner of the cage were two large bowls; one contained water and the other bore the dried and crusty remains of food.

So she was telling the truth. A bit fucking cruel on these poor things to have them like this, but at least she wasn't lying.

"What are they? Dogs?" he asked as he approached the closest cage. Mercy stood in silence.

Through the gloom and layers was a small patch of matted, black fur. He pressed his fingers to the cage and hunched down onto his knees.

"Psspsspss. Here boy," Danny said.

Mercy stared at the cage with no emotion.

There has to be a better way than this. Dogs, for Christ's sake.

This is just so cruel.

The large bundle of clothes and blankets stirred. The patch of fur moved and as it rose, the grimy face of a man looked back at Danny.

Danny leaned back, his eyes wide.

"Help me," the man pleaded. His voice was weak and gruff. His eyes were bloodshot, and grime and grease streaked his face. The stench of body odour reached Danny's nostrils.

"Dear God!" Danny whispered as he struggled to his feet.

"Please help me! I'm begging you!" the man said as he shuffled his naked body out from under the covers. His stomach and waist were heavy with stretch marks, indicating a fast loss of weight.

Danny looked away.

Mercy approached them.

The man shuffled to the rear of his cage.

"Stay away from her! She's a vampire!" the man shouted.

"Wait a minute," Danny said as puzzle pieces began to slot into place. "I know your face. You're... you're..."

"Cripple, I'd like you to meet Thomas Briggs. I take it you are familiar with the name?" Mercy asked.

"I feared that this was the case," Danny said, shaking his head. "You only feed from animals. I hoped that you were telling the truth because it made working with you easier. I feel queasy," he said and took a few deep breaths.

"Before you go breaking your heart for him, Mr Briggs," she addressed her captive, "would you like to explain why you have found yourself here? I'm sure you haven't forgotten. I told you multiple times when I took you."

Briggs stayed silent, pulling the blankets up around his neck in a defensive manner.

"No? Very well, I'll say then, shall I?" she mocked him. "See, Mr Briggs here likes girls. The younger the better. Tell me Mr Briggs, exactly how many children have you raped? But you're smart enough to make sure that you choose kids who won't be reliable witnesses when the shit hits the fan, don't you?"

Briggs remained silent.

"Aye, Mr Briggs likes them young. What was your youngest? Three-years-old, wasn't it? And you chose her because both of her parents are drug addicts, and you could make up any story you liked."

Danny's sympathy faded away and disappear like breath on a cold day.

"Even when people suspected you, you were sharp enough to avoid anything from sticking to you," Mercy said. "Unfortunately, the authorities couldn't get you to be detained at Her Majesty's pleasure. So now you're detained at mine. Only, for you, there will be no parole. No release date. You'll stay here until your heart gives out, whichever year that will be, and then you'll be dumped in the North Sea."

Mercy moved on to the next cage. Both men in the other two cages were now awake and huddled against the rear of their cages.

"Meet John Armitage. He likes to rape women, don't you Mr Armitage? Your favourite method is date rape. How many women have you raped? See, he's been in a police station before, but the issue of verbal consent was always a he-said-she-said affair, wasn't it? Over a dozen women have been brutalised and violated, haven't they Mr Armitage? Well, now you understand the importance of consent, don't you?"

Armitage continued to whimper.

"And finally," Mercy continued as she moved on to the final cage. "We have David McDonald."

McDonald looked up at her. There was no fear or despair. There was, instead, abject desolation in his eyes. Emaciated, his ribs jutted out at awkward angles and there was almost no muscular mass on his arms.

"Mr McDonald has been here the longest. I forget how many years he has been here. He is here because he loves to beat his women. Multiple partners have been battered and abused over the years with an impressive array of broken bones and internal injuries. Worst of all is the psychological torture he puts them through. He controls every aspect of their lives, from money to friends, to make sure they're totally dependent on him. Thing is, his last partner felt there was no other option. She took her own life, just to escape him. And now he's here, getting a taste of his own medicine."

Mercy then walked back through the door.

Danny shuffled after her in silence.

The three men began to beg for Danny to send help. The volume of their cries grew in unison with the increasing distance between Danny and the captives, until the door slammed shut and the men became silent once more.

Danny remained silent as he followed her back upstairs and into the kitchen.

"Tea?" she asked as she flicked the kettle on and produced a mug.

"Huh? Umm, no thanks. Look—" he began.

"I told you that I only feed on animals," she interrupted. "I was telling the truth. That's exactly what those bastards are. Animals," Mercy said as she produced sugar and tea bags.

"Mercy, I… I don't know how to process this."

"Process it however you need to."

"I can't be OK with this. I know that they are the worst kind of scum, but that's what the police are for."

"Don't get me started on the justice system. The way I see it, this serves a dual purpose. I am sustained and another piece of scum gets taken off the street."

"Yeah, but there are always going to be rapists and paedophiles," Danny argued.

"That's true I'm afraid. But at least no more kids will be raped by Thomas Briggs," she said with a smile.

"And what if they are innocent?" Danny asked.

"They're not. Trust me. Their names were recommended to me by contacts who know the cases inside out and are powerless to stop it."

The kettle clicked off and Mercy poured the boiled water into the mug.

"Alright, I need to head home and get some sleep," Danny closed his eyes and shook his head.

"You're not going anywhere I'm afraid," Mercy replied.

Danny's eyebrows furrowed. "Is this about what you just showed me? Am I your prisoner now too?"

"Don't be so melodramatic," she said. "Gabriel and his nest know who you are. Your home is no longer safe. It will be staked out and spied upon 24/7, just in case you're daft enough to return. I'm afraid you need to stay here until this is over. Gabriel will know that you are here too, but at least you'll have me, where it's safer."

"Fuck, you're right," Danny said. "I never even thought of it that way."

"I'll make up a bedroom for you. We'll buy spare clothes and have them delivered here. We'll reorder the cane you lost in Gabriel's ambush, plenty of fresh tiger's eye, galena, and anything else you need. But until this is over, you need to hunker down here for the duration."

"Fuck," Danny repeated with a whisper.

Once again, silence descended between them. After another few minutes, it was Danny's turn to break the tension.

"Look, Mercy, I don't know how to feel about what you just showed me and I might never be OK with it, but thank you for at least being honest with me," he said.

"You're welcome, Cripple," Mercy replied as she sipped at her tea.

CHAPTER 21

The group of thirty or so people mingled in one of the large spare rooms of Mercy's house. Danny yawned and sipped at his coffee. All had a cheery demeanour. As with any group of strangers meeting for the first time, there was awkward conversation and chatting about the weather. Many drank from takeaway coffee chain cups and most were bleary eyed.

I wonder if any of them are aware that directly below us three criminals are locked up and will remain imprisoned, being drained of their blood, before their bodies gives out and they are dumped in the North Sea. How many of them would still stay if they knew?

Danny had spent a sleepless night straining to make sense of what Mercy had shown him. He tried to see it from her point of view.

They are absolute scum, but they haven't been given a fair trial. Aren't they innocent until proven guilty? They've been abducted and are enduring permanent torture before receiving a long and agonising death sentence. No matter how despicable the crime, is that a justifiable punishment? What would their victims say? Is it for me to decide what is right and wrong, and what punishment is appropriate? Is it Mercy's place to do so?

After hours of inner-deliberation and soul searching, Danny still had no satisfactory answers, but it continued to play on is mind. There was no doubt he now looked at Mercy differently.

Franky had shown them into the room where Danny

stood, leaning on his newly delivered cane with one hand and clutching his mug for dear life in the other. He had been on the receiving end of a number of confused looks from the invitees, most likely wondering who he was and why he stood at the front of the room. Franky then joined Danny, leaning against the wall.

"She'll just be a minute. That's all of them apparently," he informed Danny.

Danny nodded and looked at his mug.

"Aye. Are you not having some coffee?" Danny asked.

"Nah mate. No this early in the morning. I need to wake up a wee bit before I'm able to handle caffeine," Franky replied with a smile.

"Now that's irony," Danny said, to which Franky chuckled.

The muttering died down, prompting both Danny and Franky to look in the direction of the door.

Mercy entered. She wore the same powder pink tee which got covered in blood when they visited Thompson and destroyed his face.

The group fell silent.

"Which brand of washing powder do you use?" Danny asked with a smile.

"New tee," she replied. "Hello everyone. Thank you for agreeing to come so early, and especially at such short notice. You all know me very well. I have done a number of favours for all of you. You don't know one another and that is by design. However, there have been developments recently which have necessitated this meeting."

She held the attention of each member of the group.

"I don't like calling in favours, however this is unfortunately an emergency. It is regarding the increasing numbers of people going missing in the city. I know it has been an increasing concern to all of you. You all care greatly for the people you look after in your personal or professional capacities. I have promised you help and now that time has come. However, the night is always darkest before the dawn, and we are now approaching that darkest part."

Franky and Danny glanced at one another.

"Over the next twenty-four to forty-eight hours, the amount of people likely to go missing is going to rise sharply to astonishing levels."

Mumbles and mutterings broke out. Danny scanned the faces once more. Many continued to look at him. The joviality and smiles which had been so prevalent were now gone. Some wore worried expressions, whilst others were angry.

"That is why you are all here. We are all in the same boat and we are all fighting this together. That is why I need you to spend today warning your people again to be careful. Johnny," she addressed a man who nodded. "I need you to tell your colleagues that the perpetrators of these crimes are going to go on a spree over the next forty-eight hours or so, and so they must increase patrols, especially of the places already affected."

Johnny nodded.

"Abigail, I need you to speak to your clients and spread the word that their community is about to be targeted. Tell them that over the next couple of days, they must not open their doors to anyone they don't know. Especially at night. The guilty parties are especially good at talking themselves into a victim's home. And so, they must not answer the door at all, no matter what. Spark fear and panic if you must; it'll keep them alive. June, Mark, Anne, I want you to do the same."

A few more people nodded.

"Agnes, your folks at the various elderly accommodations are particularly vulnerable, given their states, especially those with dementia. If they are targets of conmen then they will definitely be vulnerable to these people. Tell your employees and security to be on the lookout for anyone they don't know on the grounds. Phone 999 if you need to. Johnny, tell your people they may have to respond to increasing calls. They need to be on the lookout. They are unlikely to be in danger, as the perpetrators would rather not target anyone in authority, but it is not without risk."

Johnny and Agnes both nodded.

"No problem, deary," Agnes said.

"James, tell your contacts in the press that there is rumour that there is likely to be a spree over the next few days, and that official advice is to stay off the streets when the sun goes down and to not answer your door if you are not expecting company."

"Anything you need, Mercy," James replied.

"Jimmy, speak with Franky here," Mercy nodded over her shoulder, and Franky held his hand up. "Franky is already working on this, but you'll get more work done if you work together. The homeless community have been the primary targets of these bastards and they are under more threat than ever before. Get them off the street. Whatever it takes. Franky, if you need to, bring some of them here and I'll put them up for a few nights if you have no luck elsewhere."

"All of you, your primary role is to protect your people over the next couple of days. I can't promise that the problem will go away, but it will definitely die back down after a few days."

"Mercy?" a woman called out, putting her hand up.

"Aye Margaret?"

"I'll do what I can in my local area. I've never asked this before, but... the people who go missing, are they dead?"

A few seconds passed as the crowd waited expectantly on the answer to a question they had all asked themselves at one point.

"Yes," Mercy replied.

There was a collective intake of breath and murmuring. Though there were many upset faces, there was not one displaying surprise or shock.

"I know that what I'm asking will provoke a lot of awkward questioning. Try to be as vague as you possibly can, but the most important thing is saving people's lives. We can deal with the fallout later."

"Have you now got the help you needed?" Margaret asked, looking at Danny.

"Aye," Mercy replied with a smile. She looked over her shoulder at Danny. "And he's better than I could have hoped for. One way or another a lot of these bastards are going to be stopped," she finished as she turned back to Margaret. Danny's ears and cheeks began to burn.

Margaret smiled and nodded at Danny.

Danny smiled an awkward smile in return.

Every face in the group was smiling at him. Some were nodding in appreciation.

"Look," Mercy said as she momentarily looked at her feet before addressing the crowd. "Every single one of you have at some point wondered who I am and how I can manage to do the things you ask me to do. Especially when those things are not necessarily legal. I'm sure you all have your own theories. I'm happy to let those theories continue. But please trust me when I say that I will do everything I can over these next few days. Good luck everyone," she finished.

The people began to leave. Each one smiled at Danny as they passed.

Who the hell do these people think I am? Rambo? I'm an average guy with love handles, a beer belly, and a cane! Do they even know what I'm going up against?

Danny continued to smile.

Mercy turned to Danny.

"Are you ready, Cripple?" she asked.

"No," he replied with a smile, which prompted one from her. "So, what's next?"

"Another cup of coffee. Then I'm going for a nap. You have the run of the house. Just put newspaper down if you need to poo."

"You're a fucking oddball, you know that?" Danny asked as they left the room.

"Aye, Cripple. Aye," Mercy conceded.

Danny sat on the couch in front of an unreasonably large TV screen, remote in hand. He had begun with the various news channels but after a few hours he was now browsing the various streaming apps.

Why am I sitting here doing nothing? I should be doing

something. I hate being out in the cold.

The subtle creaking of floorboards announced Mercy's arrival before she entered the room.

"Well, well, well. If it isn't Sleeping Bollock," he said.

"Aye, very good," she said, then yawned and slumped onto the couch beside him.

"Is that cartoon pony pyjamas you've got on?" he asked.

"Aye. What? Want to borrow them? Just wash them before you return them," she said and grabbed the remote out of his hand.

"Christ, you're salty in the morning," he said.

"What? Oh, for fuck's sake, are you trying to be all cool, using modern vernacular? You know that in a few years no one will be using that term and you'll just look like a fucking idiot," she argued back. "Besides, I thought you didn't have any friends. How did you learn that word?"

"I *do* have the internet. I'm not *that* isolated."

"Now who's being salty?" she asked.

"You're not really in any position to talk. A few centuries ago, you would have been all 'thou' and 'dost' and 'haberdashery'."

Mercy burst out laughing.

"Seriously," he continued. "You'd have been speaking as though you were in *Pride and Prejudice*. 'Oh indeed, Lady Fotherington-Smythe. Mr Darcy-Baggington was verily vexing, and so I yeeted him out of the window. Thusly.'"

"I yeeted Mr Darcy out the window, did I?" Mercy asked, looking at Danny with a grin.

"Thusly," he confirmed.

"I was speaking more like a wildling in *Game of Thrones*. It wasn't until I reached Renaissance Florence that I developed some refinement. Seriously, keeping up with latest fads, expressions and trends is one of the simplest and most effective ways of keeping close to humans. Keeping myself..."

"Human?" he suggested.

"As close to it as I can. Now, can I turn on the news?" she

asked

"Sure."

"We should discuss what happened last night. So how do you feel about my diet then?" she asked, still staring at the TV.

"Honestly? I don't know how to feel. I appreciate you being honest with me, but I shouldn't have had to drag it out of you. I dunno, Mercy. There are three people caged like animals downstairs right now. I know they've most likely done horrible, repugnant things, but are you really the one to be judge, jury, and executioner?"

"Fair point," she conceded. "Back when I was with the vampires, I didn't care who I ate. I enjoyed it. I loved it. After meeting Josef, when I began to consider what I had become, I realised that I had lost myself. That Aurelia would be ashamed of me. That... that changed everything. I began to see myself for what I was: a vicious and sadistic murderer. I decided that I didn't have to give in to the animalistic hunter in me. That I could tame the vampire in me. But I didn't know what to do. I tried starving. I tried animal blood, but it made me violently ill. Puking up congealed blood is not nice. Weakened and wasting away, there were plenty of nights where I would hold a stake in my hand, pointed at my chest, willing myself to do it, but I never could."

Who's Josef?

"I'm glad you didn't," he said.

"Cheers," she replied. "But then I found the answer. I came across a little girl who was crying over the body of her mother. The girl must have been no older than five."

"Jesus, that's awful."

"The men who gang-raped and killed the mother had only been gone for a couple of minutes. The girl had been forced to watch."

Mercy continued to stare at the TV, but her jaw was clenched and her fingernails were white with pressure on the remote.

"I tracked them down. There wasn't anyone else around.

They would not have gone to jail. There was not going to be any justice for the slain woman or her child. I followed them at a good distance until it was night. By the time they set up camp, the sun had gone down and they were sitting by their fire. I took my time with them. Their deaths took days. I drank more blood in those few days than I had in a long time. That's when I found my answer. It wasn't a case of whether I should feed from people, it was a case of *who* I should feed from, who deserved to be targeted."

Mercy cleared her throat, but still did not take her eyes off the screen.

"Sure, I've tried blood banks since, but that didn't work. Blood which is cold stored and potentially weeks old is just as bad as animal blood. There's no cheating the system, at least not that I know. If there was a way to cheat the system then I would do it, but feeding from those who most people would consider to be scum is as elegant a solution as I can find."

"I guess," Danny said.

"So, I figured I may as well do something good with the shite situation I was in. I remember, for a good few years I used to enjoy clubbing. I saw a man chatting up some girl and when she turned away, I watched him slip a pill of some kind into her drink."

"Bastard," Danny said.

"Well, I rushed over. Told her what had happened and that I would deal with it myself. I hypnotised her to forget me and him, but to be more careful about guarding her drinks in future. That guy, however, became the first person to inhabit one of my cages."

"Is it only ever guys you take?" he asked.

"No. There are plenty of females who are just as deserving of one of my cages. There just happen to be three men in them right now. I'm an equal opportunities drinker," she said with a smile and a wink.

"But there will always be miscarriages of justice. There will always be people who get away with it," Danny said.

"And so there will always be food for me," she said with a smile.

"I can't lie, I'm not comfortable with it," he said.

"I wouldn't expect you to be. I'm sure it's a helluva shock. But it's my life, and if I must live, then I will feed off those who traded in any moral right to their own life."

Mercy's mobile phone rang.

"Hello," she said.

Danny watched the TV on mute. Mercy had not yet flicked to a news channel and so a Christmas move was playing.

Why the hell are they showing Christmas movies at this time of year?

"Good, good. Who met you?" she said.

Still, I love Christmas movies.

"Did he look ill?" she asked.

Danny's expression changed to a confused frown.

"Hmmm. Uh huh. Right… right… OK, cheers," she said and disconnected the call.

"I take it you were talking about a vampire when you asked if he looked ill?"

"Yeah. A contact of mine has informed me that the other nests have started arriving. They'll continue to arrive throughout the day. Tonight I'm going to check some stuff out, then tomorrow we'll plan what we're going to do. Right now, you just need to hold tight."

"But as soon as you leave the house tonight, they'll attack you," Danny said.

"They won't see me leave. There is a back entrance through the cellar. It means that I can escape unseen. I didn't choose this house for nothing. I've seen enough old movies with pitchfork wielding mobs. A vampire must always choose a place which can accommodate at least one secret exit in case the shit hits the fan."

"That's handy," Danny said.

"There's nothing 'handy' about it. Like I said, if I couldn't install at least one exit, I wouldn't have bought this place. Want some lunch?" she asked.

"Aye, what are you thinking?" he replied.

In the distance the front door opened then slammed shut.

"Franky's home," Danny said.

"Really? Thanks Sherlock!" Mercy quipped.

"Hey Franky, how did you get on?" Mercy asked without taking her eyes from the screen as he appeared through the door behind them.

"Aye, great. It's all sorted now," Franky said as he approached them.

"Good. Now we hunker down for the next day or so," she replied.

"So, who was this Josef? You said that you met someone called Josef and that it made you change," Danny said.

Franky walked up to the couch behind them and swung his arm down, hammering a stake deep into Mercy's chest.

Mercy let out a wispy grunt as all the air was forced out of her lungs.

"Franky!" Danny shouted. He crawled over the back of the couch and launched himself and Franky. They both landed on the ground. "Franky! What the fuck?!"

Franky struggled his hand free before producing a knife. He thrust it at Danny.

Danny blocked it in time.

They struggled, grunting and pushing. Franky rolled Danny over and straddled him. Franky used the full force of his weight and strength to force the knife blade down on him. Danny struggled with all his might, but the blade continued to lower down on him, inch by inch.

"Franky!" he pleaded.

Franky's eyes remained vacant as the tip of the blade began to press into Danny's sternum.

A thud jerked Franky and the pressure on the knife eased as Franky's eyes rolled into the back of his head. Franky collapsed, unconscious, next to Danny.

Danny allowed a couple of seconds to catch his breath

before raising his head. Above him crouched a badly bloodied Mercy. Her left hand was pressed hard against the hole in her chest. In her right hand was the butt-end of the tiger's eye stake she had been stabbed with.

She coughed and blood stained her teeth red.

She breathed long and hard. Wispy, crackly sounds escaped her mouth with each breath.

"Mercy! You're still alive!" Danny shouted.

Mercy nodded. She breathlessly mouthed the word 'blood' to him.

"Blood? You need blood! Of course, feed away!" Danny said and moved away from Franky.

Mercy shook her head.

"Your animals!" Danny whispered. She nodded, her eyes rolling upwards, and her head lolling from side to side.

He grabbed the knife and, balancing on his good leg, he lifted her up and with his head under her arm. He walked her in the direction of the staircase to the cellar.

"What about Franky?" Danny asked.

"Forget... him," she whispered in between crackling breaths.

They burst into the room with the cages. She had dropped the stake and grabbed the keys to the cages from the neighbouring room.

All three men stood up, staring at Danny and Mercy as they stumbled towards the cages.

The weakest one! McDonald! He'll put up less of a fight.

He dragged her to the door of the first cage. As blood continued to spill from her wound, she fumbled with the keys.

McDonald retreated to the far end of the cage.

The cage door burst open and Mercy and Danny stumbled in.

Sensing a moment of opportunity, McDonald rushed them, but in his weakened state, he bounced off the stronger Danny.

Danny let go of Mercy, who collapsed onto the blankets, and he grabbed McDonald. Danny headbutted him repeatedly until

McDonald's nose burst and his blood sprayed onto Danny's face.

He held the knife to McDonald's throat and pushed him onto his back, next to Mercy.

Mercy crawled on top of him and bit deeply into McDonald's neck. She began to drink. Weakly at first, but then more forcefully. The noisy supping and slurping accompanied by animalistic grunts from Mercy turned Danny's stomach.

Danny watched her slowly murder a man of Danny's choosing, and with Danny's help. The blood pulsing down the side of McDonald's neck was now on Danny's hands and would forever remain there.

Within a few moments, McDonald stopped struggling and his skin became pale.

Mercy stopped drinking and rolled onto her back. Her eyes were jet-black. Blood had poured down her chin and mixed with the blood from her own wounds. She smiled a vacant, blood-drenched smile with wet, red teeth.

McDonald was staring into oblivion. Danny closed McDonald's eyes with the palm of his hand.

The other two looked on with horror from their cages. They then stared at Danny in an accusatory manner.

"Be grateful I didn't choose either of you," he said. At that, they both lowered their eyes and looked away.

CHAPTER 22

Danny soothed the remnants of the previous night's headache by pressing a cold can of cola against his temple.

Binge watching TV had become unbearable now. Twenty-four hours had passed since Franky had tried to kill his friend, and the house had returned to some resemblance of normalcy.

Mercy was sleeping. Franky was in his room, hiding in shame, leaving Danny to once again watch TV on the now blood-stained couch.

Danny remained a supportive friend, but his mind was creaking at the seams.

Mercy's head appeared through the doorway.

"Kitchen," she said and disappeared.

Danny turned the TV off in silence.

When he arrived, Mercy and Franky were already sitting on stools.

"Pull up a pew, Cripple," she said.

Danny sat across from them and waited for someone to speak.

"Right," Mercy began. "Time for a wee debrief I think."

Franky sat with his shoulders slumped and his spine curved. He was staring at the white tiled floor.

"How are we feeling?" she asked.

There was silence in the room for thirty seconds.

"Let me start then," she continued. "I'm absolutely fucking raging."

Both Danny and Franky looked at her. Franky's expression of shame was replaced by one of fear.

"Mercy, I'm so sorry," Franky began.

"Franky, we went through this last night when you came to and I had stopped bleeding. You had been hypnotised by Gabriel. Other than me, he is the only vampire powerful enough to hypnotise someone during the day. He would have told you to come back here, pretend that everything was OK, then try to kill us. He would have given you that tiger's eye stake."

"I let you down, though," Franky said.

"Franky, it's fine. We just got lucky that you missed my heart with the stake. Although taking a stake to the lung isn't fun. But it shows that the gloves are off. It also means that any human at our door could potentially be hypnotised, so our guard has to be up at all times from now on. Door locked and bolted at all times. Vampires can't come in here, but brainwashed humans definitely can. Franky you're not leaving the house until this is over," she instructed.

"OK," he said.

"I'm also fucking raging that Gabriel would use one of my friends to kill me. That he would find a sneaky way of violating my home. That pisses me right fucking off. Anyway, how are you feeling, Cripple?" she asked.

Where do I even fucking begin?

Danny remained silent and shrugged his shoulders.

"You've been through a lot," she offered.

Danny snorted in derision. He didn't mean to, but it was out before he had the chance to stifle his reaction.

"Talk to me," she persisted.

"It's fine," he lied.

"Is it fuck. Now, out with it," she said.

"What do you want me to say, Mercy? Less than forty-eight hours ago, I find that not only has my grand plan backfired on me, but my sister, the reason why I'm doing this, is a rabid vampire who tried to kill me. Then I find out that dozens of vampires are now going to use Edinburgh's most vulnerable as their own 'All You Can Eat Buffet' and it's all because of me. Their blood will be on my hands. Then I find out that you are actually feeding off humans yourself and that they are being hidden in this very house. Then Franky tries to murder me. Then I actually help you murder a human being. Not to mention the fact that I haven't a clue what to do now that we are being targeted 24/7. We can't trust any human, and we have no plan to get ourselves out of this fucking situation. All of that in forty-eight hours! We are truly at our lowest ebb. We can't even leave the house without being killed, so as you can imagine, I'm a fucking wreck, Mercy!"

"Oh," Mercy replied.

"Wait, you feed off humans?" Franky interrupted. "Which humans? Where? Not homeless, is it?"

"No. Downstairs. Paedos and rapists," she said.

Franky was thoughtful for a few seconds.

"Fair enough," he said with a shrug.

"Franky, how are you feeling?" she said.

"Eh... uh... Just embarrassed. I'd never hurt either of yous, then I wake up with a splitting sore head, and you tell me that I tried to kill you. Both of you. I even nearly did it. I'm just... I'm sorry, lads."

"It's OK, Franky," Danny replied with a weak smile.

"Aye. Don't blame yourself. No long-term harm done," she added. "I'm going to go out tonight, like I meant to last night."

"Are you kidding?" Danny asked. "You were just run through with a tiger's eye stake which sliced into your lung less than twenty-four hours ago!"

Mercy smiled a calm and reassuring smile. She pulled her loose V-neck top down, showing that there was no injury to her sternum. Not the slightest mark.

"Bloody hell," Danny said.

"See? As good as new. Still, you owe me a new set of pony pyjamas, you dick!" she shouted at Franky, before nudging him with her elbow and winking.

"Thanks to your quick thinking with the blood, Cripple,

it allowed me to recover very quickly. If I didn't have you, it would have taken me days, maybe even weeks to recover fully," she explained. "Right Franky, get on the phone and find out if anyone went missing from last night. Do your all to make sure that people have a place to go tonight, but you're working from home here."

"No worries, boss," he said, and sprang onto his feet from the stool and trotted out of the kitchen.

"What about you and me?" Danny asked.

"We're having a coffee and a chat over a bite to eat, so get the butter out of the fridge," she replied.

Danny and Mercy sat in her library, sipping cappuccinos and allowing their recently consumed sandwiches to settle. Danny studied the room. Bookcases lined all four walls from wooden floor to the ornate white stucco-plastered ceiling. The musky smell of old books was as comforting as it was familiar.

Mercy sat in a dark green leather and oak chair behind her oversized oak desk,

"I come here when I want to read, or just for some quiet. It's the quietest above ground room in the house and the bookcases help to keep it that way," she said with her eyes closed and a satisfied smile, her head resting back on the green leather.

Danny readjusted his position into his own leather chair across the table.

"This chair is so comfortable! I need to get myself one of these," Danny said.

"If we survive this, I'll buy you one," Mercy replied without opening her eyes.

"In other words, I won't be getting one," Danny added.

"Exactly."

Danny allowed himself an ironic chuckle.

Danny studied Mercy in silence.

Without her usual half ponytail, her hair fell around her right shoulder. Her signature vivid red lipstick was immaculate as always. She wore a white cold shoulder top with a pink floral pattern in sequins. Her legs were crossed and resting on the edge of her desk.

With her eyes closed and her smile still in place, she presented the image of a woman at absolute peace with herself and with the world. A peaceful woman who did not care that they were stuck in a foxhole they didn't know how to get out of with overwhelming odds waiting for them, which guaranteed that they would not survive. Her calm demeanour had a soothing effect on him

"What is it, Cripple?" she asked with her eyes closed.

"You've changed," he replied.

At that Mercy opened her eyes and frowned, though she still smiled.

"Oh, is that right? How so?"

"Well, when we first met, you were very distant, cold, angry and scary. You were all about just looking out for you. You didn't seem to give a shit about people, or were willing to stick your neck out for them. You convinced yourself that you were only helping people because it furthered your interests, but that's not true is it? Really, you are doing all this for them. You've been looking out for them for a long time, and now you are about to give up your life for the poorest in the city. The ones who can't pay you back. And you're going to sacrifice yourself for a bunch of people who don't know you exist and won't ever thank you."

Mercy's smile faded.

"It is what it is," she replied, her eyes closing once more.

"It's just… inspiring, that's all. Quite the change," he finished.

"Fuck off, Cripple."

"You're still an arsehole, though," he added, to which they both started giggling.

"But I'm not the only one who has changed though, smartarse," she replied.

"Oh yeah?"

"Yeah. When I first saw you, you were whimpering like a bitch after that taxi tried to dry-hump you. When we first spoke, you were this little shy guy who wouldn't say 'boo' to a goose.

You had zero confidence and, to be honest, you were just a whiny wee dick."

"Gee, thanks," Danny replied with his eyes wide open.

"But now you're killing two vampires at a time, willing to submit to torture for the greater good. You've turned into quite the badass. For a human."

"Wow," he said looking down at the desk. "I didn't know I was whiny."

"Just a wee bit," she replied. "But lately, you remind me of someone I knew a long time ago."

"Oh yeah? Who?"

"You'd know him as Van Helsing."

"Wait, what?" Danny asked as he straightened up and leaned forward. "Van Helsing is a fictitious character in Bram Stoker's *Dracula*. He isn't real!"

"Of course he was," Mercy replied in a matter of fact way before lifting her feet from the desk and straightening up in her seat, leaning towards him, her hands clasped and her elbows on the desk.

"Eh? *Dracula* is my favourite book of all time, ironically," Danny said.

"Thing is," Mercy continued. "People think that the character of Van Helsing was inspired by a man Bram Stoker knew, a botanist called Georg Andreas Helwing. The truth is that the real Van Helsing was a man named Josef Von Herrig. He was the real inspiration. The original Van Helsing."

"Bloody hell! But how did Bram Stoker find out about Von Herrig?" Danny asked.

"Because I told him about Josef when I met Stoker much later," Mercy answered.

"Oh," Danny replied, his eyes wide.

"I encountered Josef in 1750, in German Prussia. He had killed seven vampires that we knew of throughout his homeland, including a nest, before I was sent after him. He was the only person I know of to have killed a whole nest. He wasn't a professor, an academic or a nobleman. He was a humble woodworker who grew a small amount of crops. He lost his fiancée to a vampire and, through grief and anger, he spent the rest of his short life studying, and subsequently killing, vampires, until he met me."

"Was she one of the chosen? Josef's fiancée?"

"No. Josef was a ferocious fighter. Even with my speed and strength, he still put up a helluva fight. However, I triumphed, I stabbed him in the chest with his own tiger's eye stake."

Mercy looked through her desk as she recounted her story. She wore a pained expression and appeared remorseful.

"I remember his last words. I was turning to leave when he called me back. I leaned over him. He asked me my name. He misheard it as 'Mercy'. With his last words, he whispered 'Mercy, losing your humanity is losing what you once were.'"

Mercy stopped fidgeting, briefly closed her eyes, and sighed before continuing.

"I didn't understand the meaning, nor did I understand *why* he chose those as his last words, but something in me awoke. It wasn't a sudden realisation. More a gradual discomfort at what I was doing and who I was, until it became overwhelming. Soon after that I decided that I wanted away from the vampire community. A new me. I took the name 'Mercy', in honour of Josef."

Danny nodded as he listened intently.

"I became a loner after that. The vampires have always considered me a legend in their eyes. The called me 'The Executioner'. Taking the life of Josef, the most successful vampire hunter ever, just added to that. But I had decided that I was done with killing for vampires ever again."

"Wow. That's amazing," Danny said. "But what did your sire think of you leaving them all behind?"

"Oh, I have no idea. He disappeared long before that happened."

"Really? You don't know where your sire is?"

"I know exactly where he is; he's where I left him," she replied with a smile.

"Wait, what? What do you mean *where* you 'left him'? Did you kill him? How are you still alive?"

"Wow, easy on the rapid-fire questions there, Tiger!" she replied. "See, you have to understand that just because I turned into a vampire and had this feral animal in me that I had to concentrate on taming, and just because I was enveloped in the community, didn't mean that I had forgotten what happened to me. What happened to Aurelia. It didn't mean I forgot the love that was stolen from me. That wrong *had* to be corrected."

Mercy shuffled in her seat. A strange look overtook her. An expression of determined anger, as though her emotions back then were every bit as raw now.

"I learned a great deal about the vampire world and the way of life from Claude. How to live day by day. How to survive. How to thrive. He wanted me to be a warrior. He taught me how to develop my powers and vampire strength right from the earliest age. It's thanks to him I'm much stronger than any vampire my age, male or female. But he made one terrible mistake," she continued as she leaned back into her chair, the leather creaking as she did so.

"What was that?"

"He told me how we are killed, then he told me about the punishment for a vampire when he breaks our only rule."

"Why do I get the feeling that vengeful Mercy made an appearance?" Danny asked with a smile.

Mercy's returned smile was half-hearted and brief.

"I waited. I gathered the materials I would need, picked out the perfect location, and waited some more until the time and circumstances were perfect. One night, when he wasn't paying attention, I approached him with sword in hand. With one swing, I took his head at the neck."

"Wow. Did you have second thoughts?"

"Every night," she replied. "I dumped his naked body, wrapped in a shroud which I ingrained with powdered galena, into a coffin and buried it. I placed his head in a small box and buried it separately. Before I did anything to his body however, I spoke to him with his head cradled in my hands. He was looking at me the whole time. His eyes burning hatred into mine. I had to tell him before the agonising melting of the galena started. I told him why I did it. He hurt her. He hurt my precious Aurelia."

Danny listened as she recounted her memory, the knuckles of her fists bone white.

Her anger has not softened, even centuries later.

"He sealed his fate the moment he touched her. So, I buried both boxes in a place no other being will ever find him. And there he lies to this day."

"So, he has been lying in the silent darkness, unable to make a sound, feeling his body continually melt and his nerve endings burning in agony, for centuries?" he asked.

"Aye."

"Bloody hell, Mercy. That's a punishment much worse than death."

"Exactly. Every now and again I'll visit the location to ensure the ground has not been disturbed."

Danny took a deep breath.

"So, didn't anyone question you on Claude's disappearance?" he asked.

"Of course they did. The elders wanted to know what had happened to my sire. I simply told them that he had disappeared without a trace one day, and without telling me. I'm not sure if they believed me, but given that I was still alive, it was clear Claude was too."

Mercy sighed and unclenched her fists.

"Anyway," she said as she straightened her posture and looked down at the front of her desk. "There's a reason I brought you in here. I have a present for you."

"Aww, babes! You shouldn't have!" he mocked her.

"Fuck off," she retorted. "I took this out of long-term storage a few days back. I wanted to present it to you before the shit hit the fan. Of all the antiques and possessions I own, this is the second-most sacred thing of mine," she said as she opened a drawer.

She produced a long thin box, eighteen inches long, four inches high, and five inches deep, and intricately carved in dark wood. She placed it on the desk in front of him.

"Seriously?" he asked, with no hint of jest or mockery.

Mercy nodded in silence.

Danny placed it on his lap. There was a clasp on the front of the box. He undid the clasp and lifted the lid. Inside was a long, thin, smooth, perfectly round stake made of amber-coloured tiger's eye which glimmered under the library lights.

Mercy smiled slightly.

He picked up the stake. There were four lines of inlaid silver running the length of the stake before converging an inch from the tip. The sharpened tiger's eye was so fine at the tip, it appeared razor-sharp.

He ran his fingers along the length of the silver lines. It was rough to the touch.

"Galena?" he asked.

"Aye," she answered.

"A galena-inlaid tiger's eye stake so sharp it could probably cut the skin by the slightest touch?" he asked as he smiled at her.

"Aye. It's a thing of beauty. And it scares the shit out of me."

"Who created this? Where did you get it?" he asked.

"It belonged to Josef Von Herrig," she replied. "You might see the carving on the side?"

Danny rolled it over in his hands. The engraved carving was rough to his fingertips. He angled it under the library lights, and read the name.

"'Ozella'. Beautiful name," he said.

"Yeah. I guessing it was the name of his fiancée. He named his stake after her."

"I'm holding the real Van Helsing's actual vampire-killing stake?"

Mercy nodded in silence.

"It's so intricate and well made," Danny said as he studied it further.

"I took it after I killed him. I didn't keep Ozella as a trophy.

I kept it because it was an expertly crafted weapon looking for a new owner. I think Josef would want you to have it. I didn't give it to you sooner because, well, I didn't know how you'd be when you were out there hunting."

"You mean you didn't know if I'd screw it up and get myself killed on the first outing, and you'd lose it," Danny replied with a cheeky grin.

"Pretty much," she replied with a smile of her own. "But you've killed four vampires already, including two at a time. You're already, I believe, the second-most successful vampire hunter in history, behind Josef, and if we *do* go down fighting, you might just break his record. I think you should be holding his stake when you do it."

"You'll take care of me, Ozella, won't you?" he asked as she studied the stake. "And I promise, I'll take good care of you. Thank you, Mercy. Seriously, no joking. I understand its importance. Thank you for giving me this."

"You're welcome, Cripple. Use it well," she said.

CHAPTER 23

The walls of Mercy's expansive home were becoming increasingly constrictive. There was one room she was always comfortable in: the study. She sat in her study, scrolling through the local news on her tablet.

The woman in the large rectangular painting which hung over the disused and blocked off fireplace smiled down on Mercy.

"If, by some terrible admin mistake I end up in Heaven, I hope you're keeping a seat for me, girl," she said, then let out a deep sigh.

Mercy had spent many months with Tiziano getting Aurelia's portrait just perfect. It wasn't just the exhaustive descriptions of her appearance, but also attempting to capture her personality, her very essence that took so much effort. It is difficult enough for artists to get a portrait just right when the subject is posing in front of them. When the subject has been dead for years and they are going purely on another person's memories, it becomes significantly more agonising.

Living in Florence at the time, Mercy would regularly journey to Rome and Venice. Over the next few months, whenever she was in Venice, he presented her with numerous updated and modified drawings of Aurelia's face – her eyes, her smile, the colour tones of her hair. They had to be perfect. With the patience of a saint, Tiziano finally had a complete drawing of Aurelia and Mercy gave her consent to begin the painting. Tiziano was known for being a fast worker with a tremendous output, and the work entitled *Aurelia* took months rather than years, however time is meaningless to a vampire.

Set in a forest background, Aurelia's green eyes looked down at Mercy with fire and compassion. Aurelia had a very slight figure, thanks to fifteenth century malnutrition and constant physical work. Her slightly coy, faintly crooked smile was captured perfectly. Her ruddy cheekbones were framed by her long light blond hair decorated with braiding and flowers. She wore a vibrant red silk dress, the kind she could only have dreamed of when alive. From the crown of her head to her feet, the painting was perfection. The world would never know of this masterpiece, but it was never meant to be shown off in a museum, it was for Mercy alone.

"I miss you so much, honey. Sometimes more than I can bear. Please wait for me."

"Right, Bride of Twatula," Danny announced himself as he walked into the study.

"Nope," Mercy said as she tore her eyes from the portrait, then cleared her throat loudly. "Shite banter. Try again."

"I haven't been in this room before. Wow!" he said and stopped in his tracks as he gazed up at Aurelia. "That painting is absolutely stunning! It's amazing!"

"I know," Mercy said as she wiped the tears from her eyes and cheeks, before turning back to face Danny.

"Is that her? Your Aurelia?"

"Aye, the resemblance is perfect. Spent a pretty penny on it. Well, a pretty Venetian ducat."

"She's beautiful, Mercy."

"Aye, she was."

"Who was the artist? It looks old," he said.

"A man called Tiziano."

"Hmm, never heard of him. Doesn't matter because he was obviously really talented."

"Yeah, he was," she replied, a subtle smile spreading across her face.

"I'm guessing this is the most sacred thing you own?" he

asked

The door buzzer went.

"I'll get it," Danny said, and left.

"Hold on," Mercy said, and followed him.

"Don't trust me to answer the door?" he asked.

"Very good, smartarse. I'm going upstairs to speak with Franky actually. I asked him to find out from his contacts how everyone got on last night. Whether anyone was taken. I ordered some things so that will be the courier."

They both walked to the open reception area. Mercy began to climb the stairs and Danny opened the door.

Standing at the top step was a man holding a mid-sized brown box.

"Hey mate, cheers," Danny said and took the box from him.

The man swiped at Danny with a knife. Danny leaned back and dropped the box. He grabbed the man's knife hand and punched him repeatedly.

Mercy came back down the steps.

Danny headbutted the man twice, swiped his feet, and as the man stumbled, Danny pushed him. He sent the courier sprawling down the steps, landing awkwardly onto the pavement below.

Mercy stood beside Danny as the man lay on the ground moaning gently.

"Oh ye of little faith," Danny said, closing and locking the door.

"Bravo, I never had a doubt. Ironically if Gabriel really wanted to screw us over, he wouldn't have hypnotised the courier to kill us, he would have stolen the box," Mercy said, handing the box over to Danny.

"How so?" he asked.

"Because I ordered a whole bunch of galena, both solid and powdered. Also, I ordered lots of tiger's eye. I'll be sharpening and sanding them down."

"Now that *is* ironic. Anyway, I'm going to open this like a wean at Christmas. I'll still be taking Ozella, but it's nice to be able to have backups," he said, looking at the box in his hands.

"Exactly."

Mercy smiled and shook her head as Danny limped down the hallway without his cane.

The doorbell rang again.

"I'll get it this time," she shouted down the hallway.

She approached the front door.

Who have they sent this time? Some poor bastard who was walking by? Well bring it.

Mercy ran to the kitchen, grabbed a kitchen knife, and ran back to the front door. She opened the door. Gabriel smiled at her.

"Hello, Mercy," Gabriel said. His breathing was laboured.

"Those stairs really take it out of you in the daytime. If you want to kill me, you'll need to send someone better than a scrawny courier."

Gabriel laughed, scratched his scalp, and wiped the sweat from his brow.

"It was a moment of opportunity. How are you?"

"All the worse for seeing you, cunt," she said. She smiled at the large black 4x4 parked on the curb. "Real subtle. Now why are you here?" she asked.

"That old Mercy charm. We drive in the daylight if we must. I am here with a peace offering. This is not you. These humans, they have made you soft. Weak. Stupid, with stupid transparent plans that were easy to foil. Then I realised that you were *deliberately* making such mistakes because you *want* to fail. You do not want to kill your brethren."

"Is that right, shit-stain?" she asked with a smile.

"Yes. Because I know the real you. You are the vampire that *everyone* fears. You are a legend. I want you to come back home to us. I have spoken to Samuel and he has agreed that as you have not murdered a vampire directly by your own hand, you will not be severely punished. However, as part of your redemption, we want the murderer. You will hand over your human and all will be forgiven."

Mercy sighed and drummed her fingers on the door.

"We are your family, Mercy, and the prodigal daughter should come home."

"That's a very kind gesture, but I'm going to have to turn down your offer," Mercy said, her smile becoming a smirk.

Danny appeared at the door and stood next to Mercy.

"Hey, fuckface," Danny addressed him.

Gabriel's smile disappearance.

"Why are you here?" Danny asked.

"I am here to resolve this situation peacefully, and to test your friendship with your mentor. My offer is thus: hand yourself over to us. If you do, we will leave Mercy alone and the other nests will leave Edinburgh immediately. You will save many of your little humans, and more importantly, you will save your mentor's life."

"That sounds like a tempting offer. And I *would* hand myself in to save Mercy. But you and I, well, we have something to settle, don't we? So, I'm going to give a counteroffer, and test your loyalty to your own kind."

Gabriel smiled.

"I'm intrigued. So out with it, human."

"You stole Aurelia away and turned her into a vampire. You turned her into something she wasn't. Before you took her, she was sweet and gentle and kind."

Mercy faced Danny. He was angry. His eyes burned at Gabriel and his voice spat venom.

"So, here's my offer. Let me kill you and I'll turn myself in. If you want justice to be done, and for me to be tortured before dying in agonising pain at the hands of your kind, then give yourself to me. After I've turned you into a little pile of dust I'll turn myself over to the vampires you brought here. If you don't, I'll kill as many of you fuckers as I can, and that will be *a lot*. You and your entire nest will be dust anyway, and you will be remembered as the hapless, idiot vampire who invited disaster upon your kind. I think it's a generous offer."

Gabriel's expression morphed in to one of outrage.

Mercy smiled.

"You know, when I saw how determined you were to get Aurelia back, I was tempted to tame her initial wild streak and give her back to you. Provided she wanted it, that is. I was willing to have a human as extended family, something which would normally be an insult. I might have even attempted to sire you, to bring you into *my* family. It's much more successful when you're experienced at it, isn't it Mercy?"

Mercy remained motionless.

"I would have even forgiven you for murdering Cassius," he continued. "I realise now that I shouldn't have wept for my beloved Ewan and Evie. I shouldn't have let you get away. I should have slaughtered everyone on that bus before killing you, so your last experience before death would be witnessing the consequences of your actions."

"Well, we've all made mistakes during this. Would you reconsider my offer if I gave you back some of your family's possessions?" Danny asked.

Gabriel frowned.

"Recognise this?" Danny asked, holding up a gold ring in his right hand.

Mercy leaned forward to see that the face of the ring displayed a lion.

"I'm guessing it's your family crest. Given all four vampires had identical rings." Danny opened the palm of the same hand to show the other three rings.

Gabriel's expression was one of naked hatred.

Danny threw the first ring at Gabriel. It bounced off his forehead and landed on the floorboards. Gabriel closed his eyes at the indignity.

"Every last one of them looked scared. Terrified, when they turned to ash," Danny said and threw the second ring which bounced off Gabriel's chest. "But if you want to know who is responsible for their deaths, you only have to look in a mirror," he continued, flicking the third ring off Gabriel, who stood motionless. "Chosen or not, when you claimed Aurelia, you doomed yourself and your whole fucking *nest*, you vulture. You don't know what love is." Danny flicked the final ring at Gabriel, who deflected it back at Danny with such force when it landed on his chest, Danny stumbled backwards by a step.

Danny steadied himself, smiled as he bent down and picked up his cane, his right hand leaning on it for extra support.

"Looks like we're at an impasse. So, get in your car and fuck off," Mercy said.

Gabriel dipped his hand into his waistcoat and produced a crumpled and folded envelope.

"Not yet. I feared that this would be your response; a pathetic display of unearned arrogance. So let me ask you, human, do *you* recognise *this*?" Gabriel asked.

He threw the envelope at the feet of Danny.

Danny picked it up, opened the envelope, and immediately dropped it with a gasp.

"Oh my God!" he whispered, an expression of horror on his face.

Mercy picked it up and peered inside. A severed finger lay inside the blood-stained envelope. Given the size, shape, and appearance, it was a female finger. On the finger, however, was a silver ring.

Mercy removed the ring. It bore an imprinted pattern of a daisy chain around the outside, studded with jade-coloured stones. Danny's expression told Mercy that it was Aurelia's ring.

"See, we *will* have our pound of flesh, one way or another. Cassius, Douglas, Ewan, Evie. They were my family. Something you have no concept of, Mercy. I loved them more than I love anything, something you are incapable of, and you both took them from me. But I have shed enough tears for them. Tears enough for a century. Now I am committed, so believe me when I say that my revenge will be horrifying, human. You see, Aurelia is little more than a feral animal right now. Barely a vampire. If you do not surrender, I'll bury her, with or without Samuel's permission."

Mercy dug her claws into the door.

"I presume Mercy has told you about our very worst punishment? Four of my family are dead. Someone *will* pay for those crimes. If not you, then Aurelia. I doubt you would want that. Aurelia lying in the dark, screaming a silent scream, burning in agony forever."

Mercy turned to Danny.

"If you touch her, I swear to God!" Danny whispered. He raised the end of his cane and prodded Gabriel in the chest.

"Thank you," Gabriel said with a smile.

"No!" Mercy shouted, but too late.

Gabriel yanked on the cane, pulling Danny towards him. Danny produced a stake with his left hand and aimed it at Gabriel's chest. Gabriel instinctively caught it.

In one smooth motion, Danny's cane split in two, revealing Danny holding a hidden blade inside. With both of Gabriel's hands occupied, Danny slammed the blade into Gabriel's heart.

Gabriel fell backwards, down the stairs and onto the pavement.

Mercy and Danny rushed down the stairs as Malcolm emerged from the vehicle, shoved Gabriel inside, and took off at high speed, tires screeching as it rounded the corner and engine revving as it accelerated away.

"Bastards!" Danny shouted after them.

"Where the fuck did that blade come from? I didn't know that you had a hidden blade in your cane!" she said.

"When you gave me that money to buy clothes and supplies, I reordered this cane. I found a seller with a faster delivery than last time. I originally had plans on removing the blade and putting in a stake instead. I just hadn't got round to it yet," he explained with his hands on his hips as he growled, frustrated. "If only I had actually got my finger out my arse and done it earlier that cunt would be dead now!"

"Well, you've hurt him. That's twice you've done it, and those rings were absolutely brutal! I'm proud of you, Cripple. That's twice he's met you, and as smart and as powerful as he is, he's not been able to get to you, or hurt you. That'll be tearing the bastard up inside. You're living rent free in his head."

"Excuse me, are you Mercy?" a voice interrupted them.

Mercy rolled her eyes as she turned around to see a man in his late sixties with a gentle face and a kind smile.

"Aye," she said.

He immediately lunged for her. She grabbed his arms and kicked him in the crotch. As his legs began to buckle and his face grew red, she kicked him in the crotch a second time, then a third. When he was on his knees, she bent down to his level.

"Look at me. You will forget any instructions you have received today. You will go home, sleep well tonight, and wake up tomorrow in a good mood. Oh, and don't forget to ice your balls often this evening," she said, before joining Danny.

"Mercy, I won't sit here while Aurelia is being tortured. If they bury her, I'll never find her, and I'll never forgive myself."

"He might be bluffing, using your love for Aurelia against you," she replied.

"Maybe, but I can't take that chance. They cut off her finger, Mercy! They actually chopped a piece of her off to send a message! Christ, the pain she must have gone through when they did that to her. We need to do something, Mercy!"

"I know. We will, we just need to be smarter for a change," Mercy said as they returned to the house. "Gimme your cane, I want to take a look at the mechanism and see how the blade fits in. I'm going to spend the rest of today preparing our weapons in case we need them. Then I'm going to go out tonight, scouting," she said.

"What are you hoping to find out?" he asked, handing over his cane.

"Something we can use to our advantage because, Christ knows, we need one."

The day turned into night and the sun drifted below the horizon.

Danny Sat bolt upright in his bed, panting and sweating.

"Fuck! I shouldn't have accepted Mercy's sleeping pills. I

should have stayed awake."

He rubbed his face

"I can't do this! I can't wait anymore!"

He touched Aurelia's ring on his right pinky finger as it pressed into his own onyx and titanium spinner ring. He began to cry. The nightmare of banging on the coffin Aurelia was trapped in. Aurelia screaming for help, with Danny scratching and clawing at the impenetrable box. For the first time in days he had slept, through sheer exhaustion, just for the horrifying dreams to torment him.

Tears rolled down his cheeks and he whimpered into his forearm as he sat up.

There was a knock at his bedroom door.

Danny quickly wiped his eyes and his face, cleared his throat.

"Um, come in," he said.

"The door opened to reveal a concerned Franky.

"You awright, mate?" he asked.

"Um, aye I'm OK. Was just managing to get some sleep."

"Aye, I just heard some noise from the room and wanted to check you were awright."

"Aye, aye. I'm fine thanks," Danny said and smiled.

"Oh here," Franky said, and stepped in the room holding Danny's cane. "Mercy told me to give this to you when you woke up. She fucked about with it and told me to tell you it's ready. Fuck knows what she's on about."

He passed the cane to Danny. Danny studied it. A screw had been drilled through it, from one side through to the other, and then sheared off at the bolt.

Danny flicked the secret release lever and the cane split in half. In place of the blade, however, was a tiger's eye stake, which was sharpened into a perfect point, and which fit snugly into the handle of the cane.

"She's screwed a hole through the stake and the cane. Clever," he said with a smile.

"That looks fucking amazing!" Franky said, looking closely

at it.

"It didn't take her long to fix it. Where is she?"

"It's late and the sun's down. She went scouting ages ago, but fuck knows what she's scouting, or where. I just wanted to know if you wanted me to order something in for us, 'cause it's getting late for dinner," Franky said.

"Aye, I could eat."

"I was thinking just a burger and chips. Is that awright?"

"Aye, lovely. Franky, how did last night go? Did everyone manage to get indoors safe?"

"Most folk, but there's a few that said they'd have trouble. I cannae get a hold of them. Nobody can. I'm fearing the worst."

"How many?"

"Eight," Franky answered.

"Fuck. I hope they're OK."

"Time will tell, but I hope Mercy's got a fucker of a plan because we cannae take any more of that."

"Were there any reports of others going missing from their homes?"

"Dunno, mate. Those others at the meeting would report to Mercy, so you better ask her."

"Aye. Did you tell Mercy about the missing eight?" Danny asked.

"Aye, I did. She said she's working on it. I hope she figures something out though."

"Can I ask you a separate question? It's been bothering my conscience since I found out about them. How can you be OK with what Mercy is doing to the three poor bastards downstairs?" Danny asked.

"It's Mercy's choice with what she eats," he replied.

"I know, but it's inhumane. Plus, is it really her place to judge them?"

Franky looked down at his feet.

"Tell me, Danny. Have you ever been raped?"

"Umm… no," Danny replied with a startled expression.

"Have you ever been abused by somebody you were

supposed to be able to trust?"

"No."

"Then you dinnae know what it's like to be brutalised, then no be believed by your family," Franky continued as he gave a thousand-yard stare at the carpet. "To be made out to be the bad one for lying about a relative. To end up homeless by fifteen and spend the rest of your life on the streets. Because of that bastard. As far as I'm concerned, what Mercy does to them is still too good for them."

"Fair enough," he replied. "Where are you initially from, Franky?"

"Leith," Franky replied. "But old Leith. Before it was tarted up enough for hipsters and middle-class types to live there."

"So, you have been homeless since you were fifteen? How long have you been homeless for?"

"Ten years," Franky replied.

Jesus Christ, he's only twenty-five! I thought he was at least forty!

"Did you ever try to get off the streets?"

"At first, aye, but I had no family support. Soon the folks out there became my family. Now I take care of them as much as I can."

"How did you meet Mercy?" Danny asked.

"I tried to steal her wallet. I was starving. I had coppers in my pocket and hadnae eaten anything for a few days. She was sitting on her own eating a burger. The corner of her wallet was sticking out of her pocket and I tried to lift it. She caught me, but instead of running away or calling the police, she asked me why I did it. I told her."

"So she didn't try to hurt you or hypnotise you?" Danny asked.

"Nah mate. She just asked why. Then she did the weirdest thing. She let me have it. She was just like, 'go on, there you go'. It was weird."

"Yeah, I'm too used to the angry, sulky, arse-skelping Mercy!" Danny said with a laugh.

"I gave it back to her, then she offered me a choice. She was staring at some random guy talking to his mate across the street. She said I could keep the money in the wallet if I found out everything I could about him in the next ten minutes," Franky explained.

"OK, that does sound like Mercy."

"So, I studied this random punter. He walks down the street. Then he meets up with his woman and they get on a bus together. I reported this to her. She asks me if there was anything which stood out as strange. I said apart from the whole fucking night, the guy had bruises on his knuckles. I thought he was just a bit of a scrapper. You know, an arsehole drunk. But then I saw a faded bruise on the girl's cheek. There's only so much that make-up can hide."

Danny nodded in silence.

"Mercy then beams this wide smile. She says, 'Here, take everything in the wallet', which turns out to be a couple of hundred quid! Then she says, 'I might have regular work just like that, and every time you do the job, there'll be more money in it for you.' So I agreed, and that was nearly eight years ago."

"Wow. Just to think. If you hadn't tried to lift her wallet..." Danny began.

"Fuck knows where I'd be, or what condition I'd be in. She insisted that I stay clear of the drugs and the drink, and when I told her that I didn't touch either of the stuff anyway, she was happy."

"So you've always been teetotal?" Danny asked.

"Aye. But a lot of folks just see a homeless guy and think 'junkie'. They don't care about whether we are or not."

"That was me until not long ago. Seeing homeless people begging on the streets used to make me feel so uncomfortable. I'd do anything to avoid them, and avoid thinking about them."

"You're no the only one, Danny. Most people are like that."

"Aye, but now I count one as my friend. In addition to that, there are so many who have been putting themselves in harm's way just to find out what I need to know about Gabriel's nest, so that I can get Aurelia back. If I manage to save her, it'll be thanks to the very people I used to always look away from; the folks I looked down my nose at all my life. I just feel..." Danny's voice faded away to silence.

"Embarrassed? Ashamed?" Franky asked.

"Aye. Something like that," Danny replied.

"Relax, mate. You're not the first arsehole to look at one of us and see whatever makes him feel better about ignoring us. The important thing is that you know the truth. We're just people. We're no scum, we're just struggling."

"Aye. I'll never forget it, and I'll never look at homeless people that way again," Danny replied and smiled. "Plus, I'll owe you all a massive debt when this is over."

"Just save as many people as you can from these vampire bastards. Help Mercy get these vampire cunts and you can consider the debt repaid."

"Aye," Danny said as he looked at his cane, then focused on Aurelia's ring. "Right, I'm going out," he said.

"Eh? Where are you going?" Franky asked.

"I can't sit on my arse any more. Standing around like a spare prick while Aurelia could be tortured as we speak. Sitting here whilst, over another night, more of the city's homeless and poor are being stolen away and murdered elsewhere. I can't sit here anymore," he said and reached for his galena gloves.

"Where are you going?" he asked.

"I'm going to Moray Place," Danny said, as he hurriedly pulled his hoodie on then grabbed Josef's ornate stake which had been sitting on his bedside table.

"Come on, Ozella," Danny said as he tucked it into his waistband.

"Who's Ozella? I dunno if that's the brightest thing to do. Mercy told me that you cannae be hypnotised which is amazing, but going there is just daft."

Danny wasn't listening. He slid the gloves on, clipped his cane together and walked towards the front door.

He placed his hand on the handle of the front door, but

hesitated.

No, wait. Be smarter. It's a trap. Of course it is, that's exactly what those bastards do. If I step foot outside, I'm dead. Right, think, Danny!

He let go of the handle and stepped back into the large stairwell.

"Franky, do me a favour would you?"

"Aye?" Franky said.

"Open the front door wide, then hide behind it. Don't announce your presence until I say," Danny instructed.

"Ohhh, I don't like the sound of that!" Franky said as he approached the front door.

Danny faced the door and placed both hands on his cane. He nodded to Franky.

Franky opened the door and stood to the side, with his back to the wall.

A vampire rushed against the door but slammed into an invisible wall. He hissed at Danny, his eyes black and his canines long. His face was new to Danny.

Danny stood in silence. Behind the vampire on the doorstep were a number of vampires down the stairs. Among the different, strange faces, one face looked very familiar.

"Is that who I think it is? Step forward, fucker," Danny said.

The man slowly climbed the steps, smiling with every step.

"Hello, Malcolm," Danny said.

"Hello human," Malcolm said. "If I'd known that you would have caused so much trouble, I'd have bitten you that night when you interrupted my dinner, regardless of what Mercy said."

"Aye, we all have our regrets about our actions, don't we?" Danny said as he readjusted his grip on the cane. "You know there's something of yours I want."

"Oh yes?" Malcolm asked, his smile widening.

"Your family ring. See, I have quite a collection. Four so far. I'd like to add yours."

Malcolm's smile faded.

"Then come and take it," Malcolm replied.

"Don't mind if I do. Malcolm, and *ONLY MALCOLM*," he shouted to the other vampires. "Please, come in."

The whooshing of wind reached Danny as fast as Malcolm's hands did. Powerful and muscular hands wrapped around Danny's neck, taking him off his feet.

Danny placed the palm of his hand in Malcolm's hand. The hissing of the skin melting was loud in Danny's ear. Malcolm began to scream when Danny punched him several times in the face, leaving four knuckle burns with each strike. Danny's feet touched the dark wooden floorboards, and he steadied himself.

Malcolm pushed Danny away with all his might, but Danny held on to Malcolm's hand for dear life. Danny bounced back at him. He slipped around behind Malcolm and placed the palm of his hand on Malcolm's throat.

With a silent, agonised scream, Malcolm sank to his knees as both he and Danny faced the shocked vampires standing on the doorstep.

Not the cane. Leave that as a surprise when needed.

Danny retrieved Ozella from his waistband and looked up at the vampires at the doorstep, each one wide-eyed in shock.

"Tell Gabriel and the others what you saw here."

With every ounce of strength he had, Danny drove the stake through Malcolm's back on the left side, breaking ribs and piercing his heart.

Malcolm's face contorted into an expression of agony as his form became a chalk-white statue which soon crumbled into powder, leaving a pile of dust with Malcolm's clothes.

Danny's eyes rose from Malcolm's remains to meet those of the four vampires who were huddled on the doorstep, peering in. Their expressions ranged from shock to fear. Franky's head poked around the door. He looked as shocked and scared as the vampires.

Danny flicked his fingers through the piles of dust until he found his prize. He picked up Malcolm's ring. He blew on it and studied it under the ceiling light.

"Another to add to the collection," he said with purposeful

volume. "That's five I have now. What jewellery do you all wear?" he asked the vampires.

They remained silent.

Danny nodded to Franky.

The door slammed in their faces.

"Fucking hell, mate!" Franky said as he slowly approached the piles of dust that had been Malcolm. "Is that what happens to a vampire when it's killed? I dinnae even know where the Hoover is."

"What the fuck is going on?" Mercy's voice called out from the darkness of the adjoining room.

Danny and Franky turn to look at her.

"Danny fucked one! He fucking killed it dead!" Franky yelled with childlike excitement.

"Where did you come from?" Danny asked.

"I was out scouting. I came in through the back entrance."

"Mercy, it was amazing!" Franky continued.

"I'm sure it was," Mercy replied as she came into the light and looked down at the dust. "My question is, how the fuck did a vampire get in here in the first fucking place?"

The anger on Mercy's face was unmistakable.

"It's Malcolm," Danny replied. "I invited him in. I live here now, at least temporarily. I figured I could take him and do it in front of any vampires watching."

"And were there any watching?" she asked.

"Another four. They will take that back to their various nests," Danny replied smiling.

"And I'm sure your bollocks feel nice and big now. Here's the thing: you invited a vampire into MY HOME!"

"Well, like I said…" Danny began.

"This is my home, Cripple! It was not your place to do that, never mind how fucking dangerous it was to do it in the first fucking place!"

"Well, I was sick of sitting around the house. I wanted to do something, so I figured that they would have some vampires waiting to pounce on us. I thought I'd use it to my advantage."

"You thought! Oh, that makes it OK then! I thought we were through making stupid mistakes and taking silly chances."

"Mercy…" Danny began before words refused to enter his mind. "I'm sorry. I can't get her out of my mind. I… the thought of her somewhere, being cut to pieces. I just…"

"Gabriel is fucking with you!" Mercy shouted. "You've got to remember, Aurelia is a vampire now. By now she will have grown a new finger! She'll be fine! I'm sure it hurt like fuck, taking the finger, but it was a dramatic prop used to fuck with you. And it's working. Just have a little faith and patience!"

"OK. I'm sorry Mercy," Danny said.

Mercy sighed, anger still in her eyes.

"Don't you *ever* fucking do it again," she replied, her tone and expression softening. She looked down at the piles of ash. "So that's Malcolm, eh? Good job anyhow. I never thought that Malcolm would end up on my floor."

"How did you get on?" Danny asked.

"Good. Very good. We're set for tomorrow."

"What do you mean?" Danny asked.

"Tomorrow we're going to take the fight to them. We attack them and kill as many of the fuckers as we can. You never know, we might just get lucky and win. One way or another, it all ends tomorrow. Right, now where the fuck did I leave my Hoover?" she asked as she walked away, leaving Danny and Franky to stare with gormless expressions.

CHAPTER 24

Danny rolled the mug of coffee in his hands, staring up at the magnificence of the portrait of Aurelia, whilst Franky slouched in the chair next to him picking at his fingernails. They hadn't spoken a word as they waited for Mercy. She had just woken and asked them to meet in the study. Danny hadn't slept overnight thanks to Mercy's bombshell that today things end one way or another. She refused to provide any further details.

Danny had spent the morning pacing the various rooms of the house while Mercy slept. Franky had been unusually quiet, his nervousness on display. Finally, at lunchtime a drowsy and flu-like Mercy stumbled downstairs and told them to meet her in thirty minutes. Danny had spent twenty-five of those minutes in the toilet through nerves alone. He just had time to make all of them a coffee and come in to the study.

"Are coffee fumes really that good for the portrait?" Danny asked.

"Dunno, mate. It's her painting I suppose. Do you know who she is anyway?" Franky asked.

"Aye, I do."

"Sorry folks, had a heavier night than usual," Mercy announced as she entered the room from behind them.

She flopped into her chair behind her desk. Her hair was wet and shaggy, having been towel-dried. She wore a white vest top and pastel blue shirt tied at the midriff. She still wore her usual vibrant red lipstick.

Danny smiled.

Priorities.

"Oooh, thanks for the coffee," she said and grabbed it with both hands. She curled her legs up onto the leather chair and sipped at her mug.

Danny and Franky exchanged expectant glances before returning their attention to Mercy.

"Is it really wise to drink coffee near the painting?" Danny asked. "And surely it will need to be cleaned. What do you do?"

"I have some of the world's best art restorers who, for an undisclosed fee, will work with absolute discretion. Now, that's not why we're here," she said.

"Yeah, the plan," Danny prompted her.

"Aye," Mercy said. "So, I know you haven't seen much of me this last day. Here's what I've been up to. Knowing that vampires always congregate in groups, I figured that they would be under the one roof. I knew that Gabriel's house in Moray Place wouldn't be large enough to house dozens of vampires. There is only a handful of places truly large enough. So I scouted out each of them. I found out where they rented out the other day," Mercy explained.

"Wait, they actually rent a house?" Danny asked, his eyebrows raised.

"Aye, what did you expect them to do?"

"I dunno. Go into a home, hypnotise the owners, or kill them and take over the building themselves. They're super powerful vampires after all," he said.

"No, they're both richer and smarter than that. There's a reason why they only invade the homes of the poor and isolated. The consequences of doing that to a rich and/or powerful family would be far too much of a headache to deal with, when they can just legitimately lease out a building for a couple of weeks over the internet and not actually meet anyone."

"Makes sense," Danny said.

"The good news is I've found out which home it is. I spent last night watching the building. More good news is there is only one elder that I know of. He unofficially rules over Scotland's vampires. He is called Samuel. Very powerful. Very old. That's the bad news. Like all other elders, he doesn't leave and has his own personal nest guarding him. I got to see who comes and who goes."

"I remember Gabriel mentioning a 'Samuel'. Do you know Samuel personally?" Danny asked.

"Aye. He was Claude's best friend. They were both elders and they were very close. Like brothers. Claude's disappearance hit him very hard."

"So he also knows you well?" Danny asked.

"Aye. But not for a long time now. But if Samuel is here then that's definitely bad news. We'll need to double team him to even stand a chance. Anyway, about Gabriel," she said.

"Does Gabriel leave?" Danny asked.

"No. As host, and as the vampire who sent up the distress signal, Gabriel follows good form by staying in the building at all times and being servant to Samuel. However, I've spotted an opportunity. I think it's our only one. We attack them at night. At about 11pm there is a small exodus from the building when many of the vampires go hunting. That means that so long as we work quickly and silently, there will not be as many of them left in the building."

"Wait, wait. At night? When they are all full strength? That sounds like a shite plan to me," Danny said.

"I know, nothing is perfect. But believe me, going in the middle of the night is definitely our best option," she replied.

"What about going in either early in the morning when they are asleep, or in the afternoon when they are weakened?" he suggested.

"It sounds good in theory, and I've thought about it, but it's actually worse in practice. Yes, the younger vampires will be weakened, but all of the older vampires will have plenty of power to deal with you, and I will be too weak to help you. Sure, attacking when they are strong sounds bad, but if we sneak in when the house is mostly empty apart from some guards and others milling about, and when I am strong enough to fight, that will be our best chance."

"Fuck," Danny said with a sigh.

"Aye, I know. It's a shite sandwich any way you slice it, but as thin as our chances of surviving this are, it's definitely our best chance," she explained.

"It's just fucked up when our best chance is to attack them when they are at their strongest," he said.

"Aye. But their guard will be down. We need to work fast and quietly. Taking them out one by one in silence is our best chance. When the alarm eventually sounds, then we're fucked, and we take out as many as we can before we go down. But at least we'll go down fighting," she said. Her furrowed eyebrows betrayed her smile.

"Right, Mercy. I've noticed you havenae taught me how to scrap with a vampire. I need a crash course," Franky interrupted.

"No crash course needed," she replied.

"What? How no?"

"Because you're not going there tonight."

"Mercy, don't bench me now. I can fight and I want to fight!" Franky replied, offended.

"I know you can. But you can't reject their hypnosis. Besides, I need you for something much more important."

"Oh aye?" he asked.

"If neither myself nor Danny come back home tonight, I need you to sort out all of my affairs."

"Fuck off, that's what a lawyer is for!"

"I need you to still look after your people," she said.

"That's still no excuse. They're no helpless wee kittens," Franky argued back.

Danny remained silent

"Fine, there's something else. I don't want you to give your life for this. I know that you won't forgive me but I'm not going to risk your neck. The Cripple and I volunteered for this and we are both trained. I'm not going to treat you like cannon fodder because that's what you'll be."

Franky sat in silence with the body language of a scolded child.

"It should be my choice, Mercy," he said.

"Not this time Franky."

Franky nodded, took a deep breath, and looked back up at her. He got out of his seat and walked towards the open door behind them.

"Franky," Mercy called out to him. Franky stopped at the doorway. "I'm only ever going to say this once, so make sure you hear it," she began. She looked awkward, uncomfortable to such an extent she found maintaining eye contact difficult.

"I'm listening," Franky replied.

"You, along with Cripple here, you're... you're my best friend. *Someone* is going to survive this."

Franky smiled.

"Awww, you have friends!" Danny said with a smile and a condescending voice.

"Fuck off, Cripple," she replied, appearing angrier than ever.

"Whatever ye need before yous set off, just tell me and it'll be done," Franky replied.

"I will," she said with a nod.

Franky smiled once more and disappeared out of the room.

Mercy and Danny maintained one of their many awkward silences, until Danny, once again, was compelled to break it.

"We're friends! Besties even!" he said, his smile reappearing.

Mercy slapped her palm down on her desk.

"I swear to Christ, Cripple. If you say that again, just one more time, I'll make sure your other leg doesn't work either."

Danny sat in silence, his grin still wide.

"Right, let's get to work. These are for you," Mercy said as she produced a brown cardboard delivery box and handed it to Danny.

He opened the box. He then looked up at her.

"Are you serious?" he asked.

"You'll be flying in the cold air with me for an extended amount of time. I'll need to fly slowly with you. Last time I went full speed, you blacked out because of the blood rushing away from your brain, so we'll need to be up there longer than normal. You need something to protect your eyes and airways. When we land I need you to still be able to see and breathe," she said.

Mercy left her seat and headed out of the door. A sullen Danny followed, still peering into the box.

CHAPTER 25

Danny readjusted his swimming goggles and the triple-wrapped scarf covering his mouth as he and Mercy soared high in the cold night air. The haar, Edinburgh's famous thick fog which creeps over the city from the North Sea eastwards, had swallowed the ancient buildings and streets below them. Lines of ethereal orange lights, the glow from the street lights, illuminated the fog which shrouded Edinburgh.

"Do you know where you are going?" Danny shouted above the wind.

"Of course," she shouted back. "You guide yourself by the church steeples and other tall landmarks that rise out of the haar. Plus, I've got my satnav on," she added.

Soon, the lighting from street lights, up-lit buildings, and occupied premises thinned out and they were over the dark of the countryside. The smooth white blanket of fog which covered the flat fields outside Edinburgh took on a silken quality. Peaceful, yet smothering. After a few more minutes silent flying, the haar eased and the fog eventually cleared.

"Right, we're nearly here. I'm going to find a place to land. When I tell you to, I want you to be absolutely silent. If we hide, they won't see us when they leave, but they'll sure as shit hear us. So, absolute silence from you when I say so, and no speaking until I tell you it's OK," she said.

She lowered her angle of flight as, in the distance behind a bank of trees, a building began to appear. As they approached, a single well-lit building in a sea of darkness grew in size. The closer they got it became evident that it was grand and imposing. They flew over a perfectly maintained golf course and touched down amongst a grove of trees.

"You know, a motorbike helmet would have done the same job as the scarf and goggles," Danny said. "The exact same job."

"I know, but I found this much funnier," she replied, stifling a laugh.

"You're a fucking prick, Mercy!"

"I know, now keep your voice down. We're here," she said and motioned over his shoulder.

Danny turned and walked to the clearing, unfurling his scarf, and gingerly removing his goggles.

"Bloody hell, Mercy!" Danny said as he surveyed the complex before them. "It's a castle! An actual complete, huge castle! It's massive!"

"I said keep it down!" she whispered in return.

"Yeah, but it's a castle! It's beautiful! How old is it?" he asked, lowering his volume.

"It was built in the late 1700's, Neoclassical style. It's a thing of beauty," she replied, a wide smile. "There was a palace before it, but it was destroyed in battle. After lying in ruins for a number of years, this castle was built using the same stones from the palace."

Before them was a large, flat freshly cut lawn with a tarmac road leading to the front gate of the castle.

A two-storey curved defensive stone wall ended in the block towers of two identical wings with turrets at each corner. In the rear stood the heart of the castle, a five-storey mansion which served as a castle keep. With defensive placements, turrets, and archer's windows, the main house looked every inch the ancient castle.

The defensive wall was up-lit and every window was illuminated.

"It must cost a fortune to keep this place lit, warm, and well-maintained," Danny said.

"Aye, but worth it none the less," she replied. "Right, we should have a wee bit of time left. Weapon check," she added.

Danny slid on his galena gloves, touched the top of Ozella in his waistband, and touched the tip of a second stake up his sleeve.

"How does the leg feel?" she asked.

"Surprisingly comfortable, although walking is weird and I doubt I could run," he replied

Under his trousers, strapped directly to the outside of his leg, was his cane. The handle jutted out of his waistband only an inch or so at the hip, allowing for the top of the cane, complete with hidden stake inside, to be released when he pressed the release button.

"I'm surprised it took this long to think this up," he whispered.

"Well, it's a clever wee idea and it should allow you to walk easier, using your cane as a knee brace, but also leaving both your hands free," she replied.

Danny pressed the palm of his hand against the bulge inside his trouser pocket; a thick bag of powdered galena. Mercy had at first been unhappy he was carrying it, however, when he reasoned there was a chance he was going to die anyway, he may as well use every option open to him.

"How are your weapons?" he asked.

Mercy had donned black leather gloves and was holding a large lump of solid galena in one hand and two thin tiger's eye stakes in the other, before tucking all the items into the inside pockets of her denim jacket.

"Ready to go. Right, let's stay in the treeline there. There will be plenty of cover overhead. Just remember: no talking, no whispering, no coughing, no sneezing, no burping, and no farting until I give the all clear."

Danny nodded, suddenly needing to clear his throat.

They stayed silent, in position for an age, before voices rose from the castle beyond – shouting, laughing, and giggling.

Danny and Mercy looked at one another. Mercy held her

finger to her lips, reminding him to be silent. Danny nodded and looked back at the castle.

Through the bright lights shining out of the castle windows, and the multitude of up-lighting lamps dotted throughout the grounds, a number of figures took to the air vertically and disappearing into the darkness of the night sky.

Danny crouched.

Dear God, please don't let them see me.

Beside him, Mercy stood tall, with her foot raised against an exposed tree root. Wisps of her hair floated in the gentle breeze as she stared ahead. Her stance mimicked age-old statues and paintings of Hellenic heroes standing victorious after battle, but Mercy and Danny's battle had not yet begun.

Over the next few minutes the amount of figures flying out dwindled.

After five more minutes, Mercy broke the silence.

"Right, I think that's them. Anyone who is going out hunting has gone, and anyone staying behind will still be in there," she whispered.

"I counted at least two dozen leaving, but my eyesight isn't so good," Danny said.

"There were fifty-one," Mercy corrected him. "Most will stay out for some time, however there will be a few coming back soon with a few victims for Gabriel and Samuel, as they are guaranteed to be there."

Danny nodded, his stomach cramping so hard he was permanently hunched.

Please God, let us survive this and if we don't, at least let Aurelia survive this.

"Right, Cripple. Hold on to me," Mercy instructed. They grabbed one another and Mercy lifted off once more.

They flew over the east wing of the castle. As they passed, Danny made out a large central square in front of the main castle house, complete with large marble fountain and surrounding topiary hedge. An internal loggia contained small marble statues on plinths running around the inside of the curved defensive wall.

Soon they had cleared the castle and landed on a large circular cement platform, with a large 'H' painted on it.

"An ancient castle with a helipad?" he asked.

"The house is from the 1700's, but below the facade and the layout, it is very much a modern building," Mercy replied as she sneaked towards the gravel courtyard of the east wing. "This was the old stables. We're going in through here and making our way to the central building through the basement corridors."

They reached a small external door nestled in the corner of the east wing. Next to the heavy-looking door was a modern keypad.

"Fuck!" he whispered. "Time to look for another entrance. Unless you can break it down quietly?"

"No need," she whispered back.

Mercy pressed a seven-digit code into the keypad and it sounded a discreet bleep. She pushed on the door and it opened. They crept inside.

"How do you know the security codes?" he asked.

"Because I own the castle," she replied.

"Wait, what?" he asked.

"This is my castle. I've admired it for a long time. Then out of the blue I got the chance to buy it some years ago. It's been mine ever since. I have all the keys, all the security codes."

"You own a fucking *castle*? I know the town house you live in is huge, but this place makes your house look like a dump! Why don't you live here?" he asked, straining to keep his volume low.

"Shh!" she insisted. "Because this place is too big, even for me. I'm its guardian. I keep it maintained and away from wealthy hands which may abuse it. It's an A-listed building, but that doesn't mean some fuckwit can't let it go to ruin. I didn't buy it to impress others. I bought it for me and to keep it in safe hands. I rent it out every now and again to people I feel comfortable having it for a while. When I found out that Gabriel had sent up the flare, I knew that they would scout for suitable locations. This place is the only one grand enough and palatial enough to hold them all. Now stop fannying around. I'll give you a tour if we survive. Let's go."

Danny followed Mercy through the bowels of the east wing. The corridors' walls were bare but when they reached the first room, the walls and the ceiling were plastered and painted a gentle off-white. Expensive and tasteful furniture decorated the bedroom. The belongings of the occupants were scattered over the room. From suits and shirts to cologne and blood-stained female clothing.

Danny picked up a white blouse with dried blood staining the neck and front, and they exchanged a glance.

"Gross," Mercy whispered, to which Danny nodded. Footsteps clumped their way down the corridor, growing louder with every step.

Danny sat on the edge of the bed and held the bloodied blouse. Mercy stood behind the door.

A man entered the room and stopped dead when face to face with Danny. Dressed impeccably in a black suit and shirt, he stood with mouth gaping open, displaying his vampire canines.

"Did she taste nice?" Danny asked him.

"Who the hell are..." he began.

Mercy stepped out and thrust at him from behind. The tip of a bloody stake appeared out the front of his chest before he turned to chalk, the blood on the stake doing likewise. He tumbled into dust, revealing Mercy, frozen mid-strike.

Her shock was evident as she stared down at the remains and the suit.

"Are you OK?" Danny asked as he got off the bed, dropping the blouse.

"Um, yeah. I'm fine."

"Are you sure?" he persisted. "You look a little... queasy."

"Um, yeah. That's the first time I've killed a vampire in a very long time and the first one without the express instruction of an elder. I always was a hunter and executioner. I was never an assassin. Plus, killing one. It just feels... wrong. It's like nature telling me that doing this... umm... I dunno."

"No going back now," Danny replied.

"Yeah. Let's just keep moving," she said with a brief shake of her head, then walked out of the room.

Let's hope all the vampires are this easily dealt with

They came to a stairwell. The staircase led both up and down.

"Right, down we go," she whispered. "This will take us to the main building."

"Wait, aren't we going to check that this whole wing is clear?" he asked.

"Of course not," she whispered back.

"Why not?"

"Because first, we don't have time for that. Secondly, we're not trying to confront every last vampire here. We're trying to get straight to Gabriel and Samuel. They're all that matters. Now come on."

Danny followed her down the stairs to the lower level. It was colder here and the air smelled stagnant. The lighting was sparser and more basic.

"Where are we?" he asked. "I'm lost."

"We're in the basement at the north end of the east wing. This is where they used to store dairy products, as it was much colder and acted effectively as an old ice house. Now it just holds some equipment. Right, there we are," she said, pointing at a stone wall at the end of the corridor.

"What? We're at a dead end."

Mercy approached the wall and began to caress every large, uneven stone. Her hand came to rest on one stone in particular. She dragged it to the left. Part of the stone slid along in front of the others and a small doorway opened.

"Are you kidding me?" he asked.

"This old building is littered with secret passageways. They were kept for a multitude of reasons. For the lords to escape if under attack, or to sneak illegitimate lovers in and out of the castle. I loved hunting for each one. I still think there are some I haven't found yet," she said with excitement in her voice.

"Can we focus please?" Danny said and closed his eyes.

"Aye, right. Follow me. This passage takes us under the main building and into the wine cellar."

Mercy pressed the torch icon on her phone and the corridor was lit. They followed the passage way for twenty yards before turning left and continuing for another thirty yards. They reached another stone dead end. Mercy caressed the wall until she found the corresponding stone and the wall cracked open. It swung inwards to reveal a fully lit wine cellar, containing numerous racks filled with wine bottles, a few barrels, and two vampires staring back at them.

"Fuck!" Danny blurted.

Mercy launched herself at the first, grabbing her, and throwing her at Danny. The second vampire took off at speed towards the open door of the wine cellar and the stone steps beyond.

Mercy caught up to him at the door and hurled him backwards.

Danny threw himself at the female who, having bounced into a rack, had slipped on her stilettos and landed on the cold stone floor. He landed on her. She hissed back at him and clawed at him, leaving four large red scratches down the side of his neck. Danny placed the palm of his glove onto her face. She began to scratch at the glove. With his free hand he reached for the stake tucked into his waist behind his back. She pushed him off with force. He was thrown upwards, cracked his head off the low ceiling, and crumpled onto the floor.

Mercy punched the man then tore the front of his black turtleneck sweater off him, exposing his hairy chest.

He swung wildly at her, but she swerved beyond his reach before punching him once more. He shoulder charged her, hitting her waist, pushing her backwards and onto her back.

He straddled her and began raining down blows.

"I was gonna run for help, but I'll be a hero for killing Mercy the Executioner!" he giggled. "Do you like thaaaa..."

Mercy shoved the lump of galena deep into his mouth. He stepped backwards, rasping and clawing at his face as a sizzling sound came from his mouth. Mercy rose to her feet and landed an almighty uppercut to the underside of the man's chin. His mouth crumbled in a melting mess, revealing his singed upper jaw and the galena still lodged in his throat, burning and melting its way down his windpipe.

She thrust the stake deep into his heart.

Deeper into the wine cellar, the woman who had attacked Danny was getting to her feet just as Danny struggled to his. With much of her face melted, she lunged at him. He swerved and punched her in the side of the head. His stake slid down his sleeve. He pulled her by hair and yanked her backwards as he bent down. She bent backwards, over his knee, exposing her sternum under her low-cut dress. He slammed the stake into her chest. She fell silent as she first turned to chalk, then crumbled into dust around him.

Danny got to his feet. His shoulders ached. His arms were weak. His neck burned raw where she had scratched him. The back of his head hurt from colliding with the roof.

"Can I just sit for a while?" he asked, puffing deeply.

"'Fraid not, Cripple," Mercy replied, fetching her galena nestled in the torn turtleneck sweater lying in the pile of dust on the ground. "Come on. I've got a new plan," she said, before heading up the stairs.

Danny sighed, rolled his eyes, and readjusted the cane strapped to his leg before following her up the stairs.

CHAPTER 26

Mercy found herself back on the ground level, this time in the main house. They headed towards the library and, after that, the first reception room. Beyond that lay the front door and grand staircase.

The majority of them will be in the grand hall, perhaps with Gabriel and Samuel. But I need to know for sure first. The hall will be empty of most furniture. Their servant put in a request for adequate dining and hosting services. Something my agent promised, but I instructed not to supply. I don't think I'm going to get a good review.

Danny hobbled behind her, tired and worse for wear.

"You alright, Cripple?"

"Aye, aye. Just slow down a wee bit," he replied.

Mercy slowed her pace as she led him towards the library.

We need to catch a vampire on their own. I should have bloody done it in the bedroom of the east wing, but nerves got the better of me and I staked him straight away. Mercy, you need to be smarter than this, you silly tart!

She crept up to the glass double doors of the library. Through the glass, a vampire sat on one of the reading desks with his back to the doors.

Thank fuck! That's perfect!

She looked back at Danny. She held up a single finger then pointed through the doors. He nodded and produced his stake.

Mercy opened the doors and as they swung open fully, a hinge squeaked.

She winced and mouthed a silent 'Fuck!'

"I thought you were going out to hunt tonight," he said without turning around. Danny closed the doors behind them. "I'm not going out tonight. I'm saving myself for the vampire hunter tomorrow. Most of all, I want the Executioner. That bitch is mine," he continued with a smile.

Mercy and Danny exchanged glances.

"After this is over I'm thinking of making an offer on this place. It's majestic!" he stated as he finally looked up from his book.

"I'm not accepting offers right now," Mercy replied.

The vampire spun around and Mercy caught him with a fist. He flew over the table and crashed against the far wall, books spilling down on him.

Mercy ran to him and dragged him up. She pressed her lump of galena hard onto his forehead. As she pressed it, she covered his mouth to muffle his screams.

"It'll soon melt through the skull and into your brain," she said. "I will spare you if you tell me what I need to know now!"

She removed the galena from his head and when his screams faded to whimpers, she removed her hand from his mouth.

"Where are Gabriel and Samuel?" she asked.

"I'll never tell you, Executioner!"

Mercy craned back to swing at him again, but Danny stepped in the way.

"Let me try," he suggested.

"Be my guest!" she said with a smile.

"See, Mercy isn't targeting the right areas," Danny said. He dragged the tip of Ozella down the centre of the vampire's face and rested it on his bottom lip. It left a burn down the centre of his face, which closed up quickly afterwards.

"I love this thing. Its true beauty is in being lined with galena. It makes even the slightest touch agony."

Danny rolled the stake across the man's face until the inlaid galena line pressed against him. The vampire grunted and tensed his posture. He then took the stake from the vampire's face.

"Think that scares me?" the vampire replied with a grin between heavy breaths.

"No, but this will," Danny replied with a smile. He unbuckled the vampire's belt and undid the zip on his trousers.

"Wait! What the fuck are you doing? What is he doing?" the vampire asked Mercy. She shrugged.

Danny pulled the vampire's trousers and boxers down, exposing his genitals.

Without a word, Danny speared one of the vampire's testicles.

The nerve-shredding scream was stifled when Mercy jammed her forearm across his mouth.

"Fucking hell!" Mercy exclaimed.

Jesus, I've turned a meek and mild-mannered guy into a complete psycho. I'm rather proud!

"Now, not only do you have the pain of a punctured testicle, you have the tissue and nerves trying to knit together, pressing against the galena on the stake. This agony can stop if you just tell us where Gabriel and Samuel are," Danny said.

The vampire nodded.

Mercy removed her mouth. The only sounds the vampire made were those of heavy panting and squeaks as tears streamed down his face.

"You heard the man. Where are they?" she asked.

"S-s-s-Samuel, is... is... in the G-G-G-Great Hall. G-G-G-Gabriel is innnnn... the study. H-h-h-he's coming... up w-w-with a p-p-p-plan to find you both!"

"And where is Aurelia, the new vampire?" Danny persisted. He then began to rotate the handle of the stake.

"I dunno! She's isss usually... oh God... with Gabriel... but hav... haven't seeeen her. Please s-s-stop!" he begged.

Danny removed the stake and the man crumpled into a foetal position, his back against the bottom of the bookcase.

Danny and Mercy exchanged glances. Danny nodded

He shoved his stake through the man's chest. He turned to a chalk statue, the agony etched onto his face.

They both turned towards the doors to see a flash of cloth disappear.

"Fuck! we've been seen! The alarm will sound now!" she said.

"What do we do?" Danny asked.

What the fuck do I do? Right, we need to keep Samuel and Gabriel apart. If they fight together we are fucked. Gabriel is on the second floor on the western end, but the Great Hall is on the first floor at the centre of the main house.

"Mercy!"

Fuck. There's no way Danny will be able to take Samuel. He's too old, too powerful. Danny has a better chance against Gabriel. I'll have a better chance with Samuel. But there will be others to fight too. Fuck!

"MERCY!"

"AYE!" Mercy snapped back. "Follow me as fast as you can," she said and they left the library. Within a few seconds they reached the expansive lobby, complete with white marble flooring, crystal chandeliers, and mahogany grand staircase. Shouts began to sound in the distance.

They both climbed the staircase to the first floor, Mercy issuing instructions as they did.

"We need to keep them apart. We need to split up. Get to the study and take Gabriel out. I'm going to face off with Samuel. It's our best chance. Right Cripple, the Grand Hall is right there," she said nodding down the short corridor directly ahead of them. "Go another storey up, then head down the corridor to your left. The study is at the end of the corridor, on your left. Now go!"

"Good luck!" Danny said and took off.

We're going to fucking need it.

Straight ahead, down the short corridor was the Grand Hall.

Right Fuckface. Time to see an old family member.

Mercy sprinted down the corridor, burst through the

double doors, and into the Grand Hall.

Fuck.

CHAPTER 27

Danny hobbled his way down the corridor, his eyes locked on an ornately carved, dark wood door at the end of the hallway. He reached the door, stopped, and took a few slow, steadying breaths.

Come on Danny. You can do this. You're living in his head. You can do this.

He reached out to the handle, but it turned and the study door opened.

Holding the door was Gabriel, looking back at another tall, muscular male vampire.

"Protect Samuel. I will find out what..." he said before turning his head and spotting Danny.

Three seconds passed as they echoed one another's wide-eyed bewilderment, before Danny pressed his palm against Gabriel's face. Gabriel stumbled back, clutching the burns. Danny connected with another punch on the other vampire, who stumbled backwards, four knuckle marks burned into his cheek.

Danny stepped inside and closed the door behind him.

They rushed Danny. He held one by the throat and the melting began. A third unseen vampire grabbed Danny. Danny let go of the vampire's throat and kicked him away with his good leg. The vampire stumbled back, clutching his throat. Danny pressed both palms into the face of the vampire, holding him from behind. He then spun around and slammed a stake into his chest.

As the vampire began to turn into chalk, an almighty blow threw Danny off his feet. He landed against the far wall of the study.

"Very good, human!" Gabriel said. "But Mercy is not here and we will settle this finally!"

Danny lay on his back, struggling to catch his breath, his body racked with pain. He was then hauled onto his feet, before being thrown onto the other side of the room. His head caught a wall-mounted metal candelabra, right at the hairline. He landed on the carpet with his senses spinning and a warm wetness trickling down his forehead.

Danny opened his eyes. The other vampire was still clutching his own throat and was sitting on the floor looking at Danny. He removed his hand; his throat was healing.

"Make him suffer, Gabriel!" he croaked.

"Oh, he shall!" Gabriel replied. He dragged Danny onto his feet. Danny swung a punch which was easily caught at the wrist by Gabriel. Danny tried the other hand with the same result.

Gabriel headbutted Danny into darkness.

When Danny came to, he was lying on the coffee table, his head bearing an intense migraine. Gabriel and the vampire stood on one side. Danny turned his head to the other side. Looking down at him was the smiling face of Aurelia.

"Did you think that I would simply let this go?" Gabriel asked quietly as he bent over Danny, his eyes burning with the purest hatred. "You murdered my family. They were all I had in the world. I loved every last one of them, more than you would be capable of in a thousand lifetimes, and you murdered them! YOU TOOK THEM FROM ME!"

Tears ran down both of Gabriel's cheeks.

"I didn't even kill your sister," Gabriel continued. "I improved her! I made her better in every possible way! I bestowed upon her the greatest of gifts. You should have been falling to your knees to THANK ME! But instead you murdered my beloved brothers and sister. Well tonight I get the ultimate revenge. No more promises of prolonged torture. Tonight you die, and the only fitting person to kill you is your precious Aurelia. You killed my family and so your family will kill *you*."

Aurelia stooped down to Danny, her hands caressing his head. She licked at the blood on his face.

"Aurelia, sis. You don't have to do this. Please. I love you."

"Shhhhh, my dear," Aurelia said as she tenderly cradled his head.

"Honey, please. Remember what Mum said to us with her last words? Remember?"

She lapped at the wound on his hairline, stinging him.

"There's no point," she continued.

"You're not wild. You're not feral. You are my big sister and I'm your baby brother. I love you, Aurelia. You can fight this!"

"There *is* no fighting this," she replied.

"Aurelia!" Gabriel interrupted. "Do not play with your food!"

"Remember when he cut your finger off? Just to taunt me?" Danny asked.

At that, Aurelia stopped stroking his face.

"He isn't your family. He hates you. But I'm your family. See?" Danny continued. He held up his left hand, showing her ring on his pinky, next to his ring.

"Aurelia!" Gabriel said. His tone was low and menacing. "Finish this!"

Aurelia bent over Danny and pressed her teeth to his neck.

"Please, honey. You have helped me so much. I'm so sorry that I took you for granted, but I'll never take you for granted again. Just fight him. I'll always be there to support you. I'll take care of you for a change. I'll help you get control of your hunger. I'll never turn my back on you, and I'll never give up on you, no matter what. But you have to fight this, Aurelia."

The pressure of her teeth on his neck lessened.

"We can still be a family, but you need to fight this. You need to fight him. He's not your master. He's your captor. You need to fight him, honey. I know that you can! I know that you're strong enough."

The pressure on his neck stopped and Aurelia slowly withdrew. She straightened up and whipped her hand across the face of Gabriel, leaving four deep lacerations from cheek to cheek

Gabriel grabbed Aurelia and threw her across the room. She hit the far wall, leaving a torso-sized dent in the plasterwork. "Useless. All this time wasted on you, for nothing!" Gabriel turned back to Danny. "I'll finish you myself!"

Aurelia appeared on his back, clawing and scratching at him. Slashes and gouges appeared on his face and neck. Gabriel struggled to pull her off, but there was no dislodging her.

Danny kicked at the muscular vampire who had been watching the scene in disbelief. He flipped himself upright and, though his head swam and his vision dimmed, Danny threw himself at the vampire. They collapsed over the couch and onto the carpet behind, Danny straddling him with one leg. His other leg, jutting outward, was incapable of flexing due to the cane.

Danny pressed the palms of his hands against the vampire's face. There was no screaming, only grimacing. Danny looked at his gloves. The two lumps of galena which had been stitched into his gloves were gone.

Fuck!

The vampire smiled up at him.

"Missing something?" he asked Danny, his smile widening.

"Fuck you!" Danny shouted. He then began to rain blows down on the vampire. Each punch left four knuckle-shaped burn marks.

"You forgot about my vampire knuckle-dusters you fuck!" Danny shouted. The vampire began to cover himself to protect himself from the punches. He shoved Danny upwards and away. Danny landed onto the coffee table, upright.

He searched his pockets and sleeves for his stakes, but they were missing. He scanned the room. His two stakes were on the mantelpiece above the fireplace. He lurched himself towards them. He laid his fingers on one, but a punch in the stomach folded him over. He fell to the side, writhing in pain, gasping for air. A kick landed on his shoulder, deadening his arm.

Danny opened his eyes. One of the stakes had rolled off the mantel and landed on the carpet behind the vampire. He crawled towards the vampire.

"There's just no quit in you, is there? You silly bastard!" the vampire said. With his one good arm he clawed himself towards the stake. He struggled between the legs of his attacker.

Behind him, the sound of grunting and snarling reached him as Aurelia and Gabriel struggled.

"No you don't, you bitch!" Gabriel said, and a loud thud was heard, accompanied by Aurelia coughing.

The vampire lifted Danny up with both hands and held him high in the air.

"Let's see how you do with a broken spine!" he taunted him.

Danny grasped one of the lumps of galena sitting on the mantel and pressed it onto the scalp of the vampire. Danny was dropped and both fell onto the ground; the vampire clutching the melted scalp on his crown and Danny on top of him.

Danny leaned forward, grabbed the stake, and clambered onto the vampire. With every ounce of energy he had left, Danny thrust his stake towards the chest of the vampire. It embedded itself less than an inch into his chest. The vampire knocked it out of his chest but with Danny's hand still clutching it.

Danny pressed the galena against the vampire's throat once more and, as a fresh wave of screaming sounded, Danny got onto one knee and fell, stake-first, against the chest of the vampire. The stake buried itself into the heart of the vampire under the weight of Danny's body.

Danny forced his head up in the direction of Gabriel as the vampire turned to dust beneath him. Danny fell through his body, coughing and spluttering for air in the dust cloud.

"MICHAEL!" Gabriel screamed at the dust and empty clothes on the carpet. "I'll fucking kill you!" he said as he made for Danny. He was stopped by Aurelia who was holding on to his ankle. Gabriel looked down in confusion, before Aurelia sank her teeth into his calf, through his trousers. He yelped in pain.

Grabbing the galena on the carpet, Danny struggled to his feet, exhausted, hunched over and flushed with pain. He grabbed the second lump of galena off the mantel and stumbled towards Gabriel.

"Fuck you!" Gabriel said and stomped on Aurelia's head, causing her to lose consciousness and a gash to appear on her forehead.

"NOOO!" Danny screamed. He thrust his stake at Gabriel, who batted it away with such force it flew out of his hand and smashed its way out of the window, into the darkness outside.

Danny took the galena in each hand.

Gabriel rushed towards him, aiming himself at Danny's neck.

Danny instinctively pressed the galena towards Gabriel's face. Each lump of galena found an eye socket. Gabriel stumbled back as Danny pushed his thumbs deeper and deeper. The galena melted through Gabriel's eyeballs and deep into the sockets. He fell onto his back. The scream was inhuman. Gabriel clawed and dug into his eye sockets but there was no retrieving the galena. Danny pressed the release catch in his cane under his trousers and the handle sprung upwards. He slid the handle, with stake attached, out of his waistband. He then mounted Gabriel's chest.

Gabriel continued to scream as the galena made its way towards his brain.

Danny looked at Aurelia. The laceration on her head was gone, she had awoken and was beginning to sit up.

Gripping the cane handle tightly with both hands, Danny plunged the stake into Gabriel's heart. His expression of agony was memorialised in chalk as his sternum collapsed into dust under Danny's weight.

Danny collapsed and rolled onto his back. He stared at the ceiling above until his breathing returned and his mind cleared. Aurelia crawled over to him and leaned in. Gone was her smooth, flawless skin, replaced by the ordinary imperfections he knew so well and loved so much.

"It's over!" she whispered and began to weep. Danny struggled himself into an upright position and held her as she sobbed on his shoulder. When the embrace finished, she looked him up and down.

"Are you OK, Danny? Are you badly hurt?" she asked as she began to fret over him.

"I'm fine, just every part of me hurts and is exhausted. Did I mention that every part of me hurts? How about you? Are you OK?"

"I'm fine, I think. I think I was all healed before you killed that bastard," she replied.

"Shit! Mercy!" Danny shouted, his eyes wide open, his back rigid. "We need to go! Mercy needs our help! Come on!" Danny said, grabbing both galena portions and struggling to his feet with Aurelia's help. Danny grabbed Ozella on the mantel on the way out.

They left the study and turned back onto the corridor. Their path to the Grand Hall was empty. With Aurelia propping Danny up, they made their way downstairs. As they progressed, the sounds of crashing, shouting, and screaming grew louder, before coming to an abrupt silence.

They moved towards the door of the Grand Hall.

"I want you to wait outside," Danny said.

"Not a chance!" Aurelia rebutted him.

"Aurelia, I've worked so hard to free you. I can't bear to see you hurt anymore," he argued.

"Honey, they have tortured me for months. I'm going to get the bastards back. I've got my own revenge to get. I'm standing with you, through thick and thin, It's *my* choice."

Danny smiled.

"Alright, take this," he said and gave her the cane-stake. "It has a longer reach. And take this," he continued, handing her one of the lumps of galena. "It causes them absolute agony. Just press it against their skin and, when they struggle with the pain, stake them in the heart. It *must* be the heart."

"OK. I love you, hon," she said.

"You too, doll. Good luck," he replied.

Danny swung the doors open wide and they stepped inside.

CHAPTER 28

"The study is at the end of the corridor, on the left. Now go!" Mercy said.

"Good luck!" Danny replied before hobbling up the next flight of stairs.

We're going to fucking need it.

Mercy focused straight ahead, towards the doors of the Grand Hall.

Right Fuckface. Time to see an old family member.

Mercy sprinted down the corridor and burst through the double doors and into the Grand Hall. She looked ahead.

Fuck.

The large hall – at least seventy by thirty feet – sported a white marble floor and dark wood joists with columns lining both sides of the rectangular room. Dark wooden ribbed vaulting was set on the high ceiling. At the far end of the Grand Hall, thirty feet from her, Samuel sat on his throne; a grand leather chair, the frame composed entirely of antlers. He smiled back at her. To either side of him was five vampires, including Hannah and Jessica.

Another eight vampires lined the hall on each side. Mercy slowly scanned the hall for others. There were four vampires behind her.

Fuck. There are so many of them here. I don't stand a chance. Shit, I really am going to die after all. There are so many more here than I thought there would be.

"Of course there are! We were waiting for you," Samuel said in his all too familiar tone of snobbish arrogance and a playful register. He slowly scratched his cheek and placed his skeletal hand back on the armrest. He had a gaunt appearance, colourless skin, and long black hair swept back, making him look like a porcelain marionette, a physical attribute all elders shared.

Mercy slowly walked further into the hall.

The vampires in front of her stepped forward. Only Jessica and Hannah stood by his side.

"I always hated that fucking chair. I'll need to burn it when I'm done here. Unless you want to stay seated and I'll go get some matches?" she asked Samuel.

"Same old Marcianne. Stubborn. Rude. Arrogant. And thoroughly delightful. You have no idea how much I have missed you and how truly disappointed I was to hear of your betrayal. My heart bled for you, daughter."

"I'm not your fucking daughter and that is not my name," Mercy barked back.

"Marcianne the Executioner, now executing her own kind. Claude would be broken-hearted."

"You haven't seen him recently, have you?" she asked.

"Please tell me you didn't have anything to do with his disappearance," Samuel said as he closed his eyes.

"No idea what you mean," Mercy replied with not a hint of jest or sarcasm. "Tell you what, Samuel. There's no need for all this fighting and ruining my house. Just me and you. We'll settle things our way. Unless you're too much of a fucking coward to fight your own battles?"

"Same old Marcianne," Samuel replied with a smile.

"Arrogant, ungrateful, and a fucking bitch too," Hannah said.

"Who the bloody hell is Marcianne?" Jessica asked.

"Why, this is," Samuel replied, pointing a long bony finger towards Mercy. "Marcianne, the female equivalent of the name meaning 'of Mars', Roman god of war. Marcianne the Executioner. Never before was there a more suitable title. You were our greatest warrior and most feared huntress."

"Once perhaps," Hannah interrupted.

"Ahh, you know Hannah of course," Samuel said. "When you left your family, we had to train another executioner, and Hannah has taken to it with great vigour. She is just as bloodthirsty as you were. Indeed, she reminds me very much of you when you were younger."

"Great, you've trained another psycho. Big deal. She'll turn into dust just as easily as you," Mercy said as she produced a stake in one hand and her lump of galena in the other.

"What did that pathetic little human do to you all those years ago?" Samuel asked. "We send out best warrior to deal with just another vampire hunter and she returns to us... different. Tainted. She abandons both her family and even her very name. Now you call yourself 'Mercy'," he said with a smile. "But you lived without mercy. You slaughtered countless without mercy. You took baths filled to the brim with blood. Just because you call yourself 'Mercy' does not absolve you of your past."

"I never thought of Mercy, I mean Marcianne, like that," Jessica said. "I mean Gabriel told us some stories about her, but I've only ever known the emo chick who lives like a hermit."

"That's because you're a young little thing, my dear," Samuel replied. "Marcianne was... truly spectacular. And now she has betrayed her family."

"Aurelia was my only family. And Josef Von Herrig taught me more in one meeting that I ever learned from you, or Claude."

Mercy approached the centre of the room.

"This didn't have to happen, Samuel. You ignored me when I sent up a flare last year. I tried to tell you that Gabriel and his nest were becoming too bloodthirsty. It was raising suspicions amongst the humans. It was threatening to reveal our very existence to the humans. If only you had listened to me, you old fool!"

"You had disowned your own kind!" Samuel shouted back. "You turned your back on us. I owed you *nothing!* NOTHING!" he rasped a croaky, hoarse scream.

"Bollocks," Mercy replied. "If only you had gotten up off your craggy old arse and…"

"Silence!" Samuel's voice boomed. "Why do you think Gabriel's brood became so aggressive? Because I instructed it! Times have changed, Marcianne, and we need to assert ourselves once again as the alpha predator in this new world."

"Madness," Mercy said breathlessly. "Absolute madness."

"There are enough humans of standing and privilege who are willing to turn their backs on their own kind for more coin. Edinburgh is our experiment. Our initial foray into playing a more dominant role. There will be no more killing just enough humans to survive without ruffling any feathers. No, we shall return to the old ways of living as nature intended vampires to do. We have begun in a city large enough to sustain us, before we adopt that existence in every city on the planet."

"And here was me thinking that vampires didn't work with humans. How wrong I was. Well, I'm happy to declare your little experiment a complete fucking failure. Now pack up your shit and go home!" she said.

"Enough of this! Kill her!" Samuel shouted.

"Dogpile her boys!" one of them said from behind Mercy.

A number of the vampires rushed her from all sides.

Mercy swerved to her left, sliding between two oncoming vampires, and tripped both of them. She approached another, avoiding his swipes, throwing him across the hall at other vampires.

In smooth motions, she weaved in between them, punching some, slamming others, and catching three cold, staking them in quick succession. Upon seeing three of their number reduced to ash piles, the others stopped. They maintained their distance, wary, looking for an opportunity.

Calm, centre yourself. Maintain awareness.

Mercy slowly readjusted her stance, until one vampire rushed her; she parried his blows. Ten vampires piled on her. She disappeared under the pile of vampires, clawing, scratching, snarling.

Samuel stood out of his seat, looking for a better view.

After a few seconds of relative calm, someone started screaming, then stopped, then another and another. The pile collapsed in on itself as someone at the side of the pile turned to ash, and then another. In the end, the final vampire fell onto Mercy, who staked him.

Mercy was lying amongst a huge mound of ash and piles of clothes. She stood up, covered from head to toe in grey-white dust, coughing plumes of dust out of her mouth, and rubbing her eyes.

"Impossible," Samuel whispered.

Mercy rubbed her eyes, and coughed her last victim out of her lungs.

"Gross," she rasped.

The remaining five vampires looked back at Samuel, unsure and scared.

Another three vampires burst through the double doors, and stopped, shocked at the amount of dust in front of them.

"You're making a total mess of my house," she croaked, shaking her hair, and brushing the worst of the dust off her favourite daisy sequinned jacket. "Worst. Guests. Ever."

"DON'T JUST STAND THERE YOU COWARDS! TEAR HER TO PIECES! KILL HER WITH HER OWN STAKE!"

At Samuel's command they rushed in.

The fight was long and hard. With every punch, scratch, and claw Mercy received, she gave out ten, but they kept coming and Mercy began to tire.

She downed another vampire with a knee to the stomach and hammered a stake through his back.

Hannah rushed from Samuel's side and barged into Mercy, sending her flying into the rear wall.

Mercy stumbled to her feet. With each punch she dealt, she received three more. Hannah knocked the galena from Mercy's hand.

Hannah punched her so hard, Mercy's ribs shattered on her left side. She fell onto her back, gasping for breath, waiting for the ribs to realign and knit together.

A vampire leaned over her. He grabbed her throat and began to pull at her neck. Mercy's spine began to stretch. She thrust the stake into the vampire and he disappeared into dust. Her ribs and spine popped back into place and Mercy shoulder charged Hannah. They both collapsed on the centre of the hall floor.

"Get her! Tear her apart!" Hannah yelled at the others as she held Mercy in a headlock.

Mercy struggled with futility against Hannah's powerful grasp. She stabbed at Hannah with her stake. Though she punctured her skin a few times; the blows were to her side.

Mercy grunted, trying to loosen Hannah's grip. Her legs were pulled away from her as the vampires descended on her. Her left leg dislocated. She yelped with the pain. Mercy's left hand came free. She stabbed at Hannah and Hannah let go.

Mercy fell to the floor, exhausted, racked with pain. She looked up at Hannah. She was clutching the side of her neck, plumes of bright red blood spurting rhythmically from between her fingers. Hannah staggered back to Samuel, who cut his wrist and fed himself to her. The wound on Hannah's neck began to close instantly.

As the pain of the hip popping back in place subsided, Mercy pulled at the foot of her closest attacker. She climbed on him and slammed the stake into his chest.

She freed herself from the grips of the others and stood hunched over, unstable on her feet, panting and sweating. Her wounds were closing but she was exhausted and growing increasingly weak.

She spun herself around to Samuel, Jessica, and Hannah.

Hannah's wound had closed and her eyes were more vibrant. She stood more powerful than ever.

"This time, bitch. I'll take your crown," Hannah said with renewed bloodlust in her eyes. She stepped towards Mercy. "I'll be the executioner you never were, then I'll..." Hannah said, then stopped. She hunched over as though punched by an invisible force.

"Oh no," Hannah whispered. She began to turn to chalk, before crumbling away to dust.

"What's happening?" Jessica said. Her expression was one of confusion, before it gave way to terror.

Her flawless skin began to appear with blemishes on it. Then wrinkles began to appear. Her hair grew grey. Crow's feet appeared at the sides of her eyes and liver spots developed on her arms. Her spine curved and stooped her over. Bags hung low under her eyes.

"Help me!" she pleaded. She collapsed onto the floor as the change continued.

Everyone stood in a state of shock.

Danny! He did it! He actually killed Gabriel!

"Well done, Cripple," she murmured.

Samuel stood over Jessica's frail body. Where there once stood a young woman in her early twenties, there now lay an old woman in her late eighties or early nineties, whimpering, looking up at them.

"Let me guess. You were turned about sixty or seventy years ago?" Mercy asked.

There was no joy in her voice, only sadness at what Jessica had become.

Samuel rubbed his head as he began to make sense of what had happened.

There was at least ten seconds' silence, as each person in that hall was unsure what to do.

"Gabriel," Samuel whispered as the truth finally dawned on him. He closed his eyes. His face grimaced in pain. He cried out an ungodly cry.

The doors burst open. Mercy spun on the spot as Danny and Aurelia entered. Danny and Mercy shared a smile.

Danny was stooped over. His head was cut; he was bruised and swollen.

"Let's finish this!" Danny shouted at which Mercy smiled and turned to Samuel.

"You murdered Gabriel!" Samuel pointed at Danny. He growled and rushed down the hall in Danny's direction.

Mercy intercepted him and barged him into the wall.

Danny and Aurelia attacked the remaining vampires.

Mercy rushed to Samuel and thrust her stake at his chest. Samuel grabbed the stake with one hand and slashed at Mercy's face with his other. Four deep gashes appeared along Mercy's face. He smacked the stake out of her hand and pushed her backwards.

Mercy slid along the floor.

Samuel rushed towards Aurelia. The vampire in front of her crumbled to dust. She pressed her galena into Samuel's cheek. He grimaced, but pulled her hand away. He threw her across the length of the hall. She flew over the antler chair, slammed hard against the wall, and collapsed behind the chair.

"I'll enjoy turning you myself! Only, unlike Gabriel, I think I shall keep you feral!" he said.

He turned to Danny who was already standing in front of him.

Danny held his hand up to Samuel's face. Samuel prepared to defend himself, however there was just powder in Danny's hand.

Danny blew the powder in Samuel's face. A fine mist of galena went everywhere. In Samuel's eyes. In his mouth, up his nose. The powder stuck fast to the skin and began to burn, Samuel's face melting. He clawed at his skin, tearing away strips of melted flesh with his nails, but the galena was stuck fast. There was nothing to push away. With Samuel blind and screaming in agony, he fell to his knees. Rasping and retching, Samuel dug his nails deep into his scalp and tore it away, revealing his bloodied skull underneath. The galena continued to eat into his face and soon the white of his cheekbones where showing.

Danny stood over him and poured the remnants of his pouch onto the top of Samuel's head. A fresh wave of sizzling and bubbling was released.

Danny pushed Samuel over onto his back. He produced Ozella and looked up at Mercy.

Mercy nodded.

A fitting end. Killed by the stake of the very hunter he ordered murdered.

Danny slammed the stake down through Samuel's chest.

The screaming became a squeal, before he stayed silent, his body crumbling to dust.

Danny didn't brag or savour the moment; he was already shuffling towards Aurelia.

Mercy helped him by placing herself under his arm and guiding him to where Aurelia lay.

Danny crouched down, stroking her hair.

"Aurelia? Aurelia! Come on, honey!"

Aurelia's heartbeat was strong in Mercy's ears. Her breathing was strong and steady. Her pulse was stable.

Mercy smiled.

"She's OK, Danny," she reassured him.

"Aye, but she might have a head injury. Brain trauma. She might…" he continued to panic until Aurelia began moaning.

They helped Aurelia sit up as she came to.

"Ouch. That was just rude," Aurelia said with a pained smile.

They huddled together, Danny and Aurelia holding one another, and Mercy hunched over them.

"What have I done? Dear God! I'm so sorry," Jessica said with a quiet and frail voice. She lay and wept a few yards away.

The Great Hall, filled with dust and designer clothing, fell silent once again.

CHAPTER 29

Mercy sipped at her cappuccino. She smiled at the mother feeding her toddler a small piece of the sandwich on her plate. The early morning sun was bright and strong as it streamed in through the café windows. Mercy didn't care that she was weak, that her scalp was sweating, yet she shivered and goosebumps prickled her skin. It was a good day. She had no idea that she had held such a weight on her chest for so long, until it lifted.

She drained her coffee.

Who'd have thunk it, Aurelia? Your Mercy has three friends, girl! THREE! Franky, Danny, and Aurelia! It's only taken six centuries, but I finally have friends! Not bad going eh, babe?

Past the mum and child, heavy traffic passed by as usual.

I think this is the happiest I've ever been, since we were together, Aurelia. I genuinely feel happy!

Danny's Aurelia appeared at the door of the cafe, spotted Mercy, and waved in an excited manner.

She came in and they hugged.

"How you doing, hun?" Aurelia asked.

"Yeah, I'm OK. Same old, same old. You?"

"Yeah, I'm OK. Just trying to sort some stuff out. Turns out that Danny didn't bother his arse doing things like paying bills. Men, eh?"

"No, just *him*," Mercy replied with a smile.

"I'm thinking of going back to work in a week's time," Aurelia said.

"That's great!" Mercy replied. "You've taken this like an absolute champ. So many people would be destroyed by what you've been through, but you've handled it so well. Now," she said, leaning towards Aurelia, "go buy me a slice of cake."

"Go buy yourself one," Aurelia replied with a smile.

"Good, good! I'm glad that you are able to block our hypnosis. It's the best way of protecting yourself."

"Yeah, Danny told me that. There have been some interesting leftovers from my wee spell as a vampire."

"How is he?" Mercy asked.

"He's good, overall. Yeah. Most of his injuries have healed. He was black and blue all over after what happened in the castle. I was so scared by the look of him. He looked so hurt; he was slow and he grimaced at doing anything. But most of the bruising is gone and his cuts and scratches have scabbed over, so he's healing well. He's even referred himself to an NHS physiotherapist to see if his knee can be strengthened," Aurelia replied.

"That's great. I think he just stopped caring about himself after you were taken," Mercy said.

"Aye, I just hope that I can convince him to go to a therapist or something," Aurelia said, her smile disappearing.

"What do you mean? Why?"

"He's not sleeping. Every single night he's waking up drenched in sweat. Sometimes multiple times. Our bedrooms are next to one another. I hear the screams coming through the wall as he wakes up."

"I'm not surprised he's having some form of PTSD," Mercy said. "What's he dreaming of?"

"He says he has all kinds of nightmares. Some of them has me dying in his arms and he's unable to save me. Sometimes it is you dying in his arms and him crying over you," Aurelia replied.

"I guess that's to be expected. He came so close to losing you and we were in a battle to the death, so having nightmares of any of us dying is understandable."

"Aye, I think you're right. Sometimes they're just

completely unexplainable. Like really weird and twisted ones," Aurelia said.

"Like what?"

"Like he regularly has nightmares of him killing people in cages. People who have been abused for years, but instead of saving them, he kills them. Weird. I think those nightmares affect him the most."

"Yeah. Weird," Mercy said. She looked down at her coffee cup. The weight in her chest began to pull Mercy downwards once again. "Do you think that, I dunno, maybe there's something stopping him from moving on?" she asked.

"I think so," Aurelia replied. "And unless it's dealt with, I don't think he'll be able to move on. That's why I hope that he goes to therapy, to try to help him get past it."

Mercy lowered her head. She took a deeper than normal breath and nodded.

Danny entered the cafe and sat down next to them.

"Alright ladies?" he asked.

"Aye. You, Cripple?" Mercy retorted.

Danny smiled and unfolded the newspaper under his arm. He held out the front page for Mercy to read.

CRISIS OVER?

The subheading read: *Missing Persons Numbers Fall Dramatically.*

"Congratulations," Mercy said.

"It's so weird to think that we have managed to help all these people, and they'll never know what we did," Danny replied.

"Aye, the lonely life of a hero, only not so lonely now," Mercy said, and Danny and Aurelia squeezed one another's hands. "But some people do know what you did," Mercy said.

"Aye, and I'm still not used to homeless people smiling and nodding at me as they pass, or randomly coming up and hugging me. It's truly lovely."

"Aye, it's a nice feeling," Mercy said, her heart hurting.

"Oh, and they found another pile of ashes with empty

clothes the other day. It was on the news," Danny said. "The theory is that it's some underground-type art installation. Really posh expensive clothes with piles of ash in them. People think it's some kind of artist's anticapitalist message about the shallowness of wealth. Others think that the artist is telling us that it doesn't matter what you wear or how rich you are, we're all headed for the same fate."

"As long as they don't suspect the truth, they can think what they like," Mercy said.

"Although there are some people who swear blind that they saw people crumble to dust in front of them. But they're just being dismissed, thankfully," Danny said. "Speaking of knowing the truth, you never told me what you did with Jessica."

"I put her in a nice care home. Told them that she's my gran. I pay her bills."

"What if she blabs about what she knows?" Aurelia asked.

"She won't say anything."

"But how can you be sure?" Danny pressed her.

"Because she has fairly advanced dementia. I doubt she remembers her life as a vampire. She certainly hasn't mentioned it to me when I visit her."

"Jesus!" Danny said.

"Aye. When she turned back, she became the age she should have been. And when you become ninety, the ravages of age and time take their toll. Turns out that she was unlucky to be destined to develop dementia in her old age."

"God that is so sad. Such a sad, sad ending to her life," Aurelia said.

"Aye."

"That was your nuclear option, wasn't it?" Danny asked.

"Hmm?"

"When our all of our plans fell on their arse, you said that you had a nuclear option. Your nuclear option was taking out Samuel so that all the vampires would die. Take out Samuel and Gabriel, and *everyone* dies," Danny said. He stayed silent, expecting confirmation of his theory.

"I wanted to keep this small and local, with only Gabriel's nest involved. When I realised that wasn't likely to happen, I had to plan for something much, much bigger," she said, then held her cup to her lips. She realised that she had already finished her coffee.

Bugger.

She watched Danny as he left the table and stood at the counter, ready to order a drink. A man cut in front of him and ordered first. Danny calmly spoke to him, and the man apologised and stood behind Danny.

Not whiny anymore.

The weight which had so quickly vanished was present once more, and pressing down on her to such an extent Mercy's smile faded.

When Danny returned to their table, Mercy pulled out her phone and stared at the black screen.

"Oh, for fuck's sake! Sorry guys, I need to go. Work demands my attention. It can't wait. Sorry folks."

"It's OK, go deal with what you need to. We'll rearrange another time," Danny said.

Mercy stood up without comment.

"Oh, I was meaning to say, Mercy," Danny said, "if ever you need our help with anything at all, just say the word and I'll be by your side, no questions asked. Balls to the wall, ride or die. OK?"

Mercy smiled and fixed the collar of her leather biker jacket.

"Take care of yourself, Danny. Take care of each other," she said before walking away, leaving Danny wide-eyed in shock.

"Danny?" he muttered.

Mercy stepped onto the pavement under the burning heat of the morning sun on North Bridge. Screwing her eyes against the sun overhead, she made her way towards the bridge. She stood by the kerb and stuck out her hand at a black cab, which turned its indicator on and steered towards her, slowing as it did.

The sun kissed both the rooftops and the heads of the people as a new hope rose in the ancient city of Edinburgh.

"Hello Marcianne," came a voice behind her.

She turned around. Before her was a man, short and slight in stature, youthful but with a gaunt appearance.

"That's not my name. Who are you?" she asked.

"Just a friend of a friend of a friend," he said in a Croatian accent; an accent from old Croatia. He aimed his face up at the sun and, with eyes closed, he smiled at its rays. Basking in its stifling, draining embrace, he was missing the sweaty scalp, pasty grey skin and sunken eyes which was normally present in a vampire in sunlight.

Just how old is he?

Eyes still fixed on the stranger, Mercy took a step towards the waiting taxi.

"You might want to hold on and hear what I have to say," the man continued before looking back at her. "I don't understand why a vampire as young as you, who is as affected by sunlight as you, continues to slog away like a human."

Around her, North Bridge was bustling with commuters, workers, locals, and tourists, just like any other day.

"We know what you did, Marcianne. You and your human. The crimes you committed in that castle of yours. We allowed you the benefit of the doubt when Claude went missing. We may even have shown mercy for your crimes against Elder Samuel, given your past service to your kind. But you have interfered in something much larger and much more important than any of us."

"Yeah, his little experiment," she replied.

"In spite of what he thought, it was not *his* experiment. A great deal of preparation and planning went into that venture. Please understand that in doing what you did, there will inevitably be consequences, for you and your humans."

A wave of dread flooded her before a torrent of anger and defiance washed it away.

"No, there won't be," she corrected him in a matter-of-fact manner.

"Sorry?"

"There won't be consequences for any of us. I have put together a team of vampire executioners unlike anything the vampire world has ever known. What happened in this city was *personal* business. That business is now over and no more vampires will be harmed."

He looked over her shoulder in the direction of the cafe, and back at her.

"But if any other elder decides that they want to try their luck, we will rain Hell down on your masters, the kind which will be the stuff of legends and nightmares. We killed almost one hundred vampires, including an elder, and we did it with absolute *ease*."

The man wore a sudden look of surprise at her response. He straightened his posture and raised his chin.

"So, go back to your masters with this message: leave us alone. If you even consider retribution, we will slaughter every last fucking one of you."

He smiled, gave a slow courteous nod, and then shot into the air, disappearing high over the rooftops.

"How the fuck?" she whispered as her question tailed off.

Two locals were pointing in the direction in which the stranger had disappeared.

We killed Samuel and his entire clan 'with absolute ease'? Best not to admit that we did it mostly through blind luck and even then, it was by the skin of our fucking teeth!

She looked back at the cafe and the friends she had just left behind.

What if the vampires don't heed my warning?

"Fuck!" she whispered.

She headed back inside the cafe. The door closed behind her as people passed, enjoying the sun, oblivious to what had just happened, and what it might mean for the future.

ACKNOWLEDGEMENT

They say it takes a village to raise a child. I would like to thank the following villagers for helping to raise this little scamp:

Firstly, to Christina O'Neill (The best mum anyone could be blessed with) and also to my late-father Matt O'Neill, who was my best friend and inspiration for writing and storytelling. Love you, Dad x

Special thanks to Kirstie Nicol for the advice and support, without which I may never have had the confidence to release this book. Many thanks to the support of valued villagers Douglas Wilson, Jackie Flynn, Boyan Atanasov, Siobhan Logan, and Frances Logan.

Finally, thanks to YOU. Yes, you reading this. You spent your hard-earned money (and God-knows, money is harder earned now that it has been before) on this book. I hope that you enjoyed it, and I would be grateful if you were to leave an honest review where you buy your books, ie. Amazon, Goodreads, Bookbub, Youtube etc.

ABOUT THE AUTHOR

Www.mtoneill.uk

M.T. O'Neill grew up in a small town outside Glasgow, Scotland in the 80's. He developed a passion for storytelling which has followed him throughout his life. Writing to maintain his sanity, he ran a comedy blog and was a guest columnist for The Glaswegian newspaper. He selflessly gave up a career in the prestigious and glamorous world of online customer service to follow his dream of writing books.

Now living in Edinburgh, he is the husband of one wife, father of one child (with another on the way), and servant of two cats. He loves football and movies, and spends far too much time playing Playstation. Visit his website for news on M.T.'s latest works, as well as exclusive content!

Printed in Great Britain
by Amazon

13509633R00163